THE BIG FIX

Tor Books by Linda Grimes

In a Fix

Quick Fix

The Big Fix

THE BIG FIX

Linda Grimes

TOR®

A TOM DOHERTY ASSOCIATES BOOK

NEW YORK

This is a work of fiction. All of the characters, organizations, and events portrayed in this novel are either products of the author's imagination or are used fictitiously.

THE BIG FIX

A Tor Book
Published by Tom Doherty Associates, LLC
175 Fifth Avenue
New York, NY 10010

www.tor-forge.com

The Library of Congress Cataloging-in-Publication Data is available upon request.

ISBN 978-0-7653-7638-1 (hardcover)
ISBN 978-1-4668-5126-9 (e-book)

Tor books may be purchased for educational, business, or promotional use. For information on bulk purchases, please contact the Macmillan Corporate and Premium Sales Department at 1-800-221-7945, extension 5442, or write to specialmarkets@macmillan.com.

First Edition: May 2015

Printed in the United States of America

0 9 8 7 6 5 4 3 2 1

This one is for my sister-in-law, Barbara, whose faith in my writing has never wavered, even when mine did.

THE BIG FIX

Chapter 1

It's not that I'm averse to holding on to something long and cylindrical, even if it does wiggle a bit. But when it hisses at me, I get nervous.

Relax, I told myself. *That snake is probably more afraid of you than you are of it.*

Yeah, right, myself answered, noting the distinctly *un*-afraid reptilian glint in its eyes. *You wish.* (Myself can be an unsympathetic bitch sometimes.)

I inhaled—slowly—fighting the impulse to gulp in air until I hyperventilated and passed out. As much as losing consciousness was starting to seem like an attractive option, it wouldn't put a paycheck in my wallet.

You need that money, you need that money, you need that money, I chanted. Mentally, of course. Saying it out loud wouldn't do a thing to enhance the image I was being paid to project. And paid extremely well, I reminded myself. Better than ever before.

The snake hissed again, its head dancing dangerously close to my own, forked tongue flicking in and out between curved fangs. *Gaaah. You need that money . . .*

(Myself took the opportunity to point out that some things are not worth the payoff. Like I said. Cold. Also, *not* helpful.)

Maybe I could get away with lengthening my arm. Just an inch or two . . .

The snake stretched.

. . . or three or four. A foot, tops. Surely no one would notice. At least, not until my sleeve suddenly appeared shorter. *Rats.*

"Don't hold it so close, Jack!" The woman glued to my side whisper-screamed at me through unmoving lips, calling my attention back to her existence. As if her chest pressed hard against my rib cage wasn't enough of a grabber. If those sweater puppies were real, I'd eat the stupid Indiana Jones knockoff hat I was wearing.

"I'm *try-ing,*" I ventriloquized right back at her, barely audible.

Holding my current self erect (all ruggedly handsome six-foot-three of me, complete with requisite three-day scruff), I tossed the snake into the murky subterranean pit situated within easy falling distance . . . only to have another one drop immediately onto my shoulder from the ledge above. *Crap.* I squeezed what's-her-boobs convulsively, but managed not to scream like a girl. Score one for self-control. Maybe I wouldn't ruin this guy's reputation after all.

At least the new snake wasn't as big. That had to be good, right?

The rattle started in the vicinity of my left ear. *Or possibly not . . .*

The new snake's head swayed in front of us, ominously close to the woman now scrambling to disentangle herself from me. I took a deep breath, grabbed the wiggly bastard by the tail (wondering fleetingly—and perhaps irrelevantly—how one was supposed to tell where a snake's body leaves off and its tail begins), twirled it twice above our heads, and sent it into the pit to join its buddy, maintaining my cool it's-all-in-a-day's-work attitude by the skin of my teeth.

Boobs Galore stopped her escape effort and wilted against me in an orchestrated flood of relieved tears. I'd worry about lipstick stains on my shirt, but I was pretty sure that stuff wouldn't come off her mouth without an industrial-strength solvent.

"Oooh, Dirk . . ." she breathed through sexy sobs.

Yeah, *Dirk.* Why was that even a name anymore?

". . . Dirk, darling, I would have been dead a hundred times over if it weren't for you! How can I ever repay you?"

I swallowed, hoping I'd get the next words right. This was the part I'd been dreading even more than the snakes. I'd never forgive myself if I screwed up the one scene I was being paid—and paid well—to pull off for my all-time favorite movie star. My *hero,* for Pete's sake.

Just say it already.

Gritting my teeth, I forced it out, making sure my gravelly voice oozed the right amount of masculinity. "Don't you worry your pretty little head about that, pussycat. I'll have you out of this hole in two shakes of that rattler's tail."

There. That hadn't sounded too cheesy, had it? Sure, I might not have elevated the schlocky dialogue to the heights Jackson Gunn was capable of, but on the upside, I delivered it without passing out. Which was more than he could have done, given the slithering circumstances. Snake phobias are no joke when you're billed as the World's Manliest Man.

"CUT!"

"Thanks a lot, Jack." The actress (whose name, I now remembered, was Sparky West-Haven—no wonder I'd temporarily blocked it) ducked out from under my arm with a shove to my kidney, and flounced off, puppies bouncing. Huh. Either she wasn't happy with my performance, or else she wanted to get as far away from any residual snakes as possible.

I was approached—with happy purpose—by the man who'd just yelled, an energetic sixty-something whose Just-For-Men black hair clashed with the Spanish moss he seemed to be growing on his face in lieu of a beard. The director.

"Perfect, Jack! I swear, when that camera is rolling you *are* Dirk fucking Dagger!"

Whew. Chalk one up to panic acting. Also, I know. Dirk *Dagger.* How could Jackson Gunn put up with a character name like that? The man was obviously a saint. (Sure, there are those who think "Jackson Gunn" is almost as bad, but it beat the heck out of his real name. I mean, if my name were Gunther Jackson, I'd transpose and truncate it, too.)

"Thanks," I said, squaring my perfect replica of Gunn's chiseled jaw.

My own chin is much more feminine, not to mention typically at least a foot lower, being as I'm usually short, blond, freckled, and female, as opposed to tall, dark, handsome, and male. Sounds strange, I know, but it's all part of my job as a facilitator.

Ciel Halligan: places to go, people to be. That's the real me.

See, I fix people's problems for a living. Not only that, but I do it as *them,* so they get all the credit. I can do that because of a special ability I share with others of my kind—i.e., aura adaptors. A quirky mutation in our genetic makeup allows us to alter our auras to look exactly like someone else. Basically, if I can touch you, I can become you, at least physically. It's a simple matter of absorbing some of your energy and redirecting it out from me.

Even if I don't touch you, I can, with enough concentration, manage a remarkably close rendition. But it's harder, and uses more of my own energy reserves, so I'm not crazy about doing it.

So what do *I* get out of the arrangement? Well, besides giving me the satisfaction of helping others (hey, I'm as altruistic as the next person), it's also a highly entertaining way to make a living. My job is a lot of things, but boring isn't one of them.

"Just a few more takes to iron some stuff out," my gushing director said. "Not you, Jack. Of course. It's Sparky who needs to tone it down. This isn't a cartoon, am I right? Anyway, another hour, two tops. Thanks for being such a champ."

Feeling pretty good about how this job was going, I smiled at his retreating back and pretended I didn't see the dirty look directed my way by the burly snake handler, who had retrieved his babies and had been crooning to them throughout my kiss-the-star's-ass convo with the big boss. He came over anyway.

"You didn't even try to aim for the mattress," he said, accusation squeezing his voice to a higher pitch than usual.

True enough. I'd been more concerned with getting the writhing, scaly tubes of poison—with *fangs*—the hell away from my face than with their soft landing at the bottom of the fake pit. I mean, sure, they were supposedly milked of their venom before the take, but they could still bite, couldn't they? I happen to have a strong aversion to having my skin pierced.

"You're such a dick," he said when I didn't deny it, and stalked off, obviously disgusted with me. I wanted to apologize—the guy obviously loved his squirmy pets—but it wouldn't have been in character. Work rule number one: never break character.

I plopped down on the canvas folding chair emblazoned with "J Gunn," spelled out in the shape of a pistol. Gotta love those graphic designers. A steaming mug of real coffee appeared in my hand (none of that froufrou foamy crap for *my* hero), courtesy of some wannabe starlet who probably only took the gopher job to get into the building. I avoided meeting her eyes.

My job was snakes, not small talk with girls I had nothing to offer.

I scanned the area while the makeup artist powdered my brow and the stylist artfully re-mussed the parts of my hair visible beneath my hat. My best-frenemy-turned-boyfriend, Billy Doyle, *had* to be here somewhere, laughing his ass off at me. I scrutinized a boisterous group of rigging technicians. There was plenty of snickering going on, but none I could swear wasn't typical of the regulars on the set, so I had to let it go. For now.

Billy had gotten me this gig because I needed the money. I had already turned down his offer of a financial bailout, primarily out of sheer stubbornness. The whole point of me having my own business was to be independent. Sure, I wasn't above getting a hefty family discount on rent, for both my D.C. condo and office, from my big brother the lawyer (trust me, he can afford it), but taking cash from the guy I was sleeping with? To me that smacked of . . . um, yeah.

Since I didn't have another job on the horizon, and some big bills were about to come due, I'd pounced on it when Billy told me about a way I could earn beaucoup bucks *and* get a trip to Hollywood. Stubborn I might be, but I do have a pragmatic side, especially where my business is concerned.

And, you know, *Hollywood.* The opportunity to meet Jackson Gunn—and walk a mile in his legendary shoes—was not to be missed.

Billy sometimes did stunt work for film actors who liked to pretend publicly they were as athletic as the characters they portrayed. Why take the bumps and bruises yourself if somebody else can do it for you? Bonus for me: threatening to tell his mom about it was part of the backup blackmail plan I hold in reserve. Auntie Mo would *kill* him if she knew what kind of risks he took. Of course,

I'd probably never be able to use it, because *he* knew stuff that would make *my* mom kill me.

Mutually assured destruction: the glue of any good relationship.

Jackson Gunn had heard about Billy through the golden grapevine—people with money who knew how and where to buy anything they wanted—and approached him with a "little problem." Seriously, what kind of action hero wanted to admit he couldn't be around a snake without peeing his pants? He'd be a laughingstock.

A throat cleared beside me. Jackson's assistant, Frannie. Cute, curvy, and in a rush. This was the first time I'd encountered her in person, but I recognized her easily from her picture in the extensive dossier I had compiled before the job. (I do that with all my clients. No room for screwups in my line of work.)

"Shouldn't you be gone?" I said, making sure I sounded concerned, not rude. According to a last-minute update from Jackson, Frannie had been called away on a family emergency.

"Come on, Ja—I mean, Mr. Gunn. You don't think I'd leave without making sure you're taken care of, do you? I got you a temp." She glanced with distaste at the starstruck girl with the black-and-white ponytail and double-hooped nose piercings. "What's your name again?"

The goth girl mumbled something I didn't bother to commit to memory (totally in character for Gunn) and took my empty cup, holding it with such reverence I was afraid she might be planning to make a shrine to it. Or possibly just sell it on eBay.

Frannie glared at her, obviously annoyed at the hero worship. "Mr. Gunn takes his coffee black, and only when he asks for it. Make sure you don't bother him in his trailer. He'll need to rest—*undisturbed*—between takes."

Goth Girl nodded, looking contrite. I split a megawatt smile between the two of them, lingering a little longer on Frannie, so she wouldn't get bent out of shape.

"I'm sure you'll do fine, sweetie," I said to the girl. I knew from his file that Gunn tended to call all women "sweetie." I supposed that spared him from having to remember names. Whatever the reason, I was glad. It made my job easier.

Frannie looked torn—she was obviously a devoted assistant—but eventually left. On her way out, she lobbed one last warning look at little Miss Black-and-White, who faded obligingly into the background, still clutching her prize coffee cup.

"Jack!" The director again. What now? Had the snakes gone on strike?

"Look, Jack . . . I don't know how to say this . . . I . . . We just heard . . . I mean . . . we have some bad news."

I quirked my mouth, shrugging it off the way I figured a superstar would. "What? Are we losing investors? Hell, let me talk to them. I'll—"

"No, that's not it, the movie is fine, though if you want . . . I mean, if you need to take some time . . ."

"Spit it out, Wally." That was his name, right? Walter Gentzner. Wally to his cast and crew, I was sure of it. So why was he looking so sick?

"It's your wife." He swallowed, his face looking as gray as his beard. "She's dead."

Well, shit. Part of my satisfaction guarantee was to never return a client's life in worse condition than it was when I got it. I could fix a lot of things, but you can't fix dead.

Chapter 2

"Tell me again, cuz . . . how is this my fault?" Billy said, pouring a hefty amount of Tanqueray Ten into a shaker full of ice. He added a much smaller portion of dry vermouth, not bothering to measure.

"You're the one who got me the job. And don't call me that," I said, not caring how unreasonable I sounded. I'd spent the last hour dodging microphones and morbidly curious sympathizers. I was grumpy.

Billy has a habit of showing up during my jobs, just to annoy me. Our moms were sorority sisters once upon a time, so they claim honorary aunt status to each other's offspring. Not only that, but Billy is Auntie Mo's stepson, so technically we wouldn't be related even if our moms were real sisters. I point this out only because a few months earlier our hormones (Billy's and mine, that is; I don't even want to think about our mothers') had taken it upon themselves to explore certain *un*cousinly possibilities. Now I occasionally like to reassure myself we aren't perverts.

Which is a good thing, because I have to admit the fruits of those hormonal explorations have been pretty darned impressive so far. But that doesn't mean we've given up on teasing and tormenting each other (I suspect that's hardwired into our personalities), only that we've added a new dimension to it.

We were holed up in Jack's luxury Fifth Wheel trailer, and Billy wasn't about to let the well-appointed bar go to waste. He filled two sturdy martini glasses. Three olives each, speared by sterling silver picks topped by tiny pistols.

"All right, then—Cielie-poo," Billy said, accommodating me with a shrug and a teasing curve of lips as he handed me one of the glasses.

I crossed my eyes and stuck out my tongue at him, as much because his glass was twice as full as mine as for the gag-inducing endearment. Normally I'd complain aloud about the lack of cocktail parity, but since I was trying to keep a clear head I let it slide.

"I only passed the job on to you because you refused to let me pay off your creditors. I don't know why you have such a big chip on your shoulder about earning your own money, anyway. Lord knows I'm happy to take it from anyone willing to give it to me."

His dark blue eyes twinkled beneath the heavy black eye shadow he still wore. The contrast was stunning, but then Billy's eyes were always gorgeous. His lashes were a source of perpetual envy on my part. Of course, now that he was officially my significant other, I didn't mind them quite as much.

He'd been the ponytailed assistant—the temp filling in for Frannie. (Three guesses who had engineered the family emergency.) Billy's two-toned goth girl was ostensibly running interference with the outside world so "poor Mr. Gunn" could rest in the aftermath of the shocking news.

Billy had dropped the aura, but he was stuck wearing the makeup until he went home for the day. Well, unless he wanted to expend the extra energy to cover it up with borrowed bits of some cosmetic-free aura. Since it was only us here, he didn't bother.

"Sweetie's" T-shirt was snug on him, and her stretch jeans too short, but the stark black clothing suited his own dark-haired coloring. Thank goodness he'd remembered to take off her facial jewelry before switching. I can never look at people with nose rings without wondering if they might sneeze and accidentally blow a snot bubble. It's distracting.

I'd borrowed one of Jack's silk robes (gunmetal gray, but the paisley print added an unexpected touch of whimsy), since the movie costume I'd been wearing swallowed my petite frame. The bronzy tone of his makeup actually went fairly well with my strawberry blond hair. It even covered my freckles to a certain degree, so silver lining there, at least.

"Of *course* you take money from anyone," I said. "*You* are a lazy opportunist."

"I beg to differ. I am a *good* opportunist. Good opportunists can't afford to be lazy. You miss too many opportunities that way." He clinked my glass with his. "Cheers."

I responded in kind and took a grateful sip. Billy's martinis were starting to grow on me. "Mmmm. You missed your calling. You should have been a bartender."

"Oh, I have been, on occasions too numerous to count. Want to see me juggle the bottles?"

"You can do that?"

He put his glass on the coffee table and returned to the bar, where he grabbed three bottles and sent them spinning through the air in quick succession, catching them over and over again with ease. "Who do you think is standing in for the lead in the remake of *Cocktail*?"

"Oh, geez. Why are they recycling that tired old thing?" Apologies to Mr. Cruise, but I am not a fan of his early work. Too many teeth.

"Because . . ." He replaced the bottles one at a time, leaving them exactly where he'd found them. ". . . recycling is the green thing to do. And Hollywood is all about the green."

I groaned. He sat beside me on the soft leather sofa and kissed my nose.

"You're supposed to laugh at my jokes, cuz. Save the moaning for when we're in bed."

I gave him a look. "I told you not to call me that anymore."

"Habit," he said. "Relax. You're not a pervert."

"Well, I suppose it's better than 'Cielie-poo.' Marginally. Still . . ."

"Never mind. Drink up. You have a call to make."

I shuddered, and downed the rest of my martini in one huge swallow. I still needed to tell the real Jackson Gunn that his wife was dead. Worse, that she'd apparently been murdered.

Okay, so there was no "apparently" about it. According to what the police had told us, she'd been shot multiple times. In the back. It sure as hell wasn't an accident or a suicide.

"Maybe I should break it to him in person," I said. Yeah, stalling. It wouldn't be any more pleasant telling him face-to-face, but at least it would allow me to put it off for a little while longer. Personally, I think procrastination is an underrated life skill.

Plus, I loved visiting the ranch. It was my favorite of the three client hideaways I kept. The lake house in upstate New York and the remote tropical island villa were nice enough, but the dude ranch had horses. I *love* horses.

The hideaways are essential to my business, because it would be awkward (to say the least) if a client were to be seen, at home or anywhere else, while I was playing stand-in. I keep three different places because the filthy rich people who can afford my services expect a certain amount of choice in their accommodations. Not that I only cater to the filthy rich. I've taken on some pro bono clients—like I said, I can be altruistic—but I've found it tends to be people with a whole bunch of money who demand my services. I guess maybe they're more used to delegating away life's petty annoyances than the rest of us are.

"You really want to risk his hearing about it on the news?" Billy asked.

"The police said they weren't going to release the details." I tried to sound positive, but from the look on Billy's face I hadn't succeeded.

"This is Hollywood. The only place leakier is D.C. TMZ is probably right outside the trailer door."

I sucked in a deep breath and let it back out through flapping lips. "All right, all right. I'll do it. Hand me the phone."

"Good girl. And afterward we can . . ." He whispered something in my ear that would make Auntie Mo wash his mouth out with soap.

I felt my eyes get big. "Are you sure the tub is big enough for that?"

"I'll go measure it while you make the call." He kissed me, doing that thing he does with his tongue that drives me absolutely crazy. After he was done stealing my breath, he worked his way up to my ear.

"I'll even be Jack for you if you want," he whispered suggestively, matching the action to his words and leaving me clinging to the physical embodiment of my erstwhile persona. Somehow, it wasn't as exciting as I'd imagined it would be during all those bargain matinees I'd spent fantasizing about him. Spending time as the man had effectively let the air out of that balloon.

Billy had made a similar offer before—to him, changing auras was like changing clothes. Assuming Jack's appearance was no different, in his mind, than dressing up as a pirate for me would be, if I happened to be into pirates. Which I'm not. (Except maybe Johnny Depp's Captain Jack Sparrow, but let's not go there.)

"Um, that won't be necessary," I said. Understatement of the year. Any "thing" I'd had for Jackson Gunn was now well and truly kaput. Just another hazard of my job. "Besides, it would be disrespectful. For Pete's sake, the man's wife just died!"

"It's not like it's really him. You know it's me, so where's the harm?"

He was going to make me admit it. "Look, he doesn't do it for me anymore, okay? I want *you*."

"Whatever you say—I aim to please," he said with a satisfied smile, and changed back to himself, leaving me to my unpleasant task.

Once again, I wondered if he really meant it, or if he was trying to be "fair." He'd told me before that while he'd sowed more than his share of wild oats, he knew I hadn't, and he never wanted me to feel like I was missing out. If I ever craved variety for variety's sake, he was able and willing to supply it. Nice offer, I supposed—especially since he'd assured me he didn't expect anything in the way of reciprocity—but Billy as himself revved my motor more than Jackson Gunn ever could, regardless of my hero worship.

I took my time dialing, both out of reluctance to impart the bad news and to give my heart rate a chance to slow down. Who needed aerobics when Billy was around?

"Circle C Guest Ranch, Dave speaking. How can I make your life more fun?"

I smiled. Dave Silverberg was the middle-aged manager of the Arizona resort where most of my West Coast clients stayed while I solved their problems for them. He was a good friend of my parents, a New York City native with delusions of cowboy grandeur (I blame his early fascination with Billy Crystal movies), and I loved him to death. Not an adaptor himself, but a trusted member of the community nonetheless.

"Hey, Dave. It's me. Can you put Jackson on? I need to talk to him."

There was a pause. "Well, darlin' "—there are those who might think it ridiculous for a man raised in Brooklyn by a cabdriver and a waitress to assume a Western drawl, but I happened to think it was adorable—"that might be a problem. It appears Mr. Gunn is missing."

"What?"

"Yup. He plum disappeared on me. I was about to saddle up and go looking for him when you called."

Crap. Just what I needed. A missing client on top of a dead wife.

"Listen, call me as soon as you find him. And, um, don't let him watch any news before I talk to him, okay?"

Billy joined me as I was hanging up. "Good news—there's a new loofah." I used to roll my eyes when Billy would tell me how wonderful he was with a loofah, but having shared a few showers with him recently, I didn't anymore. "The tub will be a tight squeeze," he added with a wink, in case the innuendo in his voice wasn't enough to carry his meaning, "but with my superior athletic ability and your impressive flexibility, I think we might just be able to manage it."

"Sorry," I said. And, boy, I really was, because Billy was an absolute virtuoso at following through on innuendo. "We have to leave for the ranch right away—Dave can't find Jack." A horrible thought struck me. "Oh, my God—you don't think he's been kidnapped, do you?"

It wasn't as if *that* hadn't happened on one of my jobs before, and Billy knew it. Seriousness wiped the fun right off his face, replacing it with speculation.

"Possibly, if whoever murdered his wife was out to get him, too. Or worse . . ."

"Or *what*?" What could possibly be worse than a kidnapped—Jesus, maybe even dead by now!—client added to the client's definitely dead wife?

"Or maybe you've provided Jackson Gunn with the perfect alibi for murder."

Bingo.

Chapter 3

"I still don't think we need to fly. We'd get there just as fast if we drove." I gave Billy a sidelong look. "Maybe faster, the way you drive."

"Not even if I were Colin McRae and had Nicky Grist as my codriver instead of you," Billy said, pulling me inexorably toward the small plane on the airfield.

The Mooney 252 was a recent acquisition of his, and as far as I was concerned he was still way too enamored with it. I had thus far avoided taking a ride in it, in spite of multiple offers. I couldn't help feeling that he was taking advantage of my current situation to force the issue.

"Who are they?" I asked, trying my damnedest not to sweat. Yeah, that went about as well as you'd expect. I had a nonsweaty aura or two in my repertoire, but none I could employ without Billy knowing exactly why I was doing it. Which sort of defeated the purpose of not letting him see me sweat in the first place.

"World-class Rally racers," he said. "Some of the best drivers on the planet."

"You have them? Maybe we should give it a shot. I mean, they sound like great auras. Shame not to make use of them—"

"Since when do auras come with a skill set? I'd say 'nice try,' but really, it was kind of sloppy."

"Maybe not the skills *per se,* but the reflexes . . ."

He gave me a look. Okay, it had been a long shot. Sure, you get the physical attributes of the person whose aura you project, reflexes no doubt included. But the instincts driving the reflexes? That was more of a psychological thing connected to the mind behind the aura.

"Trust me, flying is faster," he said. "And fast is what we need if we're going to find Gunn and get him home to Vegas—where *you* told the police he was going—before said police come knocking on his door."

That was true enough. Jack's palatial home—where his wife was murdered—was just outside the gambling mecca of the western world. And I'd *had* to tell the police he'd be going there. What loving husband wouldn't rush to where his wife had been killed? I needed to find Gunn fast, so I wouldn't be stuck standing in for him at the funeral. I was sorry for the man, but I sure as hell hadn't signed up for *that.*

I twisted my lips into a wry expression. Wry was better than scared shitless. "Aren't you the one who told me never to trust anyone who said 'trust me'?"

"I didn't mean me, twit. You can always trust me, no matter what I say." He lifted me from behind and put me on the wing, urging me toward the passenger-side door.

"Wait!" I tried to slide back down, but was prevented by two firm hands on my southern cheeks.

"No. Waiting never makes facing something you're afraid of any easier. Get in."

I craned my neck enough to see the determination on his face. It did not bode well for my weaseling-out success. Not that I wouldn't still try.

"But don't you need to, um, file a flight plan or something? I wouldn't want you to get in trouble on my behalf," I temporized.

He grinned. "Since when do I need help getting into trouble? But you don't have to worry—no flight plan required. We're good to go."

"But . . . but . . . I know! Flight check. We can't leave without a preflight check, right?" That should buy me some time.

"Very good, cuz. I will be doing exactly that as soon as you are safely buckled in. Now, get in and breathe slowly. Try not to hyperventilate before I get there."

He shoved. Frankly, there are better ways to feel Billy's hands on my ass. I sighed and climbed in, resigned to my fate.

It's not so much the flying I hate—if I could grow wings (alas, beyond an adaptor's capability), I'm sure I'd have a blast zooming through the air. But stuck inside a teensy little cabin with no way out? Uh-uh. It disagrees with my claustrophobia.

I left the door open until Billy was done with the check and ready for takeoff, closing it with a grunt and a frown when I could avoid it no longer.

Billy looked at me from his seat, speculating about God knew what. Whether or not he had restocked the barf bags, probably.

"Ciel, I'm a good pilot. I promise to get you to the ranch in one piece."

"It's not that—I know you're a good pilot. Why wouldn't you be? You're good at everything. It's just that . . ." I shifted uncomfortably in the seat. ". . . look, I don't like feeling trapped, all right? You *know* that." I knew I sounded irritated, but really I was disgusted with myself.

He continued to study my face, but thankfully didn't go into the it's-time-you-did-something-about-that-claustrophobia-thing-of-yours lecture I was expecting.

Finally, he sighed. "I was hoping this wouldn't be necessary, but . . ." He reached behind my seat and pulled out a parachute. "You can wear this, if you want. Won't make for a comfortable flight, but you *can*—technically—leave the plane whenever you want, if that helps," he said.

Yeah, right. As if I'd jump out of a perfectly good airplane. Still, oddly, it did help to know the possibility existed. My breathing slowed to something resembling normal.

"Thanks," I said quietly. "Are you going to wear one?"

"Nope," he said, showing one dimple. "I trust the pilot."

I squared my shoulders. "So do I. If you're not, neither am I."

"You sure? I braved ridicule from my fellow pilots to stow that onboard for you. Had to recalculate the weight of the aircraft and everything. It's here, so you may as well use it."

"I don't need it," I reiterated. (Stubborn? Moi? Perish the thought.) "Put it back. I'll be fine."

He complied, with an amused shake of his head, then dug into his pocket. He pulled out a miniature bottle of gin and tossed it at me. Billy's version of Boy Scout—always prepared.

"I don't need that either."

"It's medicinal. Drink it down."

I shook my head. Paused, and finally sighed. Who was I kidding. I twisted off the cap and focused my thoughts on the parachute behind me. Even if I wouldn't put it on for the world—not if Billy wouldn't wear one, too—it still made a pretty good security blanket.

Never have I been as happy to set foot on my dude ranch as when I left the plane after we touched down on the landing strip. I would have kissed the dusty ground if I hadn't been sure it would send Billy into gales of laughter. I'd had enough gales for the day, thank you very much.

Billy clapped me on the shoulder and said, "Come on, cuz. It was just a little turbulence. Storms pop up. You did great—only one bag!"

I groaned. "Don't remind me." But at least, thanks to the gin, I'd been giggling while I barfed.

He draped an arm over my shoulder and kissed my forehead. (I was sucking on a peppermint, but perhaps it hadn't kicked in enough for him to risk my lips.)

"It'll get better," he said. "You need more practice is all. Once you're used to it, you'll be fine."

I groaned again, but was spared from having to come up with a pithy rejoinder by the approach of my ranch manager, on horseback. He dismounted the palomino with ease, dropping the reins to the ground. Trigger would no more move from that spot now than if he'd been tied to a post—he was that well trained. (Yeah, Trigger—Dave's idea, not mine, but to be fair, Trigger *was* a dead ringer for Roy Rogers's horse. The big gelding and I were pals.)

Dave lifted me into a hug. He liked doing that because I was one of the few women in his life short enough to make it possible. He was not a tall man.

"Hi," I said after I sucked back in the breath he'd squeezed out of me. "What's going on?"

He shook Billy's hand as a smile spread over his face. "Cody found him out near the barn."

Cody Carmichael was the security guard for the Circle C, a younger—and more authentic—cowboy than Dave. I knew from employment records that his real name was Clarence, but he seemed to think Cody suited him better. Have to say, I agreed. He was too ruggedly western to be a Clarence.

"Seems Mr. Gunn went on an unscheduled hike and got himself lost. I already read him the riot act about heading out without me or Cody. He's taking a nap at the moment, after a busy afternoon 'rehydrating' himself. Sorry if you came all the way out here for no reason. I would have called, but I knew you were already on your way."

Whew. One less worry. "That's okay—I had to come anyway. I'm afraid I have some bad news for Mr. Gunn."

"His wife? Yeah, I saw—it's all over Twitter."

"Does Gunn know?" I said. I had Jack's smart phone (I couldn't very well "be" him without it), so, if Dave had been careful, Gunn shouldn't have been able to hear about his wife's murder from any outside source.

"Not yet. I haven't let him near a computer or the TV, and Rosa is completely tongue-tied around him."

"Rosa? Tongue-tied? I can't see it," I said. Rosa Delgado was my combination cook and housekeeper, a formidable fifty-year-old second generation Mexican American with a figure that rivaled Sophia Loren's, and who, as far as I knew, wasn't afraid of anyone or anything.

"Quivers in his presence. Can't get a word out. Funniest thing I ever saw—I'd try for a video if I wasn't so sure she'd hog-tie and geld me if she caught me. You want me to call her and have her wake Mr. Gunn up for you? I guess she can knock on his door and use sign language," he said, a tad wryly.

"Better let him sleep it off a little longer—he should be clear-headed to hear what I have to tell him."

"So, how long would you say Jack was gone?" Billy asked casually. I gave him a sharp look. Did he *really* think Gunn could have killed his own wife?

"A few hours," Dave said.

"You sure about that?" I said, sounding maybe not as casual as Billy, but I covered it by hugging Trigger's head when he nuzzled my chest. If Jack had only been gone a few hours, he *couldn't* have done it.

Dave scratched his head. "Could have been longer, I guess—he didn't come down for breakfast, so I had Rosa take a tray up. She knocked and left it outside his door. Guess she didn't want to risk catching him in his skivvies—might've made her faint dead away. I didn't get worried until he didn't come down for lunch and I found out he'd never touched his breakfast tray. But it doesn't matter now, does it? He's back, safe and sound."

I nodded. "Hey, do you mind walking back with Billy? I think Trigger wants me to go with him," I said. Also, I felt the need to ride on something I was in control of. Horses don't scare me, not one bit.

"Sure thing, honeybunch. Trigger would rather haul you than my fat ol' tuchus any day. Here, let me give you a leg up."

I laughed. While not exactly roly-poly, Dave *was* starting to fill out—and above—his jeans more than he had when he was living in Manhattan. He blamed the healthy Arizona air for stimulating his appetite, resulting in what he called "Dunlop's Disease"—his belly had "done lopped over" his belt. Which was a slight exaggeration, but after being skin and bones most of his life he seemed to get a perverse joy out of complaining about his few extra inches.

"Sure, boost away," I said. I could have made it myself, with a hop and a pull on the saddle horn, but why spoil his obvious pleasure at being a cowboy gentleman?

Once I had the reins in my hands, I was off, tossing a "See ya at the barn!" over my shoulder. Dave hadn't even had to adjust the stirrups for me. He carried his height in his torso—his legs weren't much longer than mine.

I felt mildly guilty about leaving them to deal with my luggage. Okay, not really. It wasn't as if Dave would have let me carry it anyway, and we weren't all that far from the ranch house.

Now that I knew my client was safe and sound—and sleeping—I figured taking a time-out for a short ride before dumping bad news all over his world wouldn't hurt him, and it would do *me* a world of good. It had been too long since I'd been in the saddle.

Trigger had his own ideas about where to take me. I wasn't picky, so I gave him his head. He turned west toward the pond. Good choice on his part—a quick spin around the water would be refreshing, and I should still be able to get to the barn about the same time as the guys.

It felt good doing something that didn't scare the poop out of me. Horses, I knew. I'd had some pretty wild rides in the past, even been tossed a time or ten, and once had my foot stomped on (accidentally, I'm almost certain) by a horse who'd objected to being curried in a ticklish spot, but for some reason the huge animals didn't scare me. When I was on one, I could breathe. I could *go.*

I like being able to go.

I was halfway around the pond when my cell phone chimed in with the theme from *Jaws.* My brother, Thomas, the lawyer (a legal shark if ever there was one), which immediately worried me because he never calls when he knows I'm on a job—his overdeveloped work ethic won't allow it. As an adaptor himself, he knows not to interrupt me when I'm not myself.

"You *rat,*" he said, skipping the preliminaries.

Gulp. Uh-oh. "Hi, Thomas. Listen, kinda busy here—"

"I know it was you, so don't deny it."

"I can explain—"

"I can't believe it. After everything I do for you!"

True. Home, office, business advice . . . you name it, he was there for me.

"She had my back to the wall, Thomas! There was no way out—I *had* to tell her. You would have done the same thing. Besides, it was only a matter of time before she found out anyway. I just ripped the Band-Aid off for you, so now you don't have to. When you really think about it, you should be thanking me."

Okay, that last part was a stretch.

"The *plan* was that Laura and I would tell Mom *after* we were married. Do you know what she's doing? *Do you?*"

I held my phone away from my ear. Trigger flinched. I grabbed the pommel, holding on to it and the reins both while I squeezed my legs reassuringly against the saddle. Trigger was a steady horse, but Thomas's "annoyed" voice could startle a rock.

"No . . ." *But I can guess,* I thought with a guilty wince.

"Our mother is planning a wedding. A full-on *Halligan* event. You know what that means. She's already enlisted Mo's help."

Better you than me, buddy. "Well, Auntie Mo *is* really great at organizing. I can see why Mom would—"

"Ciel, why in the hell couldn't you keep your mouth shut for one more week? Laura and I had already booked time with a justice of the peace in a town far away from everywhere, with a cozy B and B where nobody could find us. We would have been home free."

"Can't you tell Mom you've already made your plans?" I suggested hesitantly. "I'm sure she'll understand."

The silence roared in my ear. Yeah, our mother would never understand eloping. She'd take it as a personal insult. "Look, tell Mom you can't wait. Theoretically, she should be so thrilled you're finally taking the leap that she won't want to risk giving you time to back out."

"I tried that. She said fine, no waiting. The wedding is in ten days, sooner if I want."

Yeah, that was Mom all right. And she'd pull it off, too.

"By the way," Thomas continued, with a sudden, gleefully evil edge to his voice, "Laura wants you to be her maid of honor—call her. Your dress fitting is tomorrow at noon—Mom's paying the seamstress triple to squeeze you in on her lunch hour, so do *not* be late."

Well, at least *Laura* apparently wasn't mad at me. "But I'm in the middle of a job. I can't—"

More ominous silence. I coughed. "Yeah, okay. Right. I'll be there." *Or at least a reasonable facsimile of me,* I thought but had the good sense not to say.

Chapter 4

Billy was waiting at the barn. It was small—four stalls, a tack and feed room, and the wash area—but it was sufficient for our needs. Aside from Trigger, there were only two other equines in residence. One was a docile black mare named Licorice, who was a dependable mount for any of our guests, no matter their level of riding experience. If a client wanted a more spirited horse, Dave would let them have Trigger while he rode Licorice.

Then there was Eeyore, the unofficial king of the Circle C, a dapple gray Shetland pony. The nasty-tempered little thug was my childhood mount, the love of my preadolescent life, now retired. To my knowledge, of all the people who'd ever been close enough to touch him, I was the only one he'd never bitten.

I tossed Trigger's reins to Billy and hurried to Eeyore. I thought he liked it here better than his old boarding stable in the Bronx, but it was hard to say for sure. He'd earned his name—a gloomier, grumpier hoofed creature would be tough to find. But I knew he loved me in his own way.

Billy had no warm, fuzzy feelings for good ol' Eeyore. My pony's gimlet glare—backed up by bared teeth—was one of the few things I knew that could make Billy flinch. (Yeah, that had warmed my heart as a girl. Still amused me, if I was honest.)

"Eeyore, you old son of a gun, how are you?" I said, leaning over the shortened door to the roomy box stall that was his plush (by horsey standards) home. He squealed a greeting and nuzzled me as I scratched his neck.

"Hey, Billy, are there any apples in the barrel?" I knew if I didn't offer up a treat soon, Eeyore would turn his grumpy wrath on me, love notwithstanding.

"Yeah, hold on." He hung the bridle he'd removed from Trigger on a peg, grabbed a few apples, and tossed one to me. The other he gave to Trigger, who munched it with gusto. "Watch yourself with that little demon, cuz. I like your hands the way they are—with fingers."

I laughed as I held out the apple to Eeyore, but I was, in fact, careful to keep my hand flat. Eeyore snatched his favorite fruit, downed it, and nuzzled for more. "Sorry, bud. That's all." In response, my darling pony lifted his tail and dropped a pile behind him.

"Opinionated little bugger, isn't he?" Billy said as he led the now unsaddled Trigger past us to another roomy stall.

"Eeyore has always been creatively expressive," I said. "He's smart that way. Hey, wait—we should curry Trigger before you put him away." Anything to delay giving the bad news. Destroying a client's world wasn't my favorite activity.

"Dave said he'd take care of it while we're talking to Jack—special bonding time between a cowboy and his horse or some such. I told him I'd meet you at the barn and bring you back—that'll give him time to wake up Jack and make sure he's sober."

After Trigger was safely shut in his stall, Billy wrapped his arms around me from behind, bent down, and whispered, "We have a few minutes. There's a handy pile of hay in the loft—"

Eeyore lunged, narrowly missing Billy's forearm with his teeth. Billy pulled back, swearing, taking me with him. "You know, euthanasia is considered the kind option for deranged animals."

"Bite your tongue," I said, turning in his arms. "Better yet, let me do it for you." I pulled his head down to my level and followed through. But gently. I was too fond of that tongue to risk damaging it.

Billy tore himself away from my mouth and dragged me toward the loft. "Up you go. *Now.*"

As waiting activities go, sex with Billy was a way better option than currying Trigger. Still, I figured I should put up a token resistance, for form's sake. "We should be getting back to the house soon. We don't have time for—"

"Trust me, it won't take long." He lifted me to the third rung of the ladder.

"Is that supposed to be an enticement? Whatever happened to foreplay?"

Hot on my tail (so to speak), he leaned close and nipped my neck, ending with lingering lips that left me tingling. "There. Foreplay. Now, unless you're up for experimentation on a ladder, get your delectable ass over to that pile of hay."

Ten minutes later, naked and thoroughly happy, I gazed into dreamy blue eyes and wondered how it had taken me so long to appreciate this aspect of Billy. The guy had phenomenal hands, an innate knowledge of where to put them when, and what to do with them when he got them there.

"Not too disappointed, I hope," he said, voice full of lazy satisfaction, with a glimmer in his eye that dared me to lie.

"Shut up. You know damn well it was incredible. Where the hell did you learn to *do* that, anyway?" I said, trying—and failing—to hold in a clichéd sigh.

He grinned. "You sure you want to know?"

Not really. The thought of him with other women, no matter how past tense, opened an ugly little hole in my ego. But I brazened it out anyway. "Sure. Names and addresses, please."

He arched a brow. "Planning to send out a hit man?"

"Nope. Thank-you cards." I winked.

When he was finished kissing my laughter away, I told him about the wedding. ". . . and the best part is, this will keep both our moms off *our* backs for a while. It'll get the wedding bug out of their systems."

Ever since our mothers had discovered Billy and I were involved, they'd been looking at us with wedding lust in their eyes. I might have tripped and fallen ass over teakettle for my best-friend-slash-nemesis-slash-honorary-cousin, but that didn't mean I was ready to marry him. I was new to this relationship stuff, and I figured proceeding with caution was the wisest course of action.

Plus, I was allergic to weddings. It was going to be hard enough for me just being Laura's maid of honor, but I could suck it up for the day.

Billy looked at me with delighted speculation. "You totally threw Thomas under the wedding bus, didn't you?"

"Well, yeah. Of course. I mean, come on, he and Laura are planning to get married anyway, whereas *we* haven't even discussed the possibility. What's the harm in providing a distraction for Mom? It won't kill Thomas to put on his big-boy tuxedo pants and make her and Auntie Mo happy."

A softer speculation shaded Billy's eyes. "Do you want to discuss it?"

"What? Getting married? *Us?* God, no."

He laughed and rolled me onto my back. "See, that might hurt my feelings if I didn't feel exactly the same way."

Jackson Gunn was still pretty well oiled when Billy and I joined him in the lounge. Guess he'd resumed hydrating as soon as he woke up from his nap. He greeted us with a billboard smile and sauntered over to the bar. While Gunn's back was turned, Billy hastily pulled a few more pieces of straw from my hair. He'd been plucking them off me ever since we'd left the barn.

Jack put two fresh glasses on the bar next to his, added ice, and poured. "So, may I assume by your early arrival that the god-awful snakes-in-a-cave scene is complete, and it's safe for me to return to the set?" He handed us amber-colored liquid on the rocks, his voice full of his legendary self-deprecating charm. Seemed like a really nice guy—I was sure Billy was wrong about his earlier suspicions—and now here I was, about to drop a bomb on his world.

I sniffed my drink cautiously before I sipped, avoiding those friendly eyes. Bourbon. I tended to prefer my bourbon in Manhattan form (because *cherries*), but plain will do in a pinch.

When I couldn't put it off any longer, I cleared my throat and said, "Well, about that, Mr. Gunn—"

"Call me Jack. As intimately as you must know me by now, I think 'Mr.' is a bit formal, don't you?" Again with the charming smile.

I forced a return smile (only a small one, out of deference to the news I had to deliver), trying hard not to think about everything I did happen to know about him. He was a tall man, but not everything was in proportion, if you get my drift. And, no, that wasn't the reason I hadn't wanted Billy to use his aura back at the trailer. Well, not the only reason.

Ack. Stop it, Ciel. Do not go there—you'll never be able to look him in the eye.

"Jack." I cleared my throat again, focusing on his top shirt button, left casually undone to show his manly chest hair. "Um, let's sit down, all right?"

He nodded agreeably and sat on the closest overstuffed leather chair. I sat across from him, in a matching chair. Billy remained standing.

"You see, there's been a . . ." I squirmed. Being the bearer of bad news *sucks.* It was the first time I'd ever had to tell someone anything like this, and I didn't like it a bit. ". . . well, what you might call a . . ." A what? Certainly not an accident. ". . . a development."

Jack's brow furrowed, and he opened his mouth to ask a question. Before he could frame it, Billy said, "Your wife is dead."

I glared at him. "Nice, Billy. Way to break it gently," I said.

Billy gave a tiny shrug, all the while staring intently at Jack's shocked face.

Jack swallowed. "What happened?"

"Um . . . well, she was . . . it appears she was, um, looks like she was . . . murdered." Yeah, that's me. Always a smooth delivery in times of stress.

"*What?* Murdered? But when . . . how . . . ? Who would . . . ?"

"It happened when I was on set, during the snake scene," I said. "Somebody shot her at your Las Vegas home. Several times. The police are still investigating, of course. They'll be contacting you at your home tomorrow—they think you're there now, recovering from the shock—so we should get you there soon."

Jack leaned forward to rest his elbows on his knees and his face on his hands. "I can't believe it. It doesn't make any sense. Who would want Angelica dead? She's—oh, God, *was*?—the sweetest, most wonderful woman in the world."

I glanced at Billy, whose face remained carefully neutral. It was the soundless crying that finally seemed to convince him. It started slowly, tears streaming down Gunn's face, no histrionics.

"Jack, I am so, so sorry," I said, laying a hand on his shoulder. I didn't know what else to say. Nothing seemed adequate, so I just patted him.

Billy put a hand on Jack's other shoulder, offering some sort of manly support. "Look, I know it's a shock, man. But we have to get you to Vegas before the police find out you didn't go where you—or rather, Ciel *as* you—told them you were going. I'll go fuel the plane while you pack."

Crap. "It's not that far to Vegas. And, um, maybe Jack doesn't like flying. Let's take the ranch car."

Jack, still looking numb, said, "I'm fine with flying, as long as there aren't any snakes on the plane. Whatever's fastest."

I sighed and went to the kitchen for some of the candied ginger I knew Rosa kept on hand. I wasn't about to risk barfing in front of my screen hero.

Chapter 5

Jackson Gunn's face was all over the TV in the corner of the fitting room. Mom had taken me to the ultra-exclusive bridal boutique as soon as I'd stumbled off the commercial flight I'd hopped in the dark, wee hours of the morning. Other than dozing fitfully in between medicinal martinis, I hadn't slept since the night before the big snake scene in L.A. The world was starting to take on a distinct air of unreality.

I still wasn't sure why I needed to be here. Mom could have easily stood in for me—as me—and had the dress fitted to her exact specifications. But that wasn't the point, she'd explained when I'd dared to suggest it. The point was, it was my brother getting married, and if his sweet fiancée was kind enough to ask me to be her maid of honor, well then I better step up to the plate and *be* her maid of honor myself. It was the right thing to do. The *honorable* thing.

Gah. The honor argument. There was no winning with Mom once she brought honor into it.

Gunn was safely inside his Las Vegas mansion. Or, rather, he had been inside until he'd walked out his front door into the suffocating embrace of the paparazzi.

"Lift your arms, dear. Judy needs to pin you," Mom said, paging rapidly through her lengthy to-do list. Short and strawberry blond, like me, she still somehow managed to convey a large presence. Her pecan-shell brown eyes dared anyone to try and look down on her.

I complied with her request, craning my neck to see the screen when Judy blocked my view. Jack was outside his luxury Las Vegas home, looking somber against the xeriscaped backdrop. "Hey, Mom, could you turn that up for me?"

"Sure, sweetie. Just a sec . . ." She checked off two items on her list and reached for the remote. "Oh, my God, that's Jackson Gunn—your father and I love his movies!"

"*Shh.* Mom, I need to see this—ouch!" Jabbed by an errant pin. I'd blame Judy, but I was the one who'd moved abruptly.

Mom gave me a look, and automatically said, "God punishes right away."

Apparently, God did not approve of shushing one's mother. I would have rolled my eyes, but I didn't want the chandelier to fall on my head.

Fortunately, Mom was distracted enough by the news story that she didn't launch into a complete lecture. "Oh, that poor, poor man. To lose his wife that way! How awful. Ciel, turn around—Judy needs to pin the back."

I twisted my body, but left my head pointing the way it was. Gunn's voice caught on the words "my wife," and he paused before continuing. For dramatic effect? Or was I being too harsh in my judgment? Even actors didn't act *all* the time, did they?

". . . and Mark is best man, naturally, so you'll have to touch base with him about a couples' shower," Mom continued. Even a Hollywood murder couldn't distract her from her mission for long. "They're so much more fun, aren't they? And, really, why should it be all about the bride—"

I pulled my focus away from the TV. "Shower? I'm supposed to throw a *shower*?"

"Of course. You're the maid of honor, aren't you?"

"Mom, there's no time!"

"Nonsense. If I—with Mo's help, naturally—can organize a whole wedding on short notice, surely you can pull off a piddling little shower. Make it Sunday at the latest, sooner would be better—"

"*This* Sunday?" I practically screeched.

"Well, of course this Sunday. *Next* Sunday is after the wedding. You can't very well have it then, can you?"

"What about Halloween? You know you like to do it up big. Do we really have time for all these parties?" I said, grasping the first straw I thought of.

"We're skipping the Haunted Halloween hoopla this year. The wedding has to take priority. Don't worry—the neighborhood kids will survive. We'll give out full-size candy bars. They'll be fine."

Well, that was good, at least. One less production to worry about attending. "But a shower? I mean, where . . . ? Food . . . drinks . . . decorations . . . for God's sake, *invitations*!"

"E-mail, sweetheart. E-mail and caterers. Make sure Mark does his part. He's your brother's best man—I'm sure he'll be *happy* to help."

"Yeah, right. Shall I also set him up for a root canal? Bet he'd love that, too," I said.

Mom narrowed one eye in warning. "Turn."

I jerked myself around, and promptly fell off the small platform

I was standing on to give Judy easier access to the hideous maid of honor dress I was wearing. (What? Yellow is *not* my color.)

"Sarcasm, sweetie. God punishes—"

"—right away. I know, I know."

I hauled myself up, preparing to launch into a million and one reasons why a couples' shower would not be a good idea, but a sudden commotion on the TV froze my tongue. The scene had switched from the grieving widower to a woman—young, hipster-ish, and highly upset—being escorted from an apartment building by two police officers. She strained toward the reporters, who were extending microphones toward her. "Listen to me, you fucking vultures"—well, the "fucking" was bleeped out, but I could read her lips—"I didn't kill my sister!"

Her emotion struck me as totally genuine. But was the emotion because she didn't do it, or was it because she got caught?

The cops hauled her to their squad car and got her into the backseat with relative ease, their stony expressions saying it was all part of the job. The hipster girl kept screaming as her long brown hair fell over her face and her big glasses slid farther down her nose.

The camera panned over to the curvy blonde covering the story. "And there you have it—Jackson Gunn's sister-in-law, Lily-Ann Conrad, suspect in the murder of her sister, Conrad Fine Foods heiress Angelica Conrad Gunn, being arrested. Lily-Ann, you may remember from a story we did last summer, was disinherited by her father after picketing against the company's inhumane treatment of chickens. You saw it first here on STUN TV. Stay tuned for breaking details."

Disinherited? Huh. Well, that was a pretty good motive for murder, I supposed. A disgruntled sibling. Still tragic, of course, but (from my standpoint, at least) not as bad as if my client had done it. I'd have to call Jackson and find out when the snake shoot would be rescheduled so I could finish the job. With a little luck, the director would have decided Sparky's performance was acceptable after all, and I could file the job away under *Finito.* If not, I'd just have to make sure it wouldn't conflict with the wedding.

Mom grabbed her purse off a nearby heart-shaped red velvet chair and kissed my cheek. "Gotta run, sweetie. Miles to go before I sleep. Mark will pick you up here in half an hour. You can make your shower plans over lunch. See you back at the house later. Toodles!"

"Wait—what? Mark is coming here?" I said, trying to stifle the growls my stomach started emitting when I heard the word "lunch." Peanuts and martinis do not make the best breakfast. I was starving.

"Yes, right after he's fitted for a new tuxedo. He said he already had one, but I think Thomas's wedding deserves something fresh, don't you? Bye!"

I sighed. I love my mom, really I do. But sometimes I wish she'd take a nice vacation to the Thousand Islands and stay a week on each one.

What can I say about Mark Fielding?

Tall, blond, and chiseled doesn't begin to cover it. CIA operative who makes James Bond look like a wimp by comparison? Getting a little warmer. (Much like I do whenever he's near.)

The sad fact is, I've been crushing on my big brother's best friend ever since adolescence shanghaied me when I was thirteen. You know those arrows Cupid likes to shoot at the hearts of unsuspecting idiots? Well, where Mark was concerned, that rotten little cherub had zapped me with a thunderbolt. Only his aim was a little low. (Yeah, about those hormones . . .)

The thing was, now that my hormones—and, I strongly suspected, my heart—were engaged elsewhere, it still gave me a jolt when I saw him. It was disconcerting, but I was learning to deal with it. In fact, I barely even noticed it anymore.

Until he smiled at me.

"Hey, Howdy," he said, and dropped a kiss on the top of my head. (Howdy from *Howdy Doody,* which Mark picked up from my grandfather. Have I mentioned my freckles?)

Gah. I was going to have to get myself back to Billy, pronto. I hardly ever thought about Mark anymore when I was with Billy. That was progress, right?

"I see work doesn't prepare you for the really challenging stuff, like eluding my mother," I said, hiding behind wryness.

He chuckled, a gravelly, sexier-than-hell sound that vibrated right through me. "Sometimes you have to take one for the team. Besides, as much as your brother loves complaining about the fuss, I suspect he's halfway looking forward to the wedding. And I know Laura is."

Laura was a CIA spook, like Mark, and had worked many assignments with him. Things had been a little tense between Mark and Thomas for a while after Laura gave up law school to join the Agency, but they'd since come to an understanding.

"Is she? Really? Because I'd hate for her to feel railroaded into anything. Mom can be . . . well, Mom."

"Don't worry. Laura is crazy about your mother, and willing to do anything to start off on the right foot with her future mother-in-law. But I suspect it's more than that, even. A big wedding might not be her thing, exactly, but I think she's thriving on the motherly attention."

"Huh. She can have my share, too, if she wants. Lord knows I have an overabundance of it."

Mark smiled. (Yeah, I melted. Sue me.) "You'd miss it," he said.

I quirked my mouth, but didn't disagree.

"Anyway," he continued, "you don't think Tom would really allow this to go on if he didn't know Laura wanted it, do you?"

I sighed. "I suppose not. And if he can put up with it, I guess we'll have to, too." Especially since the whole thing was my fault, but no need to go into that with Mark.

After a productive lunch at my favorite dive of a deli, Mark dropped me at my childhood home, an Upper West Side brownstone still occupied by my parents. The place was way bigger than they needed now that my three brothers and I no longer lived there, but they'd never leave. They were too attached to it. My dad liked to tease us about the bodies buried in the basement—the kids they'd had before us, the ones who hadn't worked out. We were pretty sure he was kidding.

Mark and I had hammered out a crude party plan. Like the wedding, the shower would be held in D.C., since that was where both Thomas and Laura worked, and most of the friends they had in common lived there. Mom had tried to convince them to get married in Central Park with the old "It's so beautiful in the fall!" argument, but Thomas had balked, and Mom had wisely given in. Like any good tactician, she knew how to choose her battles.

Between bites of a huge Reuben (with a side of greasy fries and a giant kosher dill) I'd called the lovely Thai restaurant that occupied the bottom floor of Thomas's office building in downtown D.C. The owner had assured me that he'd be happy to provide the party space, and that the food would be his gift to the happy couple. (Thomas was apparently a really great landlord.) *Score!* Cross that off my list.

Mark would see to it that Thomas's lawyer friends were invited—

and that they *would* attend. My job was to get a list of Laura's non-Agency friends and send them e-vites, offering them whatever bribes I deemed necessary to convince them to show up on such short notice. As for her friends at the Agency . . . well, most of them were unreachable, being on assignments all over the globe, but Mark would see what he could do.

"Ciel!" Laura met me in the entry hall, enveloping me in a huge hug. My brother's fiancée and I had met not that long before, when she had been helping Mark rescue one of my clients (and, okay, me) from a neo-Viking terrorist group in Sweden. As much as I abhorred weddings in general, I was flattered she thought enough of me to want me in hers.

"I'm so sorry to do this to you, sugar," she whispered, her low-pitched Southern accent honey to the ears. "But thank you. It means the world to me."

"Are you kidding? I'd walk over hot coals to have a sister like you. A wedding can't be much worse than that," I teased, adding, "though an Aurora Halligan production might come close," as Mom joined us.

"You mind your manners, missy," Mom said, giving me a swat on the rear. Sometimes God wasn't fast enough on the draw for her.

"You sure you know what you're getting yourself into with this family, Laura? Your life will never be the same," I said, putting as much dire warning into my voice as I dared while within reach of my mother.

Laura's forest green eyes sparkled, looking at home in a beautiful face surrounded by auburn curls. Her hair had been short and black last time I'd seen her, altered for some job or another. She wasn't an adaptor, and so had to disguise herself the old-fashioned way.

"I'm counting on it," she said, smiling at my mother, who ate it up.

"Come on, you two, we have tons to decide—" Mom started.

"Ciel!" Molly's shriek arrived seconds before I found my arms full of wiggly ten-year-old girl.

"Hey, Molls," I said, nearly dropping her as I spun her around. "Geez, girl, have you been growing again?"

"Uh-huh. I'm having a spurt. Bet I'll be taller than you by Christmas!"

I didn't doubt it in the least. Doyles tended toward tall, and Molly was a Doyle through and through. She was Billy's baby sister—another of my honorary cousins—and looked just like him, other than being much shorter, having longer hair, and not sporting the occasional sexy five o'clock shadow.

"You're setting the bar kind of low there, kid. I won't be impressed until you're taller than your brother."

"That might take a little longer," she said with a giggle. Molly-giggles are infectious, so naturally the rest of us joined in. "Hey, guess what? I'm going to be a junior bridesmaid! Isn't that cool?"

I glanced at Laura, who confirmed with a smile.

"The coolest, kiddo," I said. "You can be my date at the wedding."

"I don't think Billy would like that. Anyway, I already have a date—Brian."

Brian was the youngest of my brothers, only a year older than me.

"You're rejecting me for that no-good wastrel? I can't believe it," I said, rolling my eyes dramatically.

"Don't talk about your brother that way," Mom said. "God punishes—"

"Right way!" Molly finished for her, then turned to me with a shrug. "I have to go with Brian. He's my new boyfriend."

"Does your mom know about this? I can't picture Auntie Mo approving of you dating a musician," I said.

"She doesn't care, as long as he doesn't charge her for my music lessons. Anyway, I'm not allowed to date for real until I'm sixteen. He's just my boyfriend."

Mom clapped her hands. "All right, come on everyone. Into the study. We have decisions to make. Music! Flowers! Seating arrangements! We are going to spend some of that money my eldest has been hoarding for the last decade. Laura, honey, whatever you say goes. Don't worry, Thomas can afford it. Even if he couldn't, Patrick and I would cover it. So, about venues. I've been researching what's available in the D.C. area . . ."

I hooked my arm through Laura's, and we followed Mom. "It's not too late. You can still save yourself," I whispered.

"I heard that, Ciel Halligan!" Mom called over her shoulder. "You better take notes, because you're next."

Chapter 6

I took that as my cue to leave and surreptitiously texted an SOS to Billy. If I didn't escape soon, Mom might get it into her head to make it a double wedding.

He called within five minutes, pretending to be an important client who needed my attention immediately. In those five minutes I (quite efficiently, I thought) filled Mom and Laura in on the when and whereabouts of the shower, got an assurance from Laura that she'd e-mail me her friends' contact info ASAP, and warned Molly to let Brian down easy when the time came for her to dump him. She solemnly vowed she would, but with a shine in her eyes that told me she wasn't taking anything too seriously.

After assuring Mom that I'd be there for my final dress fitting (ugh), I rushed out, barely containing my sigh of relief until I got the door closed behind me. Wedding planning made my eyeballs itch.

Once I was safely down the block, I called Billy back. "You got me out just in time—thanks. Any longer and my head would have exploded. Molly's a junior bridesmaid, by the way. You sure you haven't been roped into anything yet? Groomsman? Usher?"

"Nope. It helps to know when not to answer your phone."

"You always were the brilliant one. So, have you been watching the news? Looks like Jack's sister-in-law might be the culprit."

"I saw. Apparently she disagrees with that assessment."

"Yeah, and she seems sincere, too. Then again, she would, wouldn't she? What's she going to say? 'Oops, caught me—my bad'? It's all so sordid. I can't help hoping they find out it was one of those awful home invasion things you read about, and has nothing to do with my client *or* his family."

"It'll probably turn out to be exactly that. Try not to worry about it," Billy said.

"Believe me, I'm trying. I have enough to stress about with the wedding. Ugh. Hey, I'm heading over to your place to hide out until I can catch a train home. Please tell me you're there."

"Nope, I'm still in the land of sin. There's a job of my own I have to finish. I have a feeling Mark will be calling me in to sub for him very soon, and I want to be available."

"He didn't ask you to fill in for him at the wedding, did he? Because I was going to do that," I said. Kidding, of course. Billy would be expected to be at the wedding himself. Not that familial expectations had ever ruled his behavior.

Billy laughed, but didn't elaborate.

"Wait a minute . . . *are* you filling in for him?" That would explain why Mark didn't seem overly concerned about the wedding disrupting his work—it wouldn't.

"Shouldn't take me long to wrap things up here. I can maybe meet you at your condo tomorrow."

"Don't change the subject," I said.

"Plausible deniability, cuz. If Mommo"—Billy's name for Auntie Mo, a mashup of "Mom" and "Mo" he'd come up with as a toddler—"asks where I am, you can tell her truthfully that you don't know. Because you won't."

Maybe not technically, but I had a pretty good idea. "She'll sniff you out and you know it."

More laughter, a sound that made happiness bubble up inside me in spite of irritation at his impending ditchery. "A risk I'll have to take, if it comes to it. And it's still only an 'if' at this point, so buck up. There's every possibility I'll be there to ravish you in your wedding finery. I might even have a surprise for you."

"A surprise? Tell!"

"It wouldn't be a surprise, then, would it? You just focus on me ravishing you for now."

"Yeah, well, you might want to hold that thought until after you see my dress. It's *yellow.*" I didn't try to disguise the disgust in my voice.

"Okay, I'll take it off you first. We can burn it if you like. Toast marshmallows over it."

I laughed and hung up.

I stumbled into my condo after midnight, still groggy from my snooze on the train. I hate sleeping on public transportation—I'm always afraid my mouth will fall open and I'll drool all over myself—but it couldn't be helped. My eyes had refused to stay open. Since my shirt was dry when we pulled into Union Station, I was going to assume I hadn't embarrassed myself in front of my fellow passengers.

Home sweet home. The condo was as clean as I'd left it—in other words, not very. But it was my clutter, and nothing about it set off alarms in my head. I dropped my small suitcase at the foot of the stairs and made a beeline for the kitchen. I'd ordered a large pizza the night before I'd left for Hollywood—what was that? Three days ago now?—and I was hoping the leftovers weren't too stale.

Luck was with me—there were no science experiments unfolding amid the slices, and the crust wasn't quite hard enough to hammer nails with, so I maybe wouldn't break my teeth. There was even an imported beer left from the last time Thomas had stopped by for dinner—he always brought the good stuff.

My feast set, I turned on the TV and flipped to a cable infotainment "news" show. The Jackson Gunn story was still going strong. Lily-Ann Conrad, now L.A.'s most notorious murder suspect, had retained a lawyer. Not only *a* lawyer, but *the* lawyer of the celebrity set: Nigel Overholt. I recognized him right away because he'd worked for Thomas for a while after he graduated from law school. Thomas was always bragging about how smart his former protégé was.

In his early thirties, blessed with stunningly good looks from his Italian mother's side of the family, Overholt might have graced the silver screen himself had he not been confined to a wheelchair. He'd tried to hang glide off the Hollywood sign when he was twenty-two, and had landed badly. But he hadn't let the failure of his attention-grabbing stunt stop him from becoming one of the biggest names in Tinseltown, if not precisely in the way he had originally intended. That was probably why he was so good at his job—he never accepted defeat.

And now he was working for Lily-Ann Conrad. Hmm. Interesting. I wondered what Jack thought about that. Heck, maybe he'd hired Overholt for her—he certainly had enough Hollywood clout to attract the guy. I still had to call him to find out if we had to reschedule the snake shoot—maybe I could feel him out about it then.

Not that it was technically any of my concern. (Not that *that* has ever stopped me from being nosy, especially where my clients are concerned. Sue me. I'm a curious person.)

My cell phone rang. I picked it up without pulling my eyes away from the TV screen, where Nigel was raising one of those nifty specialized wheelchairs to a standing position. Tall guy.

"Ciel? Sorry to call so late, but I thought you should know—"

"Dave? What's up? Is something wrong? Oh, my God, is Eeyore all right?" I said, visions blowing up in my head of my beloved pony cut and bleeding from hoof strikes. Trigger and Licorice didn't always exhibit a great deal of patience with their smaller stablemate. Granted, Eeyore was as big an asshole to them as he was to people, so he probably deserved whatever equine punishment they doled out. Still, he was a little guy, and I didn't want to see him hurt.

"Eeyore is fine—as nasty as ever, and I have a new bruise on my rear end to prove it." Dave sounded resigned. I felt a little guilty about that, but not enough to rehome Eeyore. Not that any clear-thinking person would take him. "But," he continued, "I did find something interesting in his stall."

"What, a poison apple?" I said wryly. "Billy's been looking at him funny lately."

"Nope. A gun."

Well, crap. "I don't suppose it's Cody's?" I said without much hope.

"Nope again. First thing I checked. I asked Rosa about it, too. She about took my head off for daring to suggest she might own a gun, or that if she *did* own a gun, she would be so careless as to leave it in the barn."

"Any other visitors hanging around since you last cleaned Eeyore's stall?"

"You and Billy. And, of course, Mr. Gunn. But I know for a fact it can't be his—I unpacked his luggage for him myself when he got here. And his clothes were too tight for him to be carrying concealed." Dave coughed. "Not that I'd normally notice a thing like that, but Rosa's eyes got so big when she looked at him that it kind of brought it to my attention."

I bit my tongue. I'd hate to disillusion Rosa, but I knew for a fact that, metaphorically speaking at least, Gunn was packing a derringer. And maybe a few socks.

"Okay. I'll call Billy and see if by chance he dropped it while trying to assassinate Eeyore. What kind of gun is it?"

"It's a Walther PPK—you know, a James Bond gun."

The movie tie-in made my ears perk up. If anyone had a James Bond gun, it would be Jackson. I said as much to Dave.

"Yeah, that was my first thought, but like I said, I unpacked for him. Besides, it's a very popular pistol, especially with the concealed-carry set."

"But who else has been out to the ranch?"

"Well, there's the delivery people, I suppose. Groceries, hay, oats . . ." he said.

"Maybe you could call them tomorrow and ask if anyone might've dropped it."

"Will do. In the meantime, I wrapped it in plastic and put it in a drawer in the kitchen. Rosa's not too happy about that, but I told her we couldn't very well leave it in the barn."

"Why not the safe?"

"No room. Rosa's keeping all her secret family recipes in there. Damn, that woman has a *lot* of secret recipes. No wonder I'm suffering from Dunlop's."

I tried to think of what to tell him to do. I mean, a stray gun in Eeyore's stall couldn't be a good thing, but I sure didn't want to get the local cops involved. If they found out Jackson had been a guest at my ranch while he was supposedly in Hollywood filming, that would lead to all kinds of awkward questions. "Look, leave it where it is for now. I'll call you tomorrow and we'll figure out what to do about it."

As soon as I hung up I dialed Billy. Got routed directly to voice mail, left a message to call me right away, and crawled upstairs to bed. Thomas's imported beer was hitting my overtaxed brain cells and all I wanted to do was sleep.

Chapter 7

I woke to the sound of pans clanging in the kitchen. I would have been scared of a break-in, but no competent burglar made that much noise. It had to be somebody I knew.

I stumbled down the stairs, eyes half shut, still in my clothes from the night before. Changing into a nightgown had seemed like too much trouble. I ran my tongue over my teeth—my mouth tasted of stale beer and old pizza. Bleah. Apparently my usual dental hygiene routine had been beyond me, too.

I was flanked as soon as I walked into the kitchen. "Group hug!" poured into one of my ears at the same time as "It's been too long!" flowed into the other.

Sinead and Siobhan, Billy's middle sisters, who had two of the most mellifluous voices on the planet. Sometimes it was hard to listen to what they were saying because it just *sounded* so pretty.

Sinead was three years younger than Billy, and Siobhan a year younger than her. Both were still in college, and everyone who didn't know them thought they were twins. They each had the amazing Doyle eyes, which, like Billy and Molly, they'd inherited from their father. (Uncle Liam must have some powerful eye genes, is all I can say.) Their hair, long and wavy, was a light chestnut color. I suspected they got their hair coloring from their mother, though I couldn't be sure since Auntie Mo liked to appear to the world with the vibrant red hair and emerald eyes that made her resemble a young Maureen O'Hara even more than she already did.

I automatically wrapped my arms around their waists and squeezed back, trying to keep my nose clear of their chests so I could breathe. Like I said, Doyles are tall. They each had six inches on me even when they were barefoot. When they wore heels, I was a hut between towers.

"Why the hell are you here?" I blurted after they disengaged. (Perhaps not the most gracious thing a hostess can say to her guests, but it was the best I could manage in my un-caffeinated state.)

Siobhan lilted a laugh and went straight for the fancy espresso maker Thomas had left here when he'd moved on to greener pastures. She knew me well.

Sinead, always perky in the morning, said, "Not exactly our idea, shrimperooni"—Sinead was a teaser, like her brother—"but you know how it is. Auntie Ro hinted to Mom that you could use some help with this shower thing for Tom and . . . Laura, is it? Might be nice to actually meet her before the wedding. Anyway, Mom passed it along to us, and we volunteered."

"More like we were 'voluntold,' but let's not quibble," Siobhan said, and I understood completely. Our mothers' hints were not easily ignored.

"But don't you have class or something?" I asked. Granted, I was a little groggy, but I was fairly sure it wasn't any kind of holiday.

"Yeah. So? Professors don't care if you don't show up to class as long as you pass the tests," Sinead said.

"That's right. And the tests are easy if you're careful to only pick professors who care about their image on Rate Your Professor dot com," Siobhan added.

I quirked my mouth. "Don't tell me, let me guess. A little tip you picked up from Billy?"

They nodded in unison, their adoration of their brother evident by the glow in their eyes.

Then it hit me. "Shit," I said, and dug my cell phone out of my jeans pocket, where I'd left it the night before when I'd fallen into bed. Had I slept through his return call?

I scrolled quickly through a ton of wedding-related reminders from Mom until I got to Billy. Punched a few buttons and listened to him say, "Tag. You're it. I'm exhausted, lying facedown in bed. Wish you were under me." I called him and got his voice mail again. Swore.

"Oooh, that's my all-time favorite," Siobhan said as she waved a mug under my nose. "I'm a fan of strong, single-syllable Anglo-Saxon words. So expressive."

I grabbed the mug, blew across it to cool it faster, and gulped. Repeated Siobhan's favorite word after burning my tongue.

"Careful, it's hot," Sinead said. "Don't tell, let me guess. Billy."

I sighed. "Phone tag. And I can't even blame him for not answering, because I did the same thing to him last night. Slept right through his return call."

Siobhan leaned against the counter next to me and shrugged. "Don't worry. He'll call back soon. It's not as if he's avoiding *your* calls. It's Mom he's hiding from—and by extension, the two of us, because he knows we're forced to be her loyal minions until we don't need her to write tuition checks anymore. He doesn't want to be roped into any wedding duty."

That was true enough. He'd even admitted it to me. But what was he doing that had him so exhausted? He hadn't gone into detail about his side job.

Well, no sense worrying about it until I had a chance to talk to him. "Yeah, you're right. Listen, as long as you guys are here to help . . ."

I hopped the first available flight to Vegas, white-knuckling it the whole way, and rented a car at McCarran Airport. I'd hoped to catch Billy before he left Vegas, to see if he could stop by the ranch and check the gun out for me, but I still hadn't managed to connect with him. Our voice messages kept crossing in the ether. Just as well. My ranch, my responsibility. I couldn't leave Dave hanging there—it wasn't right.

Sinead and Siobhan were back at my condo, diligently going through all the contact info Laura had e-mailed me. Being dedicated web geeks, they had promised to design and send awesome wedding shower e-vites to everyone on the list, and possibly to set up a remote webcam viewing station at the restaurant for those who couldn't make it to D.C. in time to be there in person. They were even going to take care of the decorations. All I had to do in exchange was promise to get Thomas to introduce them to some of his hot lawyer buddies. (Thomas had thus far refused to do so himself, having an ironically low opinion of the species.)

About ten miles out from the ranch my cell phone played the first tongue-clicking notes of Billy Joel's "The Ballad of Billy the Kid." They sounded like hoofbeats, and indicated Billy was on the line. (He'd loaded the ringtone onto my phone himself when I wasn't looking, along with a bunch of others. I never knew which

Billy-related song would provide the ringtone when he called—he'd figured out a way to randomize them.)

I pulled to the side of the road before I answered, not out of an abundance of caution (I mean, the road was deserted) but because I'd sworn to my mother—on the urn holding my great-grandmother's ashes, no less—that I would never text or talk on my phone while driving. I was pretty sure breaking that kind of vow would result, at the very least, in a comet crashing through the top of the car (God punishing right away and all), and I didn't want to have to explain that to the rental company.

"Where *are* you?" I said, probably not as patiently as I could have.

"Hello, sweetheart. I love you, too," Billy said, laughter in his voice.

My stomach fluttered at his words. He'd only ever said them in a joking manner so far—never seriously—and I wasn't quite sure how to respond. So I deflected. "Yeah, right. Kiss-kiss. *Where?*"

"I'm at the airport, waiting for you. Your last text said you were heading this way. Where are *you*?"

"Wait a second. You didn't get my 'fuck this shit, I'm leaving' text?"

"Nope."

Crap. Who did I send it to? Please not Mom, please not Mom, please not Mom . . .

I checked my message log. *Shit.*

"Never mind. I'm almost to the ranch. Dave found a gun in Eeyore's stall. You didn't happen to leave it there, hoping he'd shoot himself, did you? You do realize he doesn't have opposable thumbs?"

"Ha ha. But nope. Not me. If I were planning to do away with the little bastard, I'd poison his oats. He doesn't deserve a fast death."

"Bill-ee . . ."

"Kidding, cuz. I'd never harm a hair on your darling's head, you know that. You'd never sleep with me again if I did."

"That's *right,* and don't you forget it. So, where are you heading?"

"Back to the ranch, apparently, to help you solve the mystery of the magically appearing gun. Shouldn't take long—I'm already fueled. By the way, how was your flight?"

I grunted and hung up.

"How many of you have touched it since you found it?" I asked, referring to the plastic-wrapped pistol on the counter.

Dave looked sheepish. "Me. Of course. I found it. I had to get it out of the stall before Eeyore kicked it to pieces."

"And?"

He gestured toward the guy next to him. Cody was tall, and whipcord thin. According to his employment records, he was twenty-eight, but his years spent outside in the harsh Arizona sun made him look older.

"I had to show it to him to see if it was his. He might've held it for a while . . ."

Cody ran a hand through thick, light brown hair. "I checked to see if it was loaded. It was empty. Listen, Ciel, I'm sorry this happened. I should've—"

"Don't be silly, Cody. You can't be everywhere at once. Besides, why would any of you expect anything like this when there's not even a client here? Now, did anyone else touch the gun?"

"Well, Rosa pulled it out of the drawer—she wanted me to get it out of her kitchen—but I'd already wrapped it in plastic by then, so I don't think she counts."

Rosa gave him a scorching look and waved a spatula threateningly. "What was I supposed to do? A gun does not belong with my utensils."

I stepped casually between the two of them. I didn't think she'd hit him on purpose, but when she got excited her arms sometimes took on a life of their own. "So only you and Cody got prints on it. And whoever left it in Eeyore's stall. If they didn't wipe it clean first, of course," I said.

"Yeah, I expect so. I just can't figure who would do a fool thing like that," Dave said.

"You got me," I said. "Why don't you show me exactly where it was in the barn?"

"Sure thing, honeybunch," Dave said with an understanding smile. He knew the real reason I wanted to go to the barn—I had to see for myself that Eeyore was okay. Poor little guy was probably upset at having his routine disrupted.

Rosa elected to stay behind and work on dinner. "I don't want my nose contaminated by the aroma of horse excrement when I'm cooking." She shook the spatula at all of us. "You don't want that either."

Dave chuckled. "Aw, admit it, Rosa. You're afraid of the little feller."

Rosa expelled a stream of Spanish, ending with what sounded like "*diablo culo de morderse,*" which I was pretty sure meant "ass-biting devil."

Um, yeah. Couldn't exactly contradict her on that. When I'd first moved Eeyore to the Circle C, I'd had the bright idea of letting him roam freely around the place, like a big, shaggy gray dog. He'd figured out how to open the back door to the kitchen and had nipped Rosa a good one while she was checking the corn bread in the oven. (I still contend he was being playful, but Rosa didn't see it that way.)

Turned out Eeyore *was* upset, and with much better reason than his default mode of annoyance with life in general. There was a sack over his head, a rope around his neck, and a strange man stomping from one corner of his stall to the next, kicking through the straw, yanking Eeyore along with him.

"What the hell are you *doing*?" I hollered as I ran toward them, Dave and Cody right behind me. Jesus, what was going on? Maybe I needed to increase my security here. Get Cody an assistant or something, because the ranch was obviously way too accessible.

The man—middle-aged, roughly groomed, and decidedly stupid-looking—assessed his situation, his eyes pausing briefly on each of us. It was like Bluto from the old Popeye cartoons had come to life. You could almost see him counting on mental fingers and figuring out he was outnumbered. But instead of making up some lie about why he was there, as any rational human being would, he pulled a switchblade from his pocket, popped it open, and held it to my beloved pony's throat.

I skidded to a halt, flinging my arms wide to stop Dave and Cody. I took each of them by a wrist and held them back. (Okay, I might have been holding myself upright at the same time. I can multitask.)

Dave spoke first (I was still gasping), temporarily forgetting his cowboy dialect. "Wait a minute. Why don't you let the pony go and we'll talk about this. What are you looking for?" As if we didn't know. "Maybe we can help you find it."

"Stand back or the pony gets it!" the man said, his gruff voice making the ridiculous words sound menacing.

Kick him, Eeyore! Kick. Him. Now.

For once in his cantankerous life, Eeyore stood still. The bag over his head must have been inhibiting his natural impulses.

I swallowed hard and found my voice. "All right, mister. Stay calm. Nobody's going near you." I spared a nanosecond to glance at Dave and Cody, making sure they were listening. "What can we do for you?"

"You can give me the gun that was supposed to be here, that's what you can do," he said, eyes getting wilder.

"What gun is that?" I asked, squeezing both the guys' wrists. They got the message and kept their mouths shut.

"The goddamn gun that was supposed to be here, that's what gun!"

Eeyore took exception to the man's tone and tried to rear up, only to be yanked—harshly—back down by the rope.

I reached for him reflexively, but halted when Bluto pressed the blade harder against Eeyore's neck. The thin cloth of the sack wasn't going to offer any protection against cold, sharp steel. I tried desperately to think of a way, *any* way to get that knife away from my pony's throat. We weren't close enough to rush the guy, even if the wall of the stall hadn't been blocking us.

"Um, why don't we help you look for it?" I said, keeping my voice reasonable. Mostly. It didn't squeak, anyway. "It's obvious the gun is important to you—maybe a gift from someone special?—and you need it back." There. If he wasn't bright enough to think of his own damn lie, I'd do it for him. Give him a credible out, and maybe he'd leave quietly. "You probably have a good reason to suspect whoever, um, stole it from you took it here. Once we find it, you can be on your way."

His mouth drooped open while he considered what I said.

Come on, you idiot. Take the opening and run.

"Uh . . . yeah," he finally said, a dim bulb lighting behind his eyes. "That's it. The gun is special. It was a present from my, uh, girlfriend. For my birthday—"

That's it, Bluto. Come on, you can do it! Now let go of my pony.

"—and her asshole ex-boyfriend, he stole it and headed this way. He called her to, um, rub it in and told her since she was into tiny things—he's a shit-face asshole jerk, is what he is, and he don't know from tiny, the pencil-dick—he told her she may as well give her present to a pony as to me. Right, like *he* was some kind of stallion."

Boy, when he took an opening, he really ran with it.

He seemed quite pleased with his embellishment of the story I'd started for him. I nodded my sympathetic understanding and kept squeezing. If I hadn't been so terrified for Eeyore it would have been tough to hold my laughter in check.

Dave pried my fingers gently from his wrist and said, "Damn, that's cold. I feel for you, buddy." He looked at me, his eyes telling me to go along with him, and then continued. "You know, I shoveled a bunch of muck out of that stall this morning. Maybe the gun was in the mess? The pile is outside, over by the corral. Why don't we go look?"

I let go of Cody, who said, "Good idea. I'll get a shovel."

The man stiffened. "Wait!" He still held the knife to Eeyore. The rest of us froze. "You go get the shovel, girly. You other two—you stay where I can see you."

I nodded. "Sure thing. Um, meet you out by the pile?" I said. With any luck, he'd leave Eeyore in the stall.

Apparently he wasn't as dumb as he looked. He took Eeyore with him, knife to throat, making sure Dave and Cody were in front of him the whole way. Even newly armed with the shovel, there was nothing I could do that wouldn't allow him time to plunge the knife into Eeyore's throat—not a risk I was willing to take.

The aromatic pile of dung and straw was percolating in the sun next to the new three-bin composting system Dave was hot to start using. I'd been hesitant to make the investment (feeling as I did that other things—say, like eating—were more important), but Dave insisted it was the green thing to do, and would pay for itself—eventually—when we started selling the finished, soil-like product to gardeners. Billy thought we should call it "Cielie-Poo." (Uh-huh, the origin of his new endearment for me.) Dave was lobbying for "Roses Are Red, Violets Are Blue, But If You Want Them to Grow, You Need This Poo." Which, granted, was a bit long, but Dave said we could always abbreviate it as "U-Need-This Poo."

Right now I needed something, that was for sure. Maybe the poo was it. It wasn't like it hadn't worked to get me out of a tight spot before, as about a hundred neo-Vikings could testify to. But I'd been told lightning doesn't strike the same spot twice, so I wasn't going to count on it.

I started poking at the pile gingerly, keeping a wary eye on Bluto.

"Hurry it up, girly. I ain't got all day."

I shoveled faster, turning over big globs of straw and manure, not really paying attention because, of course, I already knew the gun wasn't there. As I was lifting a particularly fresh bunch of horse hockey I heard a plane overhead.

Billy.

Everyone looked up, including me. Bluto didn't like it. "Hurry the fuck up! You two, start digging—hey, where the hell do you think you're going?"

Cody stopped. "To get more shovels."

"Forget it. Use your hands. Dig!"

Dave sighed. They both reached for the pile as Billy circled around. I dropped the shovel and threw my arms up in an I-give-up gesture, hoping Billy could see me.

"Listen, mister, I don't think the gun is here." I waved an arm, broadly, over the pile. For all this guy knew, I was a heavy gesticulator. "Maybe we should check the other stalls first"—I swung my other arm toward the barn—"because maybe the ex-boyfriend threw the gun in the wrong one," I said, my voice growing louder with the approach of the plane.

Bluto glanced upward, looking edgier by the minute. "You're not done here—keep digging!"

Billy flew by, heading toward the landing strip. Damn it. I'd been trying to wave him off. No telling what this maniac might do if he thought he'd be outnumbered even more. He'd have plenty of time to do major damage before Billy could land and run to us.

But Billy didn't land—he flew higher, banked steeply to the left, and came back toward us, coming in lower and lower the closer he got.

What the hell?

The plane buzzed by, probably not close enough to reach up and touch, but it sure felt that way.

I dove to the ground, followed by Cody and Dave. (Sure, the plane was already past us by then, but it's hard to stop a reflex.) Bluto tried to duck, but Eeyore, panicked into action at last, reared up, clocking Bluto's jaw with the top of his rock-hard skull. Bluto fell backward, letting go of the rope.

Eeyore, unrestrained at last, ran in circles, bucking, tossing his head until the sack came off. I pushed myself up from the ground. Dave and Cody did likewise. We all looked at each other, mentally divvying up what to do next. The pair of them made a beeline for Bluto, leaving me to cautiously approach my wild-eyed pony. Guess a crazy man armed with a twelve-inch switchblade was less intimidating than a disgruntled Shetland pony.

"Hey, sweet boy," I said softly, extending my hand toward Eeyore. "It's me. You're okay now."

Eeyore snorted twice, stamped his foot, and trotted to where Dave was bent over the semiconscious Bluto.

"Heads up!" I hollered.

Eeyore stretched out his neck and bit Dave.

Dave straightened—fast—and grabbed his ass. "Goldarn it!"

Chapter 8

Dave was sprawled on the cowhide sofa in the lounge, belly down and quietly moaning, bag of ice melting on his butt. (Yeah, I know. Cowhide. Brown and white and hairy. But it came with the place when I bought it. I'd been planning to redecorate when my finances got healthier, but now I wasn't so sure. It was kind of growing on me. I'd even given it a name: Elsie the Cowch.)

Rosa hovered over Dave, her face a mixture of sympathy and see-I-told-you-so. "Two inches lower and the tiny demon would have turned you into a woman. What would you have done then, huh?" she said.

"Become a lesbian," Dave said without missing a beat, and groaned when Rosa replaced the ice bag with a new one, none too gently.

Billy and Cody laughed while I apologized for the umpteenth time. "I'm so sorry, Dave. I thought he was going for Bluto."

Not that I could have stopped him anyway. Eeyore was fast when he wanted to be. He was safely back in his stall, munching on an extra helping of oats. The trauma of being a hostage hadn't dampened his appetite one bit.

We'd all taken to calling the guy currently duct-taped to a chair in the pantry "Bluto" because he refused to tell us his real name. Billy had checked him for ID, but came up empty.

Dave waved aside my apology. "That's okay, darlin'. The bruise will match the one on the other cheek."

"HEY! LET ME OUT OF HERE!" Bluto's voice blasted us. Again. And then kept on going until I covered my ears in frustration.

"You should've let me tape his mouth, too," Billy said from behind me. He was standing behind the leather chair I was sitting cross-legged on, massaging my shoulders. Guess I looked tense.

I looked up over my shoulder at him. "With a beard like his? That would be cruel. Duct-taping his arms and legs was bad enough."

"Cuz, the man threatened to kill your pet pony. Would a little cruelty really be out of line?"

"What do you care? You don't even like Eeyore."

He leaned over the top of the chair and kissed my nose. "No, but I like *you*. And you, for some inexplicable reason, are fond of that hoofed hellspawn. Therefore, I'm willing to be cruel on your behalf. That's just the kind of guy I am."

Even upside down, Billy's eyes were amazing. I used to think it was only because they were gorgeous (I mean, what's not gorgeous about big, dark blue, black-lashed man-eyes?), but now I thought there was more to it. Whether it was with a spark of mischief, a glint of amusement, or an ember of passion, they always glowed with life, and promised things Billy was very good at delivering.

"I could gag him with a napkin," Cody said helpfully, interrupting my reverie before I fell too deeply into the indigo-orb ocean. *Damn, girl. You have it bad.*

Rosa shook her head once, emphatically. "No. You will not put one of my good napkins into the mouth of that—"

She continued in Spanish, something along the lines of "knife-wielding, pony-threatening pig," if I caught it correctly. Not that she cared for Eeyore any more than the others did, but the pony was part of her household, and *nobody* threatened anyone in Rosa's household. Well, except Rosa. Naturally.

Cody pulled a faded, sweat-stained bandana from his neck. "I suppose I could use this."

I wrinkled my nose. "Ew, gross."

"I know what you mean. I don't like the idea of his spit getting on my favorite bandana either."

Not exactly what I was referring to, but okay.

A loud thumping noise was added to the hollering.

"What's he doing now? Is he kicking the door?" I asked.

"He can't be, not with his arms and legs taped," Billy said.

Cody nodded. "Though I suppose he could be using his head."

Rosa rushed out of the room. "*Madre de Dios,* if he has dented my pantry door with his big fat coconut of a head . . ."

"I'll keep an eye on things," Cody said, and followed her at a more sedate pace.

"Maybe we better let him out," I said, watching them go. I wasn't too worried. Even without Cody and duct tape, I'd put my money on Rosa.

"Nah. Let him stew a little longer. It'll make him more amenable to answering our questions next go-round," Billy said.

Our prisoner hadn't been at all cooperative so far. Billy had hinted that if the rest of us left him alone with Bluto for a few minutes, the man would tell us anything we wanted to know. I'd vetoed it firmly at the time, but was beginning to reconsider. He was one annoyingly loud son of a bitch.

"Can you make him shut the hell up?" I asked.

Billy nodded. "Easily."

"Without bloodshed or bruises?" I added.

He tilted his head and considered. "Well, no bruises where they would show."

I sighed. "Let him holler."

Bluto's volume increased by a few decibels, then stopped abruptly on the heels of a loud *thwack* and a stream of Spanish.

Over on the couch, Dave's eyes got big. "Holy guacamole. That's some pretty bad language, even for Rosa in a temper."

Resigned, I got up and headed for the kitchen along with Billy. Dave hauled himself up and limped along behind us, holding the ice pack to his backside.

The door to the large, walk-in pantry was open, but blocked by Rosa. Cody leaned against the colorfully tiled kitchen island, watching intently, with a smile on his face, as the housekeeper hit Bluto over the head with a spatula, apparently not for the first time.

"Ouch! That hurts! Hey, somebody make the bitch sto—OUCH!"

Rosa, still holding the spatula, yanked open a nearby drawer and grabbed a heavy metal meat tenderizer. She held it up in front of his face and said, "You *saco de mierda,* you better shut your mouth, or next time I will use *this* on your useless head. Do you understand me?"

"Anybody want to tell me what's going on?" A new voice came from behind us.

Mark.

He was standing right beyond the large dining room table (the kitchen was open to the dining area, separated only by the island).

"What are *you* doing here?" I asked.

Cody raised one hand about halfway up, looking guilty. "I contacted him after Dave called to tell you about the gun."

"Why the heck did you do that? Did I *say* to contact him?" I said.

Red crept up the security guard's neck. "No, ma'am. But when Mr. Fielding got me the job here, he told me if there was ever any trouble I was to let him know right away. When nobody knew who the gun belonged to, I figured that qualified as 'trouble.' "

Mark had vetted the security guards at all three of my client hideaways. Guess I should have known he'd use them to keep tabs on me. He'd picked up Thomas's overprotective tendencies when they were roommates at Harvard, and hadn't let go of them since. It was annoying—but somewhat understandable—when I was in high school, and maybe even college, but now that I was a businesswoman I was trying to break him, along with the rest of the men in my life, of the habit.

Mark crossed the space between us, kissed the top of my head, and said, "No need to bite his head off, Howdy. Aren't you glad to see me?"

Then he smiled at me and, okay, I still melted. Speaking of breaking bad habits . . .

Of course, melting at another man's smile is a little awkward when your new boyfriend is standing a few feet away. I glanced at Billy, who had a rueful half smile on his face and a knowing look in his eye. Damn. He'd noticed, all right.

Nothing I could do about that now. So I coughed and plowed ahead. "That's beside the point. Cody is *my* employee"—I cut the employee in question a stern glance—"and he should check with me before he contacts someone else."

"Yes, ma'am. I'll remember that from now on," he said. But he still looked at Mark for confirmation, which Mark gave with an all but imperceptible nod that almost set me off again.

"Hey, Mark. Good to see you," Billy said, defusing the tension with his trademark affability. "If I'd known you were coming I would've offered you a lift."

"I believe I'll wait until you log a few more flight hours before I take you up on that."

Billy laughed. "Wuss. Even Ciel has been up with me, and you know how she—"

"EXCUSE ME!" the voice from the pantry rudely interrupted. "I can have you arrested for kidnapping, you know. You can't hold me against my will. I know my rights!"

Mark zeroed in on me right away, for some reason. "Aren't you usually on the other end of things in these situations, Howdy?"

Billy put his palm over my mouth. "Ciel, I *understand.* You can stop trying to explain. Trust me, you're not helping your cause."

I pulled his arm down, but held on to his hand. "I want you to know . . ." Oh, hell. What did I want him to know?

I'd dragged him out to the barn with me on the pretext of checking on Eeyore, which I really did want to do, but mostly I wanted to get him alone so I could reassure him about the Mark-melting thing. Eeyore eyed us malevolently from his stall, munching on hay.

Mark and Cody were hauling Bluto to the local sheriff's department. We'd discovered through persuasion ("we" being Mark, and "persuasion" being something I'd rather not dwell on) that Bluto was a Las Vegas parking lot attendant with an oh-so-clichéd gambling problem. He'd been contacted by an anonymous source and told where he could find the gun. All he'd wanted to do was retrieve it, drop it at a prearranged location, and pick up the money that would be waiting there for him. When I'd interjected that that was mighty trusting of him, he'd said if there hadn't been money there, he wouldn't have left the gun. Guess he wasn't totally stupid.

Of course, he swore up and down he thought the gun had been stolen from the person who hired him, and therefore it wasn't as if he was stealing it himself. He was only *retrieving* it.

Yeah, right. But Mark was sure the guy was at least telling the truth about not knowing who'd hired him. The plan was to let the local sheriff deal with the man while Mark followed through with the drop. Using Bluto's aura, naturally, in case anyone was watching.

I swallowed and looked beseechingly into Billy's eyes. "I want to be sure you know I'm not still hung up Mark. I'm *over* him, really I am. Only sometimes, when seeing him catches me off guard . . . well, the best way I can explain it is, it's a reflex. Like a . . . a sneeze. Or something."

He grinned, the twinkle back in his eyes, and tugged a lock of my hair. "Gesundheit."

I laughed. "Okay, maybe not like a sneeze. More like a bad habit. One I'm trying my best to break," I said sincerely.

"I almost wish you'd gone ahead and had a fling with him and gotten it out of your system. Might be easier for you to forget about him if your curiosity didn't keep poking you," he said, still teasing me.

Frankly, I wasn't so sure that would have worked, but I wasn't going to say that to Billy. "Well, that boat has officially left the dock. No flings for me. I'm sure my Pavlovian response to Mark will fade away to nothing soon, and *you* will be the only one I drool over." I smiled as engagingly as I could.

"Ciel, it's not wrong to respond to other men. It's normal and healthy. Do I like it?" One corner of his mouth lifted in a wry smile. "Not a bit. But as long as you come to me to act on those responses, I'm not going to complain."

He pulled me to him and kissed me in a way that made me wonder what in the heck I had *ever* seen in Mark.

Chapter 9

Finding myself on a plane for the fourth (or was it the fifth? I'd lost count) time in three days was not the highlight of my week. But at least the first-class accommodations Billy had insisted on springing for helped somewhat. And, yes, I let him. My independent, pay-my-own-way streak is severely weakened by altitude.

If Billy had been with me, it would have been even better, but alas. He was with Mark, monitoring the drop to see who *else* was watching.

It was killing me not to be with them, but if I didn't get back to the East Coast for my final dress fitting, and other assorted wedding stuff, Mom might send her favorite celestial hit man after me with (pardon the expression) God knew what. I'd already had a heck of a time explaining how I'd come to leave such an unladylike text message on her cell phone. For some reason, she did not appreciate being told to "fuck this shit" by her daughter.

To make amends, I was going to have to do a spectacular job on the shower. Billy's sisters could handle it, but if I didn't figure out a way to put my own brand on it, they'd take all the credit and bank the brownie points themselves. (Not that I'd blame them. I'd do the same thing. Brownie points are essential currency in our great big happy adaptor family.)

There were fifteen texts of escalating urgency from Mom waiting for me when I got off the plane. Since I was already in the doghouse, I didn't dare not respond. I formulated a shower update in my head as I waited for her to pick up.

"Ciel? Have you landed? Of course you have, you wouldn't be calling otherwise. But you're still at the airport, right? Because your brother—Brian, I mean—will be landing there in about twenty minutes. He has Molly with him. She wants to help you and her sisters with the shower."

"Doesn't she have school?"

"Please. She's so far ahead, her teacher will be happy for the time to help the other kids catch up. Now, I know you have everything under control already"—*Ha! Good one, Mom,* I thought wryly—"but try to find something she can do, all right? It's so important for her to feel needed. And Brian has to check out the wedding venue for his band—did I tell you he's playing the reception? Isn't that wonderful? Such a nice thing to do for his brother—so Mo and I thought we'd kill two birds with one stone by sending them down together. They can stay with you, right?"

"But Sinead and Siobhan are already staying at my place—"

"That's okay. Molly can share your room and Brian can sleep on the couch. It'll be fun, like a slumber party."

I sighed. "What's their flight number?"

Brian walked from one side of the stage to the other, stopping at various points along the way to say a few words.

"The acoustics in this place are *amazing,*" he said, a big, goofy smile on his face. "I can't wait to play here."

The Barns at Wolf Trap, a rustically charming theater constructed by combining two eighteenth-century barns that had originally come from upstate New York, had been suggested by Thomas as a possible spot for both the ceremony and the reception. It was where he and Laura had gone on their first date, and was still one of their favorite places to see musical talent from all over the world. And then there was the New York connection—Mom liked that.

We'd learned from an employee that the larger German barn was the actual theater, while the smaller English barn served as the bar. The lovely space wasn't often available as a rental on a weekend during the show season, but Mom had wangled it somehow. Probably made a large donation to the foundation that ran the place, knowing her. Or else made Thomas do it.

Molly was onstage with Brian, helping him check out the acoustics using an odd assortment of Taylor Swift and Justin Bieber lyrics, while Sinead and Siobhan were busy snapping pics of every corner of the place with their phones, and sending the images to our mothers.

I had slipped into the alcove in the back and was doing my best to connect with Billy, so I could see what was going on out west. I'd watched an interview with Nigel Overholt back at my place before we'd all piled into a hired van to get to our current northern Virginia locale, and I couldn't get the situation off my mind. Not that I didn't appreciate Molly's musical offerings (she was actually pretty good), but I was anxious to see if Billy and Mark had come up with any info on the gun's owner. I had a bad feeling about it.

Billy answered after my third attempt. "Really, sweetheart, such language. My voice mail is blushing."

"Well, answer faster next time and you won't hear it again. Now, what's up with the gun? Did you figure out who owns it?"

"Sadly, no. The gentleman I caught watching the drop had been hired—again, anonymously—to pick up the gun and dispose of it. Mark and I, of course, being extremely good at what we do, stopped the guy before he managed to get rid of it. So, we're back at square one—we have the gun, but with no proof of who's interested in its whereabouts."

"Are you *sure* the guy didn't know?"

"Gosh, no, Ciel. Mark asked him once, nicely, and when the guy said he didn't know, we apologized for interrupting his job, patted him on the back, and sent him on his merry way. Now we're kind of worried he may have been having us on."

"Okay, okay . . . no need to get snippy. It's just that . . . well, did you see Nigel Overholt on TV? The way he's talking, it's obvious he believes Lily-Ann is innocent. Billy, what if you were right? What if Jack set me up as an alibi?"

There was a long pause. "That's pure speculation on our part. The gun might not be related to Angelica's murder at all."

"Oh, come on. Don't you think that's a bit too coincidental?"

"Coincidences *do* happen."

"Maybe, but . . . hey, I know—can you or Mark find out what kind of gun Angelica was shot with? Maybe we can rule out the one we found."

There was a big sigh. Billy hardly ever sighed like that.

"What?" I said.

"Same caliber," he admitted.

"He *did* it," I whisper-shouted. Who knew how well voices carried in this place? "Jackson Gunn committed cold-blooded murder while I was him!"

"Calm down, cuz. We don't know that. It's a common caliber. We have to approach this carefully—"

"Oh. My. God. What if I'm an accessory to *murder*?"

"You are not—"

"But *what if*? Just because I didn't know it at the time doesn't mean I didn't make it possible. I could be a . . . a . . . a murder *enabler*!" My head felt like it was going to explode. My heart was pounding and my breath was coming too fast. Was it possible God was striking me dead as I spoke?

"Ciel . . . *Ciel.* Listen to me. Breathe slowly. This is *not* your fault."

"But he couldn't have done it without me. That *makes* it my fault," I said. Well, gasped. But quietly, because of the acoustics.

"Ciel, if Jackson did it—*if*—then he would have found a way even without you. In fact, I would have done the snake job myself if you hadn't. And I sure as hell wouldn't be taking the blame for murder if I had."

"Of course you wouldn't," I muttered.

"What's that supposed to mean?" Billy said, sounding a trifle peeved.

"Nothing. I didn't mean anything." *Much.* "Listen, Siobhan found me. I have to go. We'll talk later."

"Slow breaths!" was the last thing I heard before I disconnected.

I was too distracted to pay much attention during the rest of our tour. Brian worked out the details of his band playing the reception, and Sinead provided our guide with name of the caterer Mom had hired, along with the requisite insurance information. (I supposed if any of the wedding guests got food poisoning, Wolf Trap didn't want to be sued.)

Back in the car, Brian looked over the top of his seat at me and said, "You sure you're okay, sis? You look kind of pale. If you're feeling queasy, I have something that might help." He reached into his shirt pocket.

"No!" I said quickly. I knew what Brian's nausea remedy was, and I didn't think the driver would appreciate the aroma. Plus, I didn't want to get arrested. "I'm fine. Really."

Siobhan leaned close and whispered, "That was Billy you were on the phone with earlier, wasn't it? You're not upset with him, are you? Is it the other girls? Because—"

"No, honest, I'm okay," I said.

"—you know it doesn't mean anything when he flirts with other girls, right? He's a friendly guy," Sinead finished in my other ear.

I was sitting between the two of them in the backmost seat of the hired van. Brian and Molly were in front of us, occupying the two seats in the middle row.

"Sociable," Siobhan continued.

"Exuberant." Sinead again.

"Ebullient." Back to Siobhan.

All the Doyle kids had great vocabularies, thanks to Auntie Mo refusing to "dumb down" her conversations with them when they were little.

"Wait, what? What other girls?" I said.

"I'm sure it's just habit. He loves *you,*" Sinead said.

"Billy still flirts?" I said. How had I not noticed this?

Brian twisted in his seat to join our little huddle. "Not cool, Sinead. Billy doesn't mean anything by it, sis."

"Siobhan said it first, not me. I was only elaborating," Sinead said.

"Well, I figured Ciel already knew, and I wanted to reassure her that it doesn't mean anything," Siobhan said.

Molly, who'd been looking out the window at the subway train passing us on the track in the middle of the highway, poked her head between the seats. "Billy doesn't flirt with other girls, Ciel."

"Thank you, Molly," I said. You could trust kids, right? Weren't they always the bearers of awkward truths? Surely *she* would have told me if—

"*They* flirt with *him*. He only talks and smiles back at them to be polite. He's an extremely courteous guy, you know," she added.

Brian nodded. "Hey, me too. I'm courteous."

Well, wasn't *that* reassuring? Brian changed girlfriends every other week.

On the other hand, worrying about my boyfriend flirting with other girls beat the hell out of waiting for God to smite me for aiding and abetting a possible murderer.

Thomas was waiting for us at my condo, complete with a take-out feast from a local gourmet fried chicken place. My stomach released an unladylike growl at the delectable aroma of deep-fried goodness emanating from the spread laid out on my dining room table.

I hugged my oldest brother (extra-tight, because that tends to make him squirm). "Does this mean you've forgiven me?" I said.

By the time the driver dropped us off I had convinced myself I'd overreacted to the news about the gun. Like Billy said, it was a common caliber. Unless the bullets taken from Angelica matched the gun barrel precisely, and unless the gun could be proven to belong to Jack, we couldn't be sure of anything. It might just be some freak coincidence.

I was *really* hoping it was a freak coincidence.

"I might forgive you," Thomas said, still sounding a little grudging, "if you'll do me a favor."

"For chicken like this I'll cut your lawn with manicure scissors. What do you need?"

"Eat first. We'll talk after."

He didn't have to say it twice. I let go of him and elbowed my way in between Brian and Molly. Grabbed a golden-crusted leg, beating Sinead and Siobhan by a fraction of a second.

Thomas looked on as a tangle of arms swarmed the food. "I brought paper plates," he said to everyone. "You guys might consider using them."

We all paused, eyed each other, then raced to the counter. Molly got there first, raising her plate triumphantly over her head before scrambling back to the table. The rest of us weren't far behind. Well, except Thomas, who waited patiently until all our plates were full. Which meant he was still chewing on his chicken when the rest of us started arguing over the last piece of chocolate pecan pie.

"Back off, ladies. I'm bigger than all of you and I need more sustenance," Brian said.

Molly stuck her tongue out at him. "I'm having a growth spurt—I need the calories."

"Hey, it's *my* condo. Ergo, *I* should get the last piece," I tried. Lame, I know, but worth a shot.

"But I had the tiniest first piece!" Sinead said.

"Whose fault is that? You snooze, you lose," Siobhan said, reaching for the pie tin only to have it snatched away by Thomas in a truly impressive sneak move. No one had even seen him approach.

Holding his prize high, he said, "Possession is nine-tenths of the law. I now possess this last piece of pie." He gave me pointed look. "*Ergo,* it's mine. Besides, I haven't even had one piece yet, and I bought the damn thing."

Molly batted her eyelashes up at him. "But you haven't had any watermelon yet either. It's really good." She grabbed a slice and bit into it. "Mmmm. Don't you want some?"

"There's plenty of watermelon. I believe I'll eat *my* pie first." He was reaching for a fork when a small, black oval appeared on his forehead.

"Molly! Did you spit a seed at Thomas? What would Mom say?" Siobhan's shock was exaggerated, and the glint in her eye gave her away as the culprit.

"No, I didn't!" Molly protested as a seed landed on Siobhan's cheek.

A quick look at Sinead revealed from whence it had come. She was reloading her mouth with juicy red ammo when a whole slew of seeds pelted her. Brian. He'd mastered rapid-fire watermelon-seed spitting when we were kids.

And he'd taught me everything he knew. I reached for the seediest piece left and loaded up. Felt a splatter of seeds hit my neck. Apparently Brian had taught Molly his technique, too.

"I can't believe I'm housing you guys!" I mumble-shouted around a mouthful. It's possible I sprayed Molly's garishly printed hot-pink sweatshirt with more than just the seeds.

"Eeew!" she said with a giggle.

I shrugged. "Nobody will notice stains on that shirt."

"Sloppy, sis. I taught you better than that." Brian demonstrated by machine-gunning my entire torso. Molly joined in, as did her sisters, covering my face and hair. When they were done, I looked like a demented dalmatian.

"Mmm. That was tasty," Thomas said from across the room, where he'd retreated to eat his pie and watch the battle. His plate was empty.

"Coward!" I said.

He smiled and let the shark show behind his eyes. "The key to winning any fight is knowing the proper time to exit the fray."

"You're still working your Hollywood job, aren't you?" Thomas said once the uproar died down.

Sinead and Siobhan were putting away the remains of our lunch while Brian and Molly diligently gathered the watermelon seeds from floor, walls, and furniture. I'd brushed myself off and joined Thomas for a quiet talk on the sofa.

"Yeah. Unless the director decides Sparky's overacting in the snake scene isn't as heinous as he first thought. Then I'm done, which I am sincerely hoping is the case. I was planning to call Jack after his wife's funeral."

"When is that, do you know?"

"No clue. I suspect the murder investigation is holding it up."

"Yeah, about that . . . you know Nigel Overholt is representing Lily-Ann Conrad—you remember Nigel, don't you?"

"Of course," I said. "He's—and I'm quoting *you* here—brilliant. I saw him on TV talking about the case."

"He called me for some advice—it's not looking good for Ms. Conrad. I mentioned you had done some work for Gunn in your capacity as professional problem solver, and he'd like to meet with you as soon as possible."

"Does he know about us?" I asked. Thomas knew I was referring to adaptors.

"No. Never had occasion to tell him." Thomas was almost as tight-lipped about our kind as Mark was.

"So what can I do for him?"

"I told him Gunn hired you to help him cope with his snake phobia, and that you probably learned quite a bit about him and his family in the process." Thomas knew how thorough my client questionnaires were—he'd helped me draft them. "In cases like this one, information gathering is key. You never know what might prove crucial to your defense. So, will you meet with him?"

"Sure. When? After the wedding?"

"Tomorrow."

"*What?* Thomas, I can't go back to L.A. now—what about your shower? If I screw that up, Mom will fricassee me."

He held up one hand in the universal calm-down gesture. "Relax. Nigel's coming to D.C. tomorrow. You can meet with him here"—he looked around—"or maybe my place would be better. I'd suggest my office, but the fewer people connecting you to him, the better."

Sinead and Siobhan, finished storing the leftovers, joined us and started talking excitedly about a shopping expedition they wanted to drag me on.

"We found the best store," Siobhan said. "Four whole floors of nothing but wedding paraphernalia."

Gah! Kill me now.

Molly plopped down beside me. "And then we're going to the comic book store for the new Spider-Man. I brought the rest with me—we can stay up all night reading them again!"

More fun than wedding shower shopping, granted, but all night?

Before I could temper Molly's enthusiasm, Brian wandered over and plucked a stray seed from my hair. "Hey, you guys almost done talking? The rest of the band will be here to rehearse soon, and I need to move the couch to make room for the drums."

I felt my eyes widen in horror. Stood up, grabbed Thomas by the hand and said, "Um, yes, of *course* I'll meet with Nigel for you. Let's go!"

"But it's not until—"

"Now or never, bro," I said, narrowing my eyes at him. He got the message.

Chapter 10

Nigel Overholt was even more impressive in person than he was on TV. His smile was blindingly swoon-worthy. Think a young George Clooney, with a touch of Karl Urban. My first thought after being flashed by those pearly whites was, *I'll bet you don't have a bit of trouble convincing the ladies to go for a ride on your chair.* But I repented immediately.

I'd stayed the night on the love seat in Thomas's living room. It was comfortable, and I'm short enough that I wasn't too compressed. But honestly, how can you live in a million-dollar-plus home in D.C. and not have a guest room? I suspect it's intentional on my brother's part. I mean, did he really need a library, a study, a music room, *and* a sitting room, on top of the living room? It was just his fiendish way to avoid playing hotel every time a friend or family member came to town.

Nigel had been waiting for me in Thomas's study when I finished showering and changing into the clothes I'd hastily packed the day before (good pants, nice shirt, not-sneakers—it was a business meeting of sorts, after all). He'd rolled over to greet me, adjusting the height of his wheelchair so that we were eye level. I thought it was thoughtful of him not to try to intimidate me by towering over me, though he easily could have with the flick of a switch.

"Miss Halligan, so nice to finally meet you. Thank you for agreeing to speak with me."

I returned his smile, hoping I didn't have any stray poppy seeds stuck in my teeth from the bagel I'd just devoured in the kitchen. I held out my hand, and was pleased to note he had a firm grip. "Please. It's Ciel, and I'm happy to help a friend of Thomas's."

"If I call you Ciel, I'm afraid you're stuck with calling me Nigel. Not nearly as pretty." Again with the smile. Almost made you forget about the wheelchair, because honestly, who wanted to look down when you could stare at that face?

"Coffee?" he asked. "Thomas left the pot."

So that was where it was—I hadn't been able to find it when I was scarfing my bagel. "Coffee would be great. Where is my brother, anyway?"

"He had to make a quick visit to his office, but should be back soon," Nigel said, and handed me a beautifully crafted pottery mug. "What can you tell me about Jackson Gunn? Other than that he's afraid of snakes." Guess he didn't believe in wasting time on chitchat.

"Well . . ." I said after a fortifying sip of the strong brew, and then paused, considering how best to answer the question. I sipped again. And again, figuring it was probably best for me not to engage fully until I'd been properly caffeinated, or no telling what might spill out of my mouth. Besides, this was the good stuff. French-pressed dark roast, possibly Hawaiian, and smooth as silk.

I put the cup down and pulled myself back to reality before I got lost in the flavor. "Snakes were mainly what I worked on with him. I'm not sure what else I can tell you about him that isn't general knowledge."

"Did he talk to you at all about Angelica? Are you aware they were having marital difficulties?" Boy, he really didn't beat around the bush, did he?

"On the contrary, I was under the impression he was very much in love with his wife," I said. Which was true—nothing Jack had told me in our prejob interview led me to believe he was anything other than the most adoring of husbands. "Look, my job was to help him get through the snake scene without embarrassing himself in front of all his fans." Absolutely true, on the face of it. "We really didn't talk about much other than, um, coping mechanisms."

Nigel looked at me thoughtfully, and seemed to come to a decision. "I know you're a busy person, so I'm going to speak plainly to you about some of my client's private matters. Maybe it will trigger a useful thought or memory. Anything. Of course, I'm hoping what I say won't go any further."

I raised an eyebrow. "Not even to Thomas?"

"I've already discussed it with him. I know he would never be the source of any embarrassing leaks." There was the slightest emphasis on "he," which I supposed was his subtle way of letting me know if anything got out, he'd know it was me.

I nodded. "There won't be any leaks from me either. You might say discretion runs in our family."

"Ms. Conrad feels there's a strong possibility that her brother-in-law hired someone to kill her sister, and has set her up to take the fall."

My heart started beating faster. If Jackson had motive to want his wife dead, it wasn't out of the realm of possibility to think maybe he *had* used me as an alibi. My fix-it-fast instinct revved into high gear. I could *not* have that on my conscience.

"Why on earth would she think that?" I said, hoping like heck Nigel was grasping at straws.

"Because she was having an affair with him, and he promised her Angelica would be out of the picture 'soon'—which Lily-Ann assumed meant a divorce was imminent."

Shit. An affair with his wife's sister? My idol? That was low. "Even if that's true, why *not* a divorce? Why would he have her killed?" I said.

"Angelica found out about the affair and confronted Lily-Ann. There was a huge blowup. Angelica told her sister she'd been collecting information about Gunn since early in their marriage, to use in case of a divorce, as proof he broke their prenuptial agreement. She intended to use it to destroy him. Apparently—again, according to Lily-Ann—Angelica had quite the dossier built up."

I shook my head and lifted my hands slightly. Put them back on my lap when I saw they were trembling. "I still don't know how I can help you with your case. It seems to me, if Jack really were having an affair with Lily-Ann, he must care for her. I'd think he'd be the last one to want to set her up for murder."

"Lily-Ann broke it off with Jackson after Angelica found out about them. He didn't take it well, told her women did not leave Jackson Gunn, *he* left them, and only when he was through with them."

"That doesn't sound like the man I met," I said carefully.

Nigel shrugged. "I can only report what Lily-Ann told me. She thinks he might be afraid Angelica showed her the dossier—though Lily-Ann claims she never saw it—and that it has him spooked. She thinks this might be his way of getting rid of them both."

I thought back to the hipster girl I'd seen yelling and cursing on the TV screen. Somehow, I couldn't picture her paired up with Jackson in the first place. "And do you believe her?"

Nigel cocked his head. "That's where I'm hoping you can help me. Lily-Ann is, I believe, innocent. But her public persona is . . . prickly. Put her up against a likable celebrity like Jackson Gunn, in a he-said she-said situation, and she won't stand a chance. Especially when my sources at LAPD tell me they haven't been able to find an iota of evidence to show Gunn, or anyone else, tried to hire a killer."

Judging by the little I'd seen of Lily-Ann on TV, he was right about her prickly nature, and about the public—from whom the jury would be pulled—being much more likely to sympathize with Jackson.

I screwed up my eyebrows. "This may sound like a silly question, but why doesn't Lily-Ann just tell the police about the dossier? Wouldn't that provide motive for Jack and, at the very least, reasonable doubt for Lily-Ann?"

"Frankly, she's afraid of what the dossier might say about her—that it might appear to give her even more motive for the murder herself, and I have to say I agree. I'd prefer to leave the dossier—which, at this point, is only a matter of hearsay, in any case—out of the equation if at all possible. Any insight you can provide into Jackson Gunn—anything at all—would be very much appreciated."

I shifted uncomfortably in my chair. "The thing is, there's this small matter of confidentiality. My setup with my clients isn't all that different from yours—there's trust involved."

He nodded, understanding. One look in those expressive eyes and I felt terrible for letting him down.

"Look," I said, "if it's any help at all, I'm not holding anything relevant back. I honestly don't think there's a thing I learned about Jack that would be of use to you."

Now, the fact that what I *did* for Jack might be extremely relevant was another thing entirely. But not practical, since it wasn't something Nigel could use in court, not without outing adaptors to the world. And what would be the point of doing that if it turned out Lily-Ann was spinning bullshit in order to save herself from prison?

He shrugged. "You never know what might prove useful. But I understand your reluctance to divulge a client's secrets. Though, in the case of a murder, one might expect a certain flexibility in such ethical matters would be equally understandable . . ."

I felt myself getting sucked into Nigel's imploring gaze. The pull wasn't in any way sexual—it was more like I suddenly felt compelled to do everything I could to *help* him. Boy, he was good. Where the hell was Thomas? I could use a little brotherly support.

"Listen," I said, breaking eye contact, "did you ever consider that Lily-Ann might be playing you? That *she's* the one who's trying to set up Jackson? Who inherits Angelica's estate if Jackson is convicted of her murder, anyway?"

Nigel shrugged. "It's possible Lily-Ann is trying to do that, yes, but my instincts tell me otherwise. And my duty is to my client. At the very least, I'd like to get her out of jail until her trial. Jail can be a very unpleasant place for a young woman."

No shit, I thought, swallowing hard. *Especially if she's innocent.*

I'm no idiot. I knew exactly what kind of subtle pressure Nigel was applying, hoping to get me to say more. Engage my sympathy, get me to help him deflect the assumption of guilt from his client to mine. Fortunately, I'm stubborn enough to dig in my heels when someone is trying to get me to do something before I'm good and ready. And I wasn't ready yet, not before I'd had a chance to talk to Jackson myself.

Besides, I couldn't fail to notice Nigel hadn't answered my question. Who would inherit?

After Nigel left I cornered Thomas in the kitchen, where he was cleaning up after the light lunch of crab salad on toasted croissants he'd prepared for the three of us when he returned from the office. (Thomas loves to feed people. Which is handy, because I love to be fed.) I'd avoided answering any more of Nigel's questions about Jackson, and he'd been too polite to push it.

"What the hell, Thomas? Do you think my client did it? Do you think I helped somebody commit murder?"

"Jesus, Ciel, of course not. I'm just trying help Nigel with his case. That's *all.*"

"Well, who do *you* think did it, then? You're always right," I said, grabbing some plates from him and putting them in the dishwasher. I might not particularly enjoy food preparation, but that didn't mean I couldn't be helpful in the kitchen.

He hesitated. I could see he didn't want to answer me. "I'm not *always* right," he said eventually, relocating the plates to a better position on the bottom rack.

"Oh, yeah? Name a case you weren't right about."

"O. J. I totally thought he did it."

I rolled my eyes. Big-time.

"Hey, he wasn't convicted," Thomas said. "Sis, it doesn't matter whether Jackson did or didn't do it. *You* are not responsible."

Okay, so he obviously assumed Jackson was guilty. And I hadn't even told him about finding the gun. Should I mention that? Nah, he'd only worry, and he already had enough on his mind with getting married.

He gave me a peck on the cheek. "Thanks for meeting with

Nigel anyway. Now, get out of here. I have a hundred and fifty things to take care of at work before the wedding. And *you* have a shower to orchestrate. If I have to interrupt my schedule to show up for it, it had better be a damn good party."

My condo was blissfully empty when I returned home. The Doyle sisters, according to a text from Sinead, had gone to haul a load of party decorations to the restaurant, and Brian, according to the note he'd scrawled on a paper towel (he probably forgot to recharge his phone), had gone to the grocery store to restock my sadly empty larder. Huh. That probably meant I was out of Cheetos.

I was debating whether it was too soon to call Jackson and confront him about the gun and his possible affair with Lily-Ann—after all, if he wasn't the murderer, he could still be recovering from the shock of his wife's death—when he decided the issue by calling me.

"Ciel? I need your help," he said without preamble.

My stomach gave a small lurch. "Hey, Jack. Do we need to schedule a repeat performance with the snakes?"

"What? No. Maybe. But not now. Listen, I can't even think about that now—the movie's on hold, with Angeli—" His voice broke.

There was an excruciatingly long pause, during which my mind raced to find the right thing to say, finally stumbling upon, "Jack, I'm so sorry."

Which, I suppose, beat other relevant options like "Did you kill your wife?" or "Were you screwing Lily-Ann and are you setting her up now?" Still, it felt inadequate to the emotion flowing through the phone.

"Thanks," he said after taking a deep breath. "I appreciate it."

I cleared my throat. "So, then . . ."

He took another deep breath. I hoped he wouldn't hyperventilate, because I had no idea how to handle that long-distance. "Listen, Ciel, I need a favor. Two, actually, and not really favors—I'd pay you for your time. More like an extension of our business arrangement."

"Shoot," I said, and immediately winced. Had that really come out of my mouth? "I mean, go ahead. What do you need?"

"I need you to go to Angelica's funeral for me. I just don't think I can face"—it sounded like he swallowed another sob—"face the public yet."

Crap. Crappity, crappity, crap-crap-crap. If there's one thing I hate more than weddings, it's funerals. "Ummm . . . well, you see, Jack, my brother's wedding is coming up in a little over a week, and I'm in the wedding party, and there's so much I have—"

"That's okay—I don't know when the coroner will release the body, anyway. I can make sure the service is planned around your schedule."

"But—"

"Please, Ciel. I need you," he said, his voice gravelly with suppressed emotion. How could I ignore an appeal like that?

I sighed. "As long as it's after the wedding, I suppose I could—"

"Thank you, Ciel. You don't know what this means to me. Angelica's parents are insisting on making a huge production of it, and I'd never be able to keep up a strong appearance. The fucking paparazzi would have a field day."

"I understand," I said. And I did. It must be horrible to have your every public move under such intense scrutiny. "What was the other thing?"

"The Conrads are on their way to D.C. Joe—that's Joseph Conrad, Angelica's father—told me it was for a business meeting, but I'm pretty sure it concerns her sister, Lily-Ann. I'm hoping they're making arrangements to transfer the capital to bail her out of jail, but maybe not. She's been estranged from her parents for years, and I'm starting to think they might really believe this nonsense about Lily-Ann murdering Angelica."

My ears perked up at once. "And you don't?"

"Of course not. Angelica and Lily-Ann were very close, in spite of Lily-Ann's falling out with their parents. But the Conrads don't know Angelica kept in contact with her sister—it would have made the family board meetings awkward. Anyway, I'm hoping you might be willing to watch the Conrads and tell me where they go—which banks or lawyers they visit, stuff like that—and most importantly, who they have lunch or dinner with. If they see who I'm hoping they will, I can relax about Lily-Ann."

He paused, clearing his throat, and sounded less agitated when he began again. "Angelica wouldn't want her sister sitting in jail. I'd hire a private detective, but frankly I don't know one I can trust. Too many people are willing to let things leak when celebrities are involved."

Okay, this was getting weird. Did Jackson have no clue that Lily-Ann suspected *him*? Why was he trying to protect her when she was ready to throw him to the wolves?

I made an executive decision to cut through the bullshit. I couldn't tell Jackson anything Nigel had told me in confidence, but that didn't mean I had to keep him in the dark about everything. "Jack, there's something you should know. I found the gun."

There was a longish pause. "What gun?" he said. I couldn't decide if he sounded guarded or genuinely clueless.

"The one you left at my ranch. The one that happens to be the same caliber as the murder weapon."

"Look, I don't know what you're implying"—indignation now;

not tough to recognize that—"but there's no way that could possibly be my gun."

"I don't know how else it could have found its way to my ranch," I said. "It's not like I have a lot of guests there."

"Ciel, you have to believe me—I don't know anything about it. If it's the murder weapon, I don't know how it got there." The desperation in his voice was pitch-perfect, but was it real? Jesus. Actors. Who could tell?

"Who besides you has access to your guns?" I asked.

"Angelica." Well, that was hardly useful.

"No one else? Maid, butler"—did Hollywood stars have butlers?—"other household"—were they called servants anymore, or had I been watching too much *Downton Abbey*?—"um, household help?"

"No. The gun safe is hidden behind a hinged bookcase in our—my—bedroom. I doubt any of the staff even knows it exists. We—Angelica and I—felt that would be best."

I gave myself a mental head-slap. *Staff.* I should have known that. But never mind. "Think, Jack. Anyone else? Anyone at all?"

"No! Unless . . . well, Angelica and Lily-Ann used to go to the range together sometimes. I suppose—but no. Lily-Ann wouldn't be capable of . . . of . . ."

I decided to hit him again. "Jack, were you having an affair with Lily-Ann?"

An even longer silence, followed by a deflated sigh.

I took that as an affirmative. "Does Lily-Ann know about my ranch? And what I did for you?"

"Look, I didn't tell *anyone* about our arrangement, I swear. Just as our contract stipulates. But . . . I was with Lily-Ann the night before I left for the ranch, to break it off with her. The whole affair was complete idiocy on my part. I should never have given in to . . . listen, it wasn't her fault. She wanted a taste of what her sister had—that's how she put it—and I was stupid enough to think it would be harmless to give it to her. When I left Lily's place to meet your driver, I was careful to make sure I wasn't followed, but . . . oh, hell. No. No, she couldn't have."

"Forget how unlikely it is. Is it *possible*?" I pressed.

"I suppose. Technically," he said, sounding irritated at where my focus lay. "Listen, you *have* to watch the Conrads for me. I need to know if they're going to post bail for Lily-Ann. I'd do it myself, but if the press got wind of it, it might look like . . ."

Like exactly what it is? I thought wryly.

I wasn't sure why I agreed to do it. Jackson sounded not-guilty enough to me, which ought to be enough to let my conscience off the hook. But something still niggled at me. Nigel—and Thomas—seemed to buy Lily-Ann's story. I couldn't let it go yet.

I sighed. *Bye-bye, shower brownie points.*

The lobby of the Jefferson, a luxury boutique hotel in downtown D.C., was a nice place to hang out while waiting for Joseph and Elizabeth Conrad to make an appearance. Bright and cheerful, it was busy enough that I could blend in without attracting too much attention, especially with a judicious application of my ability.

I'd changed auras four times already, so the staff wouldn't get suspicious about the same person sitting in the lobby for so long. Having taken the precaution of wearing nondescript clothing—nothing that would etch itself into the average observer's awareness—I only had to switch flashy accessories with each new aura in order to cement the appearance of being a completely different person. I used female auras—different ages and hair colors, but of similar size, so my clothes would fit—and an assortment of bright scarves, chunky jewelry, and prescription-free glasses, which I kept in a plain, small bag tucked beside my chair. A nearby potted plant was tall enough to provide the necessary cover for quick changes when no one was looking. Jane Bond, at your service.

The Conrads had arrived late the night before, and hadn't settled into the hotel until after eleven, which I knew because I'd watched them check in. Assuming they wouldn't be handling any business at that time of day, I'd gone home and grabbed a few hours' sleep, but I was back by seven a.m., in case the they proved to be obnoxiously early risers. Pushing noon there was still no sign of them. I suppressed a yawn. Sheesh, the things I do for my clients.

I recognized the Conrads at once when they exited the elevator—their images had, of course, been splashed all over the news along with Angelica's and Jackson's. Joseph—Joe—was short, bald, and stocky, but not to the point of stoutness. Elizabeth was dark-haired, tall, and expensively thin. Both were well dressed, but in an understated fashion. More burnished gleam than flash.

Not looking directly at them, I put my unread magazine back into my bag and casually left the hotel right ahead of them. (Clever, huh? No one would suspect the person in front of them was following them.) Once outside, I dug into my pocket for my cell phone and pretended to text someone while waiting for the Conrads to pass me. When they got into a limo, I hopped into the nearest taxi. And, yes, I said, "Follow that car!" Got an eye roll from the driver, but he snapped to when I waved a bunch of twenties in his face.

Many hours, several cab rides, and a hundred-dollar bribe to a bored restaurant hostess later, I was sitting at a table inside a pricy French bistro in the Upper Northwest part of town, next to Joe and Elizabeth's booth, wondering if Jackson would be able—or inclined—to reimburse me for my expenses if he wound up behind bars.

The Conrads had visited the Smithsonian (Elizabeth had seemed fascinated with the gem collection at the Museum of Natural History, while Joe was more taken by the exhibits at the Air and Space Museum), a bakery (for which my stomach was eternally grateful), and the Capitol building (where they took a tour). The day struck me as oddly touristy for freshly grieving parents. Over the course of the afternoon I hadn't seen them communicate with anyone other than each other, and even that was the bare minimum.

I'd been growing less patient as the hours passed. Tracking down restrooms and peeing at warp speed so I wouldn't risk losing my quarry while on a call of nature was getting really old. Not only that, but the shower was due to start in less than an hour, and I still hadn't found out anything that could be considered significant.

Damn it. If I left now, the whole day would have been a great big waste of time. But if I didn't get to the shower, my mother would kill me. Or worse, sic her pal the Big Guy Upstairs on me. I started to gather my belongings.

A man in a dark business suit, his gray hair and mustache impeccably groomed, approached the Conrads' table. He smiled tightly at both of them as he sat. "You have the certificates?" he said.

Bingo. I settled back onto my chair and sent Billy a rapid-fire text that started out "I need a huge favor" and ended up "I'll make it up to you, I swear!"

Then I laid the phone on the table next to my plate. With a few taps of my finger, I set it to record a video. I'd wind up with a movie of the ceiling fan above me, but with a little luck, I'd also have intelligible audio of the highly interesting conversation starting to unfold next to me.

Chapter 11

"Are Sinead and Siobhan mad at me?" I asked Billy as I helped him change out of my clothes and back into his own.

We were in my office, on the third floor of Thomas's building in downtown D.C. The shower was reaching a crescendo in the party room of the restaurant on the bottom floor, and, to the best of everyone's knowledge (well, everyone except Billy), I had been there all along, and was currently taking a bathroom break.

"Nope, not at all. They're quite pleased to have you owe them a future favor of the unspecified sort."

"Should I be scared?" I asked.

"Shouldn't be too horrendous. What you should be afraid of is the favor you now owe *me,*" he said, and paused to nibble my neck.

"Oooh," I said with a shiver. "Scare me again."

"Later," he promised, and resumed dressing.

I'd sworn I would explain everything to him, along with Mark, after the shower. I really didn't want to go over everything twice.

"Why'd you have to pick this one?" I said, putting on the dress he'd been wearing as me. "And, come on, heels?" I knew I shouldn't look a gift horse in the mouth, but ugh.

"I happen to like you in that dress. It's short."

"It's too low cut." Not to mention clingy. I'd bought it for a party back in college, egged on by my roommate.

"Funny, that's what your mom said, too. That's why she gave me this." He handed me the lightweight, lacy jacket I recognized as one of Mom's favorites.

"She just happened to have it with her?"

"She was wearing it herself, but said you needed it more than she did."

I slipped the jacket on and let Billy pin it closed at the neck with the accompanying cameo brooch. When he was done, I reached up and pulled his head down to kiss him. "Seriously, Billy. Thank you for this. You're the best boyfriend ever. Even if you do still flirt with other girls."

"*What?*" he said.

"According to your sisters. But it's okay. Molly assures me that you're only being polite," I said.

He shook his head. "Ciel, I don't 'flirt'—"

I lifted one eyebrow. "No?"

"*No.* I may *smile* at people, some of whom happen to be female. But smiling is not flirting."

"It is when you have a smile like yours," I teased.

"Thank you. I think," he said. "Tell you what. For you, I'll make an extra effort to be surly to all the other girls from now on."

I was at the shower in time for the opening of the gifts, and was as surprised as Thomas and Laura were to see the assortment of flavored body oils "I" had given them. Siobhan and Sinead looked on like two saints, but I could see the horns beneath their halos.

Doyles. They were always there in a pinch, but they could never resist making sure you felt it.

After everyone had a good laugh (especially Laura, who seemed to enjoy Thomas's initial scandalized reaction), Billy made an entrance, apologizing for being late. Auntie Mo admonished him, Billy dimpled away her frown, and all was well.

The room was a gloriously kitschy mess of heart-shaped balloons, silver streamers, and cheap paper bride-and-groom decorations. Looked like the trip to the wedding store had been a success. It was *perfect.* Kudos to Billy's sisters.

I *was* disappointed to see the spread of Thai food had been decimated before I got there. Only the tantalizing aromas lingered, jabbing my empty stomach. I'd barely taken a bite of anything at the bistro, intent as I was on the table next to me.

"What did I eat?" I whispered to Billy when he came to greet me with a kiss, as everyone naturally expected now that our relationship was out in the open.

"More like what didn't you eat," he said. "You were ravenous."

I groaned. Quietly. "Was it good?" My salivary glands were tingling at the thought.

"Succulent. The drunken noodles were particularly tasty—so soft on the tongue, with just the right amount of heat," he said.

I groaned again, and not entirely from hunger. "You are a cruel man."

Mark joined us in time to hear my stomach growl, which he graciously ignored.

"Billy," he said. "Glad you could make it. Ciel, thanks again for taking care of the details. Great party."

Billy nodded to Mark and grinned at me. "Need a tissue, cuz?

You look like you might be about to"—there was an infinitesimal pause—"sneeze."

I gave Billy a dirty look before answering Mark. "Well," I said, wobbling, which I chose to blame on my heels. "I can't take all the credit." Or any of it, really. "Sinead and Siobhan were a huge help."

The two of them were currently holding court at the center of a crowd of young lawyers, under the scowling eye of my big brother. Now that Thomas considered me to be Billy's problem (yes, that made Thomas a chauvinist, but that was Laura's problem), he'd shifted his protective tendencies to Billy's sisters. Laura finally drew his attention back to the presents when she held up matching his-and-her honeymoon underwear—a thong for Laura and baggy boxers for Thomas.

"Jesus," Thomas muttered after he read the card that had accompanied the gift, and shoved them back into the festive, heart-covered tissue-stuffed bag Laura had pulled them from. "Um, thanks, Mom."

"What? You need to give the boys space to breathe—I want grandchildren," Mom hollered across the room, and then joined my little group, putting one arm around Mark and one around me. I suspected she may have had a glass or three of wine.

"You two did a marvelous job on the shower. See, honey? I told you it would be fine."

"I'm afraid I left it all on Ciel's shoulders," Mark said. "All I did was show up—she took care of everything else."

"No, I didn't. Really. Sinead and Siobhan deserve the credit," I said.

Mom beamed at me, obviously not listening, lost in a happy haze now that one of her children was finally getting married. "I'm proud of you, sweetie." She let go of Mark and tugged on the hem of my dress with both hands. Didn't help the length at all. "Billy, you put what I said about grandchildren on hold. You got that? First things *first,*" she said meaningfully.

"Mom!" I said, giving her my I'm-shocked-you-said-that look, which she ignored.

Billy nodded dutifully. "Whatever you say, Auntie Ro."

After Mom wandered off to mingle, Mark said, "So, are you going to tell me where you were for the first half of the shower, Howdy?"

Ack. "I . . . um, I . . ." Damn, I couldn't flat out lie to him.

"What gave me away?" Billy asked.

"You're better at walking in heels than Ciel is."

After the party, Mark, Billy, and I went up to my office. I sat behind the antique wooden desk, borrowing confidence from its size. Billy sprawled in one of the burgundy leather chairs I have for clients, and Mark perched on the edge of my desk.

Fortunately, no one else had noticed my switch, not even the other adaptors. Guess Mark was just extra observant, probably because of all that spy training.

Thomas and Laura were on their way to Thomas's D.C. house with a trunk-load of amusing gifts. The out-of-town guests, including Billy's parents (with Molly) and mine, had retired to their respective hotels to get some sleep before their early flights home the next morning.

Sinead and Siobhan were being shown around town by two Thomas-approved (and appropriately terrified) young lawyers from his firm. Thomas had given their names and addresses to Auntie Mo and Uncle Liam right in front of the girls and the two gentlemen in question. And gentlemen they would be, I had no doubt, considering the look Uncle Liam had given them. He was every bit as charming as his son, but tended not to waste it on the young men who wanted to date his daughters. The girls would meet me at my condo later. (Brian had decided the second queen-size bed in James's hotel room beat the couch in my living room, and was bunking there.)

"Okay, gather round," I said after giving the guys an account of my day up until my text to Billy. They both joined me behind my desk, standing on either side of me.

"I started recording right after Mr. Conrad—Joseph or Joe, depending on who's talking to him—handed a large envelope to the gray-haired guy. His name was never mentioned, but I got a picture of him before I left the restaurant. Well, kind of." I showed them the blurry image on my phone, a side view of the guy, with the top of his head cut off. I shrugged off the poor quality. "It's not easy taking a picture one-handed and without being noticed."

"It helps if you're smarter than your phone," Billy said, patting my head. I tried to elbow him in the gut but he was ready for me, blocking my arm. "*Kidding,* cuz. You did great to get a picture at all."

Mark took the phone and studied the screen, making a few adjustments with some apps I didn't know I had. "I can work with that," he said after forwarding the photo somewhere, and handed it back.

I started the video. All three of us stared at the spinning fan on the screen as if it would offer insight into what we were about to hear.

"The handwriting samples?" came the voice of Gray Hair. The audio wasn't bad, considering how softly they'd been speaking and the background noise of the other diners.

"I don't know why a business document wouldn't do. She signed those, too." Elizabeth's voice.

"What I do is an art. If you want a copy, use a machine," Gray Hair said, disdain coloring his words.

That was when Joseph had taken the letters from Elizabeth and handed them to Gray Hair. "We'll need those back, along with the certificates," he said.

I paused the video. "They were letters from Angelica to her mother—I caught a glimpse of the return address."

Mark nodded and started it playing again.

"Those are very important to me." Elizabeth's voice. If she felt any overwhelming grief for her daughter, she controlled it well.

"Of course." Gray Hair's voice. "I can assure you they won't be damaged in any way."

My waiter's voice intruded, comparatively sharp and clear, asking to take my order.

I reached over and stopped the video. "That's pretty much all there is. The man left, and the Conrads ordered dinner. They didn't say another thing about the transaction. I slipped away as soon as I could to get here. So, what do you think it all means?"

Mark picked up the phone and replayed the video, holding it closer to his ear. When it was done, he tapped a few spots on the screen. "Just sending it to a guy I know in acoustics."

"Well?" I prompted. "Those certificates—stock certificates of some sort, I assume—why would the Conrads be handing them over to this guy? Could they have been trying to sell them to raise money for Lily-Ann's bail? But in that case, why the samples of Angelica's writing? Is this as shady as it seems to me?"

Billy looked thoughtful. "Sounds to me like the Conrads don't like where some of their daughter's assets were allocated. What do you think, Mark? Are dear old Mom and Dad trying to fabricate a retroactive stock transfer before the will is read?"

"Could be. I'll know more after I find out the background of their companion."

"Could this mean the Conrads are involved in their daughter's murder?" I said. Horrible as that sounded, it would at least clear my client. And my conscience.

Billy, quick to guess my underlying reason for the question, gave me a reassuring look. "Wouldn't surprise me in the least. They do strike me as the sort to eat their young."

Happy as I was that Jackson might not be culpable, it made me more concerned about Lily-Ann. Was an innocent woman in jail? Maybe she *wasn't* trying to frame Jackson—maybe she thought it must be him because she couldn't imagine her parents doing such a thing.

I chewed my lip, but only because I didn't want to bite a fingernail in front of the guys. "I suppose I ought to talk to Thomas about it. He's consulting with Nigel Overholt on Lily-Ann's case. I hate to think of her sitting in jail if she didn't do it."

"You really want to drag Thomas into this a week before his wedding? Even if he could help—which is doubtful—can you imagine what your mother would do if he's distracted?" Mark said.

"But," I started, and then stopped, because he was right. Mom would freak if anything threatened The Event. And it wouldn't be fair to Thomas, who was having a tough enough time coping with the wedding as it was, or to Laura either. She deserved her big day to be as free of outside problems as possible.

"Okay, I won't drag Thomas into this"—*yet*—"but I have to do *something.*"

"Look, Ciel, I'm on a tight schedule this week, a job that can't wait." *So, what else is new?* I thought, but resisted rolling my eyes. "After the wedding—which I'm hoping like hell I can make, because disappointing your brother is not high on my list of favorite things to do—I'll look into the Conrads."

"Don't worry, I won't let you disappoint Tom," Billy said.

Uh-huh. I knew it. But that wasn't my concern now.

"Look, I talked to Nigel yesterday—he thinks Lily-Ann is innocent, and Thomas trusts his opinion. I can't just let her rot in a jail cell all week."

Mark's eyes bored into me. "What did you tell Overholt?"

I huffed an exasperated sigh. "Relax. Nothing about adaptors. Thomas told him I was counseling Jackson through his snake phobia, and Nigel wanted to pump me for any info I might have learned about him and the Conrads. Oh, yeah, and he told me Lily-Ann and Jackson were having an affair."

"Well, there you are," Billy said. "The other woman. Maybe the police have the right person after all."

I shook my head. "Before this thing with the Conrads, I was leaning"—hoping—"that way, too. But now . . . listen, maybe I *should* run this by Thomas."

Mark shrugged, looking deceptively sanguine about the whole thing. "Go ahead. I'm sure Ro will understand if he gets distracted by the case. Which, being Thomas, he would."

I gave him a dirty look. "I can't just do *nothing.*"

"For now, what if *we* post Lily-Ann's bond?" Billy suggested. "Then at least she won't be sitting in a cell until her trial."

"The judge set an enormous bail," I said. "Way too much for me, and probably too much even for you. But thanks for the offer."

"I'll take care of it," Mark said. "*If* you'll promise to stay out of it and focus solely on your brother's wedding for the next week. Laura could use your help. All the special-ops training in the world couldn't prepare her for Ro and Mo in a frenzy."

"Really? You can afford it?" I said.

"Let's just say I have access to special funds to use as I see fit," he said.

I jumped into his arms on a springboard of relief, hugging him tightly, without a second thought.

Until I heard Billy's voice behind me: "Gesundheit."

Chapter 12

It had to be the longest week of my life.

Sure, I wasn't—for the time being—worried about Lily-Ann. Mark had been as good as his word, and she'd been released the morning after the shower. She had to wear a tracking anklet—he'd made sure of that—and her passport had been confiscated, but it was way better than sitting in a cell. Especially since Nigel was letting her stay at his place in the Hollywood Hills, which from all accounts (i.e., star tours of celebrity homes) was one damn fine place. That made me think more than ever that Nigel truly thought she was innocent. Surely he wouldn't let her stay with him if he was at all doubtful.

Then again, this was the guy who'd tried to hang glide off the Hollywood sign. He obviously wasn't risk-averse. Also, I suspected he hated to lose as much as Thomas did. If he thought letting her stay with him showed his confidence in her innocence, and would help her case, he might do it for that reason alone.

And then there was Jackson Gunn. What had he wanted me to find out about the Conrads? Was it really if they were going to post bail for Lily-Ann, or had it been something more, something to do with those stock certificates, perhaps? What would he do if he found out the Conrads had them? If he *had* murdered his wife, no telling what he might be capable of where his in-laws were concerned.

Ultimately, I'd decided not to tell him about the stock. I'd assured him Lily-Ann's bail would be posted, implying that I'd heard the Conrads talking about it. So, yeah, I'd officially lied to my client, breaching our trust. But I'd been crossing my fingers at the time, so maybe God would understand.

The whole situation was twisting in my brain like a nest of adders. (And thank you for inspiring *that* lovely analogy, Mr. Jackson "Quakes-at-Snakes" Gunn.) But I couldn't do anything about it now, so I pushed it to the back of my mind and let my subconscious chew on it, because I was sick of it.

Mark had been gone the whole week on some pressing assignment involving matters of national security (really, did he have any other kind?), and Billy was with him, subbing for Laura. Which was nice of him, and I understood completely, but I did miss him. Some parts of him even more than others.

The real problem was that Mom had put her own work on hold until after the wedding. She and Auntie Mo had a boutique modeling agency that specialized in models who looked almost exactly like the industry giants from bygone eras. More accurately, they *were* the agency—they adapted their auras to be whomever the client wanted. I sometimes helped them out in an emergency, either theirs or mine—they paid well, and when you're perpetually low on cash, every little bit helps.

So, not only was Billy not around to distract me from the horror that was wedding prep, but Mom was in the perfect position to run my ass raggedy doing this, that, and the other thing "for Laura." She knew I couldn't, in my time-honored MOH position, refuse to do anything she asked as long as she tacked that onto the end of the request. I did get a little suspicious when she told me to give my own condo a good cleaning "for Laura," but at least it kept me busy. By the end of the week, I was kicking myself for not having the foresight to schedule another job for myself. Too bad I hadn't known the Hollywood job would be cut short.

Thank God Laura had insisted she didn't want a big bachelorette party—she'd said the wedding following the shower so closely was more than enough excitement for her. But since Brian and James were taking Thomas out after the rehearsal dinner for one last evening as a single guy (with the understanding that Mom would kill them all if Thomas was hungover at the wedding), I felt like I should do something with Laura. We'd finally decided to just hang out together, nothing fancy. Laura had been planning to stay overnight at a hotel, so Thomas wouldn't see her on the big day before she walked down the aisle. I suggested she might as well stay at my place instead. Since it was clean and all.

Sinead and Siobhan had moved their things over to the hotel where all our parents were staying, so Laura and I had the place to ourselves. The rehearsal had been chaotic, but it was a happy chaos, full of joking and laughter, and followed by good Italian food, which Laura only nibbled, saying to Thomas, "Hey, I can't adapt away a belly pooch tomorrow."

Billy and Mark had missed it, not being able to take that much time away from the assignment, but no one doubted their skill at improvising. They could be told what to do and where to stand the next day, right before the ceremony.

Back at my place, Laura and I changed into pajamas, made

mimosas, and settled in front of *The Princess Bride* (hey, I can get with a theme if I have to), reciting the lines along with the characters as we giggled our way through a bottle of Moët drowned in orange juice.

After the first glass, we'd decided the vitamin C in the OJ should counteract any possible negative effects from overindulgence in champagne.

"And if it doesn't, then fuck it," Laura said, her Southern accent somehow making it sound genteel.

I clinked my glass with hers. "*And* the horse it rode in on! Hey, did Thomas ever tell you I have a pony? Eeyore. He's the best pony ever."

Laura scrunched up her eyebrows (they were dark auburn, like her hair, and beautifully shaped). "He mentioned something about an Eeyore, but I was under the impression it was a donkey."

I sighed, and sucked down more vitamin C. "He probably told you Eeyore was an 'ass.' He *happens* to be the world's cutest Shetland pony. Also kind of an ass . . . hole"—she almost spewed her mimosa at that—"but he's still the love of my life."

"I thought Billy held that position. Unless you've decided . . . never mind. Here's to Eeyore!"

"No, wait—what were you going to say?"

"I shouldn't . . . look, you and Billy are great together."

"But?" I said. Because there was no denying the invisible "but" at the end of her statement.

"But nothing, sugar. If Mark's nose is a little bent out of shape by your relationship with Billy, well, it's his own fault, isn't it?"

"Mark is bent out of shape?" Damn. I did not like the way that made my chest clutch.

"Never mind. I'm sure it's only a little macho pique." She stopped for a second and studied me. "Oh, hell, Ciel. I probably shouldn't say this, but we *are* going to be sisters. Sisters have to look out for each other, right?"

"*Yes.* We *do.* Say it, Laura."

Still she hesitated.

"Lau-*ra* . . ."

"All right. Sugar, are you sure Billy is the one? That you're not . . . well, settling for him because you think Mark might never come around?"

"Of course not! I *love* Billy. I think. No, I mean, I *know* I love him—I always have. He's my honorary cousin, for God's sake. But . . ."

She looked at me intently, the "But what?" there in her eyes.

"But . . . this romance part is new. *Could* I just be infatuated? Is it possible to love someone platonically and be infatuated with them at the same time?"

"Isn't that what romantic love is? Loving someone like a best friend and wanting to jump their bones every time you see them?"

"Is that how you love my brother?" I asked. *Ew. My brother.*

"Sure it is. Only the friendship part came *after* the initial burst of lust."

"Crap. I got the order wrong!" I stood up. Not because I had anyplace to go, but because I couldn't *sit.*

How *did* I feel about Billy? We'd only been together romantically for a short time. It sure *felt* real, but would it last? Or would the fire fade, leaving me—and maybe him, too—stuck, pretending to feel something that wasn't there because we couldn't bear to hurt each other's feelings?

I wandered to the kitchen on autopilot, and found myself in front of the freezer.

Laura came up behind me. "Oh, honey, I'm sorry. I shouldn't have said anything—it was stupid of me to bring it up."

"No, it's okay. Really. But . . . out of curiosity . . . why *did* you ask that?"

Uncertainty clouded her face. "Mark's become a good friend of mine. We talk sometimes. There are these long, boring stretches on assignments, and . . . well, I'm not so sure Mark *wouldn't* come around. Eventually. Because he does love you."

My heart clutched again. I couldn't tell if it was because what I heard made me happy, or supremely uncomfortable. Kind of made me long for the days in the not so distant past when my love life was purely imaginary.

Laura reached around me into the freezer for a pint of ice cream. I automatically got two spoons from the drawer and followed her to the table. *The Princess Bride* droned in the background.

After we each had a couple of fortifying bites of B & J's Chocolate Fudge Brownie, Laura continued.

"The thing is, sugar, I don't think Mark's exactly come to terms with his feelings yet. And who knows if he ever will? It's hard for him to let go of this image of himself as some sort of . . . not superhero, exactly, but close. He has a stupidly strong sense of duty. The job is so important to him, and the idiot seems to think it's not compatible with a personal life."

I smiled ruefully. I could hardly complain about the hero complex—it was one of the things that had always attracted me to him. "Maybe he's right," I said. "Maybe it doesn't pay to get close to a guy like him."

She shook her head lightly, agreeing, if reluctantly. "Can't deny that. Hell, maybe I'm being too romantic, here on the eve of my wedding. I want everyone I care about to have the same kind of love I do. And I can't help feeling it would be a shame if you and Mark *were* meant for each other, and then it was too late because . . ." She shrugged.

"Because I was with Billy," I said. "But aren't you the one who told me what I had going with Billy was special and that I shouldn't—and I'm quoting you here—'fuck it up'?"

"I did. God, I feel like such a rat. I *adore* Billy. He's a fantastic guy, and it's obvious he's crazy about you. If that's mutual, then I'm thrilled for you both. But if you . . . well, I think every man deserves a woman who feels about him the way I feel about Tom."

I couldn't think of a good response, so I dug into the ice cream. From across the room, the vocally challenged clergyman from the movie proclaimed, "And wuv, twue wuv, will fowwow you fowevah . . ."

I had never been able to watch that scene without cracking up. Until now.

Mom's hired decorators, under her and Auntie Mo's madly annoying supervision, had turned The Barns from a rustically warm and inviting theater into a rustically warm and inviting wedding chapel, festooned with sheaves of wheat and yards of colorful grosgrain ribbon. They'd lined both sides of the aisle with tall, thin terracotta pots of fall flowers—chrysanthemums, pansies, and asters being the only ones I could put names to, if pressed. It was simple. It was colorful. It was gorgeous.

As I walked down the aisle I tried to focus on my handsome brother and how happy he looked, instead of staring at Mark in a tuxedo, but it wasn't easy. What was it about a spy in a tux?

Molly, in a wispy tea-length dress the exact blue of the asters, had led the way down the aisle, rocking her debut wedding with the classic Doyle swagger. She'd given me a thumbs-up and a broad smile right before she took off (she obviously liked weddings more than I did). Sinead (same style dress, only matching the bronze mums) and Siobhan (the red mums) had followed her, one at a time. Beautiful, the both of them. I brought up the rear, unfortunately having been chosen to coordinate with the bright yellow pansies. I felt like a walking banana as I made my way down the aisle.

To the right of the temporary altar were Thomas, Mark, Brian, James . . . and still no Billy, not even sliding in at the last possible second, like I'd halfway expected.

Damn. Where the hell was he? He'd finally been roped in by Mom to balance out the wedding party, so he was supposed to be there. There'd been a minor kerfuffle downstairs in the dressing room when Mom and Auntie Mo couldn't track him down, but everyone was so used to Billy breezing in at the last minute that no one had gotten too upset about it.

But if Billy wasn't here, then . . .

I looked sharply at Mark. If it *was,* in fact, Mark.

Passing the front row, where my parents sat with Auntie Mo and Uncle Liam, I shot Mom a panicked look. She shrugged and shook her head, looking exasperated but not surprised. As long as Thomas was married by the end of the ceremony, she'd be fine.

Auntie Mo flashed me a peek at her smart phone, where I could see a picture of Billy's smiling face. He must have contacted them with an excuse.

I couldn't say I wasn't halfway expecting this. The question was, if the job Mark and Billy had been working were at a critical point, would Mark have left it to be in a wedding?

Or would he be more inclined to have another good friend fill in for him as best man? Someone (Billy) who wouldn't himself be missed, because he was known for being less than reliably present at family functions? Someone (Billy) who, while he would catch some shit from the parental units for missing the wedding, was more than used to letting parental shit roll off, and quite frankly, due to his well-known charm, wouldn't be in the doghouse for very long anyway?

Or would Mark instead trust Billy to handle the critical job so he could be there for arguably the most important day in his best friend's life? Would Mark ever put *anything* over his job? Laura was right—he did have a stupidly strong sense of duty.

The answer probably depended entirely on how critical the job was.

I found my spot without tripping, and turned around in time to see everyone in attendance stand to watch the bride. When Laura stepped into view, all thoughts of Mark and Billy (and who was who) fled. Her utter and absolute radiance as she caught sight of Thomas didn't leave room for any other thought. She made the vintage gown she was wearing even more beautiful.

I'd helped Laura change into her wedding finery—another of my MOH duties—so the dress itself wasn't a big surprise to me. It had lacy cap sleeves and a V-neck, and was belted at the waist by braided satin ribbons the same colors as the flowers in the simple bound bouquet she was carrying. Layer upon layer of gossamer silk swayed close to her curves as she walked.

A circlet made of the same type of flowers as her bouquet sat atop a cap of soft, auburn curls. The elegant simplicity of the whole ensemble was perfect for both her and the setting. In the soft lighting, she looked as if she could have walked out of a tinted daguerreotype.

She was walked down the aisle by Harvey Smith, her boss and mentor at the CIA. I'd met Harvey over Laura's hospital bed a few months earlier, and had liked the heavyset, avuncular man at once, despite Thomas's antipathy toward him at the time. (Thomas got over it.) Harvey looked every bit as happy as Laura, proud of his position as substitute father of the bride.

I glanced at Thomas. If he had any remaining objections to Harvey, you'd never know it. Heck, I doubted he even saw Harvey. He was obviously blown away by the sight of his bride. My heart filled for him. He was a great brother, and deserved all the happiness I was sure Laura would bring him.

As Harvey placed Laura's hand into Thomas's, I glanced at Mark. He was looking at me, his gray eyes softer than I'd ever seen them. I just wished I knew for sure who was behind them.

Chapter 13

"Ciel!" Auntie Mo cornered me at the bar.

All the wedding guests had gathered in the smaller English barn to await the changeover of the German barn from chapel to party central. The catering staff was well trained and efficient, so it wasn't supposed to take long. In the interim, the bar was open, and appetizers were being passed around by servers dressed in black pants and white shirts with button-down collars. More flowers adorned every flat surface, from the bar itself to the tall tables scattered throughout the room to catch empty glasses and hors d'oeuvres plates.

The wedding party and the family members had finished the posed pictures in front of the altar. Thomas and Laura had gone with the photographer, who was hot to get some outdoor pictures with the fall foliage before the sun set.

I smiled my extra-bright, nothing-wrong-here smile at Auntie Mo, waiting to be grilled.

She engulfed me in a hug. "Honey, first of all, let me tell you how beautiful you look. That dress is gorgeous on you. Ro said you hate yellow, but that's utter nonsense. It makes your hair look like a titian halo—positively lovely."

Note to self: look up "titian."

"Um, thanks, Auntie Mo. You look marvelous, too." And she really did. The deep green of her below-the-knee dress set off her Maureen O'Hara coloring to perfection, and coordinated beautifully with Mom's dark burgundy mother-of-the-groom dress.

"Thank you, darling. Now, second thing"—her eyes captured mine and didn't let go—"where exactly is my son?"

Crap. She'd never believe I didn't know, even though it was the God's honest truth. I *didn't* know, not for sure. But more and more I suspected Billy was right here among us, playing Mark to perfection, being the best man so the real Mark could finish his job with peace of mind on the home front. Something about the way Mark had smiled at me as we walked back down the aisle together after the ceremony had given me a Billy vibe.

I didn't think that would fly with Auntie Mo, though. She would be really put out with Mark if she thought he'd put his job ahead of his best man duty, and so would Mom. I didn't want either of them to hold it against Mark.

I sighed. "You know Billy helps Mark on some of his jobs, right?"

"I do," she said. She wasn't pleased about it, but she'd come to terms with it once she'd realized that helping Mark was probably less dangerous than some of the jobs Billy took on his own, not to mention a whole lot more legal.

I lowered my voice. "Billy's been filling in for Laura on a really sensitive job all week, and he and Mark couldn't both leave without it falling apart. Since Mark is the best man, Billy volunteered to stay on the job for him." I held my stemmed wineglass between two crossed fingers and my thumb (not easy, but doable), in case I was lying, which I highly suspected I was. "I think that was really thoughtful of Billy," I added.

Mo agreed, if reluctantly. "I suppose so . . ." She hugged me again. "Well, I'm sorry your date isn't here. Try to have fun anyway, okay?"

Mark—Billy?—caught my eye from across the room, where he stood chatting with my dad. The intensity of his look warmed me even from a distance. "I'll try my best," I said.

The transformation of the German barn in such a short time was amazing. The chairs that had been set up in rows now surrounded tables covered by cream-colored muslin tablecloths embroidered with golden stalks of wheat. The flowers that had lined the aisle for the ceremony served as centerpieces. Tea candles set in short glass vases half-filled with river rocks provided a warm glow in the romantically lowered lights of the room.

Space had been left open in front of the stage for a dance floor. Brian's band, looking remarkably unscruffy, was playing softly enough that the guests could hear themselves talk. That was a minor miracle—Mom must have laid down the law ahead of time.

Molly was hanging out at the foot of the stage, staring dreamily at the band, telling anyone who'd listen that the lead guitar was her date. Of course, everyone there knew Brian and his dating proclivities, so Molly was getting a lot of pats on the head and indulgent smiles.

Brian tapped on his microphone. "Everyone . . . if I can have your attention, please . . . it gives me great pleasure to announce Mr. and Mrs. Thomas Halligan. Hey, Laura, it's great to have another sister!"

They entered from the alcove in the back, looking flushed and a little windblown. The photographer tailed them, snapping photos like a mad paparazzo. Thomas (who normally had no patience at all for that sort of thing) and the new Mrs. Halligan ignored the man elegantly.

Have to admit, I was a little surprised when Laura decided to take the Halligan name. She was so independent that I'd thought surely she'd keep her own, but while Mom and I were helping her dress earlier, she'd told us that, all things considered, she'd rather share Thomas's last name than her asshole father's. (Well, she hadn't said "asshole" in front of Mom, but I could read between the lines.) Mom had teared up, and told her she couldn't be happier to have another Halligan in the family. In fact, she wouldn't mind *many* more Halligans in the family. Laura had smiled and hugged her, but made no promises. She obviously knew how to handle Mom.

"Oh, dear," Mom had said, "I've wrinkled your dress. Ciel, get the portable steamer."

Laura had laughed and reached for me, hugging me tightly. "Never mind the steamer—I'm hoping to gather lots of these kind of wrinkles today."

Looked like she was making headway on her goal. Instead of a formal reception line, she and Thomas were circulating through the room, stopping to say a few words to everyone, upping the hug tally by the minute. But the wrinkles accumulating were minor and only made her dress more beautiful.

Mark came up to me as I beamed at the happy couple and said, "I believe you're my date for the evening." His eyes were soft, not a hint of the spook. Not that I'd expect there to be, even if it was the real Mark. He was too good at compartmentalizing his life.

I searched his face for a clue. Surely Billy would give me some sign if it were him . . . or perhaps not. Not with so many knowing adaptor eyes around. He wouldn't want to take a chance that someone else might notice he wasn't the real deal.

"Best man, maid of honor . . . it does make sense," I said, taking a drink from the tray of a passing waiter.

"Careful with that—it tastes like apple cider, but I have it on good authority that it will knock you on your butt."

I sniffed the contents of the sturdy goblet. "I'll keep that in mind. Wouldn't want to stumble into the wrong limo later." Mom and Dad had hired drivers for the whole wedding party.

"Don't worry. Since Billy got held up, I'll give you a ride home."

Was there an odd inflection when he said "Billy"? Could that be my clue?

Before I could dig for more hints, my brother James approached with his boyfriend, Devon. He and Devon had been through a rough patch, but had recently agreed to give their relationship another go. When I looked at Devon, I could certainly see why James had been willing to summon up a little forgiveness of spirit—the man was gorgeous, with platinum blond hair, pouty lips, and violet eyes.

James was no slouch himself in the looks department, with his longish strawberry blond hair and pale green eyes. Kind of a male version of me, only without freckles, the lucky bastard. Looked better on him.

"Ciel, there you are. You look lovely," James said, and gave me a rather stilted kiss on my cheek. He'd never been terribly comfortable with public displays of affection. "Mark, good to see you. Have you met Devon?"

Mark shook Devon's hand. "Devon. It's a pleasure . . ."

Devon smiled, and a flash went off nearby. I'm sure he was used to it. The photographer's assistant was wandering freely, taking candid shots of the guests. Coming across a face like Devon's was something that didn't happen every day, and he was taking advantage of it.

"Ciel," Devon said after shaking Mark's hand, "your brother is the master of understatement. You are beyond lovely—a piece of summer sunshine. Totally gorgeous." He kissed both my cheeks, European style.

Was everybody blind? Or being kind? The fact is, yellow washes me out, highlights my freckles, and makes my hair look like a Dreamsicle. But I murmured a thank-you anyway, and was spared from further embarrassment when an announcement from the band instructed us to take our seats for dinner. Mark guided me to our table with his hand at the small of my back. All the members of the wedding party were seated together, so it wouldn't seem strange to anyone for me to be with him.

Thomas and Laura had their own small "sweetheart" table near the stage, and seemed oblivious to the crowd as they gazed adoringly into each other's eyes. (Gag me. No, wait . . . that wasn't very nice, was it? I mean, everyone's entitled to be sickeningly sweet on their wedding day. It wasn't their fault weddings made me cringe.)

The menu was as rustic and simple as the wedding: a hearty vegetable soup served in hollowed-out miniature white pumpkins, with a sliced beet salad (not nearly as disgusting as I'd feared it might be) and crusty bread on the side. There were crocks of hand-churned butter and mason jars of local honey, complete with honeycombs and wooden honey dippers. For those who preferred more protein, there was grilled salmon or tender filet of beef. Or, if you happened to be starving, like me, all of the above. Mom and Auntie Mo knew how to put on a spread.

The wineglasses were a pale bottle-green, thick and sturdy, and etched with Thomas and Laura's names and the date, so the guests would have a memento of the occasion. I planned to make off with as many as I could get my hands on—my stock of stemware at home was in dire need of replenishing.

I sat between Mark and Brian, who had joined us after announcing the band would be taking a break to "get some food, man." James was also with us, Devon having been seated at a table reserved for the dates of the wedding party and the other band members. He'd have fun entertaining the two young lawyers who'd escorted Sinead and Siobhan around town the previous evening. Apparently they'd behaved themselves, seeing as how they were here and, you know, still alive. They cast wary glances in Uncle Liam's direction, but seemed to be having a good time otherwise.

All through dinner I tried to watch Mark without looking like I was watching him. The more wine I had, the harder it was. (Hey, I knew I wouldn't be driving, so why not? Wine is the anesthetic that makes weddings bearable. Even Jesus knew that.)

I was still running about fifty-fifty in my head as to whether my date was Mark or Billy. Talk about déjà vu. The last wedding I'd attended—that time filling in for the bride—I hadn't been able to tell if my "date" (aka the groom) was Mark or Billy either. Now, *this* guy was quintessentially *Mark.* Of course, Billy could pull that off without a blink, knowing Mark as well as he did. But I thought maybe some of the looks he gave me were . . . well, more *knowing.* Or something.

Mark caught me looking, and gave me a long, slow smile. I looked away, feeling myself blush. *Oops.* Was I staring at him too much? What if it was Billy, and he didn't know I knew it was him and thought I was ogling Mark? That wouldn't be good. On the other hand, if he knew I knew it was him, but didn't know *I* knew he knew I knew it, then maybe he was . . . oh, hell. This was getting confusing. I signaled the waiter for another glass of wine.

Brian excused himself as the dessert cheese platter (complete with wedges of dark chocolate—*way to go, Mom!*) was being served. He whispered something to Molly, rounded up the band, and started the dance music going. According to Mom, who had of course grilled him on it prewedding, he'd actually put together a nice, romantic playlist, ranging from Frank Sinatra to Michael Bublé. He'd also included a few zippier numbers from They Might Be Giants and Train to keep things upbeat and spirited.

The first postdinner song was one Brian and James had written especially for Thomas and Laura's first dance as man and wife. James joined the band onstage for the number. He and Brian harmonized the sentimentally mushy lyrics into a work of transcendent beauty, judging by the tears streaming down our parents' faces. Yes, my dad can be a crier. (Okay, I may have leaked a few drops, too. Sue me.) Thomas and Laura loved it, that was the main thing.

As we'd been preinstructed to do, the wedding party members—other than James and Brian, of course—joined the happy couple on the dance floor about halfway through the song. Sinead and Siobhan laughingly pulled their unsuspecting lawyer dates onto the floor with them. Mark guided me into the dance so expertly I almost felt coordinated. I guess I was still leaking, because he let go of my hand for a moment, and gently wiped my cheeks with his thumb, without ever missing a step.

"You okay, Howdy?" he said, taking my hand again and pulling me closer to his chest, but not inappropriately close. It was a slow dance, after all.

"Yeah, I'm fine. Stupid wedding song." I sniffled. "Remind me to slug James and Bri when I get a chance."

He chuckled, a low rumble in his chest that made me want to lay my cheek against his lapel. If I'd been dancing with Billy—Billy in his own aura, I mean—I wouldn't have hesitated to do it.

But almost everybody here knew about my long-standing crush on Mark, so if I were to do that, they might think I was backsliding.

I looked up into dove-soft eyes. Hell, maybe I *was* backsliding . . .

No. I dragged my eyes away from his and gave myself an infinitesimal shake. *Ciel Halligan, you will not backslide.*

"Something wrong, Ciel? Are you cold?" His quiet voice vibrated into my ear.

I shivered. "No. I'm not," I said, and looked boldly into his eyes.

They gave nothing away. Damn it, I had to figure out if this was Billy. It would be like him to delay letting me know for as long as possible, just to tease me.

"So," I said, "it was awfully nice of Billy to fill in for you on the job." There was a slight edge to my voice.

"You annoyed about that, Howdy?" he said.

Maybe. "No, not a bit. Of course, it might have been nice if *he'd let me know,*" I said meaningfully. It's possible I also stepped on his foot. Maybe I could tweak him into giving me a proper hint. There were too many ears around to ask him outright, but surely he could come up with some sort of subtle indicator.

He ignored my clumsiness. Probably didn't realize it was intentional. "We didn't know until the last minute that we couldn't both come," he said. "I'm sure he figured you'd understand."

Not enough to go on. "Yeah, well, he figured wrong," I said, and searched his face for a sign, getting zip. Not a wink, not a hair tug. Only a blandly understanding smile and nothing more.

Damn it. I should be able to tell.

Billy would tease me unmercifully if it turned out I couldn't. He was probably seeing how long he could keep me guessing—that would be just like him.

"He could have *called,*" I said, and then decided to up the ante. "I'm beginning to wonder if it was such a good idea to dive into a relationship with him." I stepped on his other foot. Could he not *see* what I was asking him?

I *know.* I wasn't exhibiting a lot of finesse. But after the hard apple cider and all the wine with dinner, my tongue wasn't exactly on its best behavior. My feet either.

At least I'd succeeded in wiping the bland off his face. He pulled me closer still. "I think you know where I stand on that," he said.

Like *that* helped. I knew where Billy stood on the issue—he'd made it plain enough he wanted me. And I knew where Mark stood—he'd made no secret of the fact that he didn't think Billy was right for me.

Ugh. I was just going to have to drag him someplace private, admit defeat, and ask him outright.

But then the music stopped. Mark let me go and we both joined in the applause. When I turned back to him, I was startled to see a familiar face behind him.

"Nils!" I said. How had I missed that flaxen head in the crowd?

Nils was an agent with the Swedish National Security Police I'd met on one of my jobs. He worked with Mark and Laura as a liaison on some of their overseas ops.

His crystal-blue eyes crinkled at the edges, and he lifted me into a bear hug. "Ciel! It is so good to see you again." He put me down and shook Mark's hand. "You too, Mark. But I don't think I can pick you up so easily."

Mark didn't look quite as happy to see Nils as I was, but he kept a pleasant enough expression on his face. "And I thank you for that."

"What are you doing here?" I asked. Yeah, I know. How rude. But when I'm surprised, I blurt.

"Laura invited me. I couldn't pass up the opportunity to visit your country. Under better circumstances this time."

His quirky half smile reminded me of when I'd last seen him. He'd been in full Viking regalia then, which had been an impressive sight to behold. The expensive suit he was currently wearing wasn't hurting my opinion of his looks any either. He and Laura had become good friends when she'd worked an extended assignment in Sweden. I had to wonder if Thomas knew he was here, but before I could think of a tactful way to phrase that question, the music started again.

"May I?" Nils said, reaching for my hand.

Mark nodded once, looking as if he would have refused if he could. Billy hadn't been thrilled with Nils over in Sweden—he'd thought my inexperienced head was being turned by the big Norseman—so that was one more check in the "Billy" column. As far as I could remember, Mark had had no problem with Nils.

Hmm. Maybe I could manage this without admitting defeat. Which would be good, because there's nothing I hate more than admitting defeat, especially to Billy.

The band played an old Frank Sinatra tune as the big man led me into an enthusiastic, if inexpert, two-step. If I'd been trying to follow his sometimes unexpected moves in heels, I probably would have been on my ass, but Laura, bless her sweet Southern heart, had left the footwear selection entirely up to her attendants. Mom had lobbied heavily for heels ("Only three or four inches, honey, so you won't get lost in the pictures."), but I'd told her comfortable feet were more important than looking taller. Besides, I was wearing yellow—I *wanted* to get lost in the pictures. Thank God for understanding brides and kitten-heeled dress shoes.

Nils laughed, and apologized when he stepped on my foot. (Karma is a bitch.) I told him not to worry about it, that I had a spare. It really was good to see him again, and reassuring that friendship was all I felt toward the handsome Swede. Maybe my hormones weren't as out of control as I thought.

Thomas cut in, sending Nils in search of another partner. Judging by the way Sinead and Siobhan were ignoring their lawyers and giving him the eye, it wouldn't be difficult for him.

"Mark sent me to you," Thomas said. "Told me it was time for the bride and groom to dance the customary dances with their attendants, or some such nonsense."

I glanced at Mark, who was dancing with Laura, chatting pleasantly, keeping a respectful distance between them. When he caught me looking, he nodded his head once, with a highly satisfied look on his face. For what, separating me from Nils?

"Wouldn't want to fly in the face of tradition, would we?" I said to Thomas. "Speaking of which, don't forget Mom, or you'll be paying for it the rest of your life."

He smiled down at me. "Don't worry, I won't. Bri's going to play something special for that one. Guaranteed to make her cry."

"Good thing she wore her heavy-duty waterproof makeup," I said. "By the way, I'm sorry I set you up for this. That was bad."

He looked down at me. "Yeah, right. As you can see, it's killing me."

"You're welcome," I said, grinning up at him. I love it when my nefarious plots work out for the best.

"Don't press your luck. And don't do it again."

I laughed. "Better make sure this one takes, then."

Our song ended, and Thomas excused himself to find our mother. When Brian started singing Lucero's "Mom"—sounding even better than the original—I knew Thomas was right. Sure enough, it didn't take long for our mother to start the waterworks. Even Thomas's eyes were glistening.

See, this was the problem with weddings. If you aren't all that close to the couple, they bore you silly. And if you are, they squash your heart. Stupid song.

A strong pair of arms hugged me from behind, pressing a cocktail napkin into my hand. I dabbed my eyes with it.

"Thanks, Dad," I said, leaning into his embrace. The first man I'd ever loved, and the only one I could count on not to drive me crazy.

"You're welcome, sweetie pie. I'm feeling a bit damp-eyed myself," he said. "May I have the rest of this dance?"

We made it through with minimal tears, thanks mostly to the truly horrendous knock-knock jokes Dad kept whispering in my ear. He'd used the same tactic on me when I was little and had needed distraction from one of my endless crises. After the song, he gave me a squeeze and said, "I better get over to your mother before I have to mop her up off the floor."

"And now an antidote to all that sentimental stuff . . ." Brian announced from the stage.

Thank God, I thought, and took another goblet of cider offered by a passing server, both of us almost getting knocked over by Molly as she whizzed past. She didn't slow down until she was onstage. The drummer vacated his seat for her. After a sign from Brian, she hit her drumsticks together three times. Brian let loose a crazy laugh, culminating in "*Wipeout!*" The band dove into a rousing rendition of the Surfaris' classic instrumental, dominated by the ten-year-old on the drums.

After a few seconds of stunned silence, the whole crowd was up and moving. Molly was *good,* and, like any Doyle, she knew it. The look of utter concentration on her face as she beat the hell out of the drums was exhilarating to behold. She must have been practicing with Brian.

I hopped around throughout the whole thing. But at least I wasn't the only one. Heck, even Auntie Mo got into the act once she was over her shock. When the tune was played out and Molly took her bow, it was Mo who added a piercingly appreciative whistle to the thunderous applause.

After the cake was cut and served (the one part of any wedding reception I looked forward to), things moved along at a brisk pace. We had to vacate the premises by eleven, thank goodness. A Halligan event could easily go on until dawn if not strictly reined in by the rules.

When it came time for the bouquet toss, Laura exhibited deadly aim. Even though I was standing as far on the outskirts of the group of giggling singles as I could get away with, the bundled bunch of fall flowers hit me right in the middle of my chest. I grabbed it reflexively, some part of me thinking it would be a shame if the pretty arrangement hit the floor. Mom and Auntie Mo clapped their hands and hurried over to me.

"Oh, honey, what fun!" Mom said.

"I wish Billy were going to be here for the garter toss," Auntie Mo said, as if I couldn't already read their collective mind.

I felt myself blushing, and looked at Mark, who was grinning broadly. Much more characteristic of Billy than the spook. And when Thomas tossed the garter, he was front and center, surreptitiously elbowing Nils out of the way to catch it himself, after which he made a crack about his training making it impossible for him not to jump in front of a bullet to protect his fellow man.

As maid of honor, it was my job to help Laura change into her travel clothes and pack up her wedding dress for her. She thanked me profusely for all I'd done to make her day so perfect, which made me feel kind of guilty about all the inner bitching and moaning I'd been doing.

While she was in the restroom, I checked my cell phone to see if Billy had ever left me a message. It was possible—just barely—that he'd spent this whole evening thinking I knew he was playing Mark and had just been giving him a hard time for the fun of it.

No such luck. I slipped my phone into my bra (the top of my dress was blousy enough that you couldn't tell), figuring it didn't hurt to keep it close. Sometimes texts got delayed.

Back upstairs, waiting for the bride and groom say their farewell to the crowd, I felt my boob buzz. *Aha!* I edged to the side of the room and dug my phone out. A text from Billy after all. Better late than never.

Hey, cuz, it read, *are you ready for me to rip that yellow rag off you?*

Trust Billy to understand my feelings. I automatically searched the room. Sure enough, Mark was slipping something into his pocket. Billy's phone? He smiled when I caught his eye.

I walked deliberately over to him, passing through a group of elderly ladies laughing it up over the questionable dance moves of one of my great-uncles. Some of the ladies were distant relatives, some of them were friends of the family, and all of them were wearing way too much perfume. I sneezed, absently took a tissue one of the ladies handed me, and held to my path.

Mark's eyes were hot on me by the time I got to him. "Gesundheit," he said.

Bingo.

Chapter 14

If I hadn't already figured out it was Billy at the wedding, I would have known it for sure when I saw the Chevy in the parking lot of The Barns. I raised my eyebrows at Mark. Because he was, of course, still Mark. Billy wouldn't drop the aura until completely free from prying eyes.

"My car is still on the job with Billy, so he let me borrow his."

Ah. So, that was how it was going to be, was it? We weren't through playing games.

I finally realized what Billy was doing. Or, rather, what he thought he was doing. He'd mentioned, back at the ranch, that he wished I'd gotten Mark out of my system before we'd embarked on our own relationship. He'd also once told me he was afraid my lack of experience with the opposite sex would make me wonder what I'd missed, and had offered me, on more than one occasion, a "safe" way to experiment. Putting two and two together, I was guessing this was supposed to be my safe opportunity to satisfy any lingering curiosity about Mark.

If I dared. I mean, it was wrong, wasn't it? It was at the top of the adaptor No-No list to use another adaptor's aura without permission. Of course, Billy *had* permission. Technically. Mark had to have asked him to fill in, right? You can't specify every little thing you're going to do ahead of time—that wouldn't be practical. Given the circumstance, Mark had to know there would be social interaction involved. Not that we'd be telling Mark the extent of the interaction. What he didn't know couldn't hurt him, right? Or piss him off.

The question was, what the heck did I want to do? Was Billy right? Did I still melt around Mark only because a decade-long crush had been cut short just shy of its ultimate fulfillment? Would acting out my fantasy somehow exorcise it?

Gah. I didn't know. It felt wrong, but . . . well, was it really so very different than the role-playing games non-adaptors played to spice up their love lives? Adaptors just had access to more realistic "costumes."

The thing was, my love life with Billy didn't need any spicing up. When I was with him, he was the only one I wanted. He got me revved up like no one else could. But I couldn't deny that Mark did still have an effect on me. If Billy was doing this, *he* must have thought it would help somehow, and he had a hell of a lot more experience with sexual matters than I did.

Whoa . . . wait a second. Was *this* the "surprise" he'd told me about? Hmm.

Maybe I should see how far *he* wanted to take it before I backed out entirely. Right before the first time we made love, he'd called me a chicken. Teasing me, like he always did. He wasn't being mean. He'd suspected—rightly so, as it turned out—that goading my temper would make me forget my fears. He knew me that well. I didn't want him clucking at me over this, though—I should be past silly sexual fears with him, shouldn't I?

The ride back to my place with Mark (it was easier to think of him that way as long as he was wearing the aura) was filled mostly with chitchat about the wedding. I tried not to roll my eyes when he called me "Howdy"—I thought Billy might be overplaying it a little because I hadn't let him get away with calling me that since the time he'd called me "Howdy-Doody-In-Your-Pants" when we were eight years old.

When he got a small overnight bag out of the trunk, I raised my eyebrows again.

He looked a little sheepish—well, as sheepish as anyone wearing Mark's aura could look—and said he was hoping his old room was free, since Tom and Laura were borrowing his boat for a few days. They didn't have time for an extended honeymoon, but both loved sailing. The use of his boat was part of his wedding gift to them.

The room that had been his when he'd shared the condo with Thomas after they graduated from college *was* free, as Billy well knew. His sisters were staying at the hotel with their parents, and catching an early flight back to New York the next morning.

"Sure," I said. "You know you're always welcome to sleep over."

Okay, I admit it. I laced it with a hint of innuendo. If Billy wanted to play, I could play. I thought he looked mildly shocked (again, hard to tell—Mark's aura didn't show shock easily), but not displeased. I guessed he was happy I was going along with the game.

Once inside, I took his bag, dropped it on the entry hall floor, and pushed him back against the door. Before he could say anything, I pulled his head down to mine and put my mouth on his. We'd see who veered off course first in this game of sexual chicken.

He froze, but only for a moment. An instant later, our positions were reversed, and I was against the door, lifted to his level, his lips moving on mine, his tongue exploring my mouth as my feet dangled off the floor. My shoes fell off. Or maybe I kicked them off. Who needed shoes?

My arms clung to his neck, more to hold him closer to me than to hold myself up. I knew he wouldn't let me fall.

He pulled his lips away from mine, kissing his way closer to my ear. He was breathing hard. "Ciel . . . are you sure?"

I forced myself to take a steadying breath. Billy did tend to push me into things I might not otherwise do, but he always gave me the opportunity to back off if I needed to. Like the parachute in his plane. Well, I hadn't needed it then, and I wasn't going to wimp out now either.

I focused on his eyes, trying to read what lay behind the aura. Did *he* really want this? I was met with intense gray. The color might be different, but the desire was there, same as always.

"I'm sure if you are. I trust you," I said.

With that, he hooked one powerful arm behind my knees, leaving the other supporting my shoulders, and carried me up the stairs. The door to my room was ajar. He kicked it the rest of the way open and crossed to my bed in the dark.

Holy crap. I'd been Rhett Butler-ed. And, my God, it was every bit as exciting as I'd imagined it would be the first time I'd seen Clark Gable carry Vivien Leigh up that grand staircase in *Gone with the Wind.* I felt dizzy with the memory of it.

Instead of laying me on the bed, he stood me next to it. My hands slid from his neck down his chest, stopping at heart level. Impatient with the feel of cloth, I pushed his tuxedo jacket from his shoulders and tossed it onto a nearby chair. He yanked his tie loose and dropped it to the floor while I started undoing the tux buttons on his shirt. The cuff links were next, and then, like magic, his shirt was gone.

It was too dark for me to see his chest clearly, but I could picture it as I ran my hands over it. Lightly covered in blond hair, well-defined pecs, and a six-pack—no, make that an eight-pack—that wouldn't quit.

I felt his hands at the back of my dress, searching for the zipper.

"There's a hook-and-eye fastener at the top . . ." I said, and sucked in my breath when he found it.

He unzipped me in one swift motion, and swept the cap sleeves off my shoulders, letting the dress fall to the floor. My bra was next, undone in seconds and gone even faster. When he kneeled to slip off my lacy underwear, I had to hold myself upright by gripping his shoulders. His (I reminded myself to breathe) *very* well-muscled shoulders.

Before he stood, he kissed me lightly, right below my belly button. And that's when my legs buckled. Man, I was never going to hear the end of that . . .

He caught me beneath my arms as he straightened. "Easy there," he whispered, sitting me on the edge of my bed, and leaning down to find my mouth again with his own.

"Wait," I said, pulling back a little. "You're really okay with this? I wouldn't want you to . . . I mean, just because you know I—"

"Ciel, if you want this, *I* want this."

Okay, then. My hands reached out to unhook the waistband of his pants. He got the idea, and took them off, along with his shoes and socks.

My eyes were getting accustomed to the dark. I could see well enough to notice the impressive bulge in his boxer briefs, at any rate. I swallowed hard.

He kneeled in front of me, parting my legs so he could get closer, wrapping his arms around me in an embrace that nearly overwhelmed me with its skin-to-skin contact. He rubbed his chest lightly against mine, until my breasts ached with the need to feel more. As if he knew what I was thinking, what I was feeling, he kissed his way from my shoulder to the hollow of my throat, and then downward, until I felt the hot, wet suction of his mouth on one breast.

I cried out. He moved to the other side. I moaned, trying my best to keep it inaudible. Not succeeding.

When he moved lower still, I bit my lip against the sound I was afraid I would make next. He eased me back until I was lying down, my knees bent at the edge of the bed. He spread them farther apart, and then . . . then I stopped thinking at all.

The next few minutes were pure sensation. I would have jumped right off the bed if he hadn't been holding me down. As it was, I was pretty sure the bedspread I was clutching would never be the same again.

He didn't allow me any time to recover before he was on the bed next to me, cupping me gently but insistently with one broad, strong hand as he kissed me deeply, until I felt the tension start to build again. I scooted farther up onto the bed, pulling him with me.

He settled on top of me, between my legs, kissing the most sensitive places on my neck as my hands played over the muscles of his back. Reaching lower, I was annoyed to find he was still wearing his boxer briefs. I slipped my hands beneath the cotton jersey and let them glide over the hard, smooth muscles, pinching to test their firmness. With a harsh sound in his throat, he ground himself against me, giving me a good idea of what was in store for me. I grabbed the waistband and yanked his briefs down, leaving it to him to kick them off entirely.

Finally as naked as I was, he rolled onto his back and pulled me on top of him. His hands slid over me, from shoulders to hips, heating every bit of skin they touched, until I was shivering from the contrast with the cool air. His fingers paused briefly over the small birth control patch I wore on one hip, circling it a few times before squeezing my ass with both hands. He sat me up and adjusted my position until my still ultrasensitive flesh settled against the hard length of him lying flat against his belly.

And then he started rocking his hips, ever so slightly at first, until I was gliding back and forth along him, so wet I would have slipped off if he hadn't been holding me upright. It felt so . . . damn . . . *good* . . . that I thought I'd go crazy with it. But I needed more. I needed to feel him inside me.

I gripped his shoulders, sliding up until I felt the tip of him at my entrance. A shaft of moonlight from a gap in my curtains fell across his face, delineating his hard-chiseled features, highlighting the intensity of his dark gray eyes. A tiny droplet of sweat made its way down one temple, with more of them spiking the wisps of new growth at his hairline.

He was holding himself in check, waiting for me. And it wasn't easy for him.

In for a penny, in for a pound, I thought, and reached down to adjust his angle. I watched his face intently as I lowered myself, taking his fullness into me slowly, until I had him completely engulfed. He held himself still as stone until I began moving.

Leaving me to set the pace of our lovemaking, he stroked my breasts, alternately kneading them with his palms and flicking his thumbs across the tips. When I started whimpering, he reversed our positions and stopped holding himself back.

If I'd had any fingernails to speak of, he would have had stripes on his back by the time we were finished. Lying there in his arms, too bemused to speak, I wasn't sure if Billy had exorcised my fantasy of Mark, or had only succeeded in entrenching it more deeply.

Chapter 15

I excused myself to go to the bathroom, and then, needing more time to sort out my feelings, decided to put on my robe and go downstairs.

"I'll be back in a sec—just getting us something from the kitchen," I said, hoping he'd take the hint and give me a minute.

Staring into the freezer, trying to decide which flavor of ice cream the situation called for, I couldn't help wondering if this whole thing had been a supremely bad idea. Sure, it had been exciting as hell, but—

No. That kind of thinking was puritanical, wasn't it? Nobody was more comfortable with what it meant to be an adaptor than Billy was. Changing our appearance was a core part of who we were—shouldn't we embrace that part of ourselves along with everything else?

Or was I over-rationalizing?

I was reaching for the Rocky Road when I heard Billy's voice.

"Hey there. Couldn't wait to get out of the dress, huh? Too bad. I was looking forward to ripping it off you with my teeth."

I froze, suddenly colder than the ice cream in my hand.

Oh, God. *NO. No, no, no, no* . . . It couldn't be.

He hugged me from behind.

"Billy?" I said weakly.

"Who else?" he said, and kissed my neck.

Normally, that particular action would make me turn around in his arms, ready, willing, and happily anticipating anything he might have a fancy to do. All it did now was paralyze me with guilt. My mind went numb, absolutely refusing to consider what his presence here in my kitchen, at this moment, meant.

No, I thought again. It had to be a joke. He'd put on some of the clothes he kept in my spare room, and followed me downstairs. He was teasing me again. Please, God, he *had* to be teasing me. He *always* teased me.

"Ciel? Are you all right?" He turned me to face him, concern filling his gorgeous eyes. "You're not sick, are you? The caterers didn't give you food poisoning, did they?"

I shook my head. He wasn't teasing me. He just got here. Which meant—

"Everything okay, Howdy?"

I spun my head around to see Mark had come down. My one reprieve from total fucking disaster was that he was dressed. Maybe he'd heard Billy come in—his hearing had always been incredibly sharp. His collar was undone, and his tie was hanging out of his tux jacket, but Billy wouldn't think that was strange. Ties were a pain.

"Hey, Mark," Billy said matter-of-factly. He knew Mark often stayed in his old room when his boat wasn't available for whatever reason. "I got everything finished up, no problem. Subject showed up shortly after you left, and has been safely delivered to your bosses. He's singing like the proverbial canary."

"Great. Thanks again," Mark said, a bit stiffly, I thought. He had his "assessing" face on, sizing up the situation, and, I was terribly afraid, coming to the correct conclusion. "It means a lot that I didn't have to miss Tom and Laura's wedding. I'm sorry you did."

Billy, still oblivious to the load of shit that was about to be dropped on his head, draped one arm casually over my shoulders and pulled me away from the fridge.

Mark's eyes narrowed.

"No problem," Billy said. "I'll catch it on video. I'm only sorry I didn't get to see Ciel in the infamous yellow dress in person. But no doubt there'll be plenty of pictures."

I felt a little sick, remembering exactly where the dress was, and whose hands had removed it from me. "Trust me, it's not a look I wanted to have commemorated," I said, my voice hollow.

Billy tugged my hair. "Bet you were beautiful, cuz."

"She was," Mark said. "The prettiest one there."

He seemed to be waiting. For an explanation, probably. A confession. Something. I stared into his eyes, silently begging for understanding. For time. Because I had no fucking clue what to say that could possibly make this situation all right.

How could I ever explain this to Mark? Right now, either he was thinking I was a duplicitous bitch for throwing myself at him with no intention of breaking up with Billy—and maybe feeling guilty for participating—or else he'd figured out what had actually happened, in which case he would be feeling used and maybe even violated.

Neither option left me smelling like a rose.

When no words found their way out of my mouth, Mark smiled—it didn't reach his eyes—and said, "Well, I better get going." He dug into his pocket for the car keys and laid them on the closest table. "Here you go, Billy. Nice ride, as always. Mine out front?"

Billy tossed him the set of keys he still had in his hands. "Yeah, right behind the Chevy. Thanks for seeing Ciel safely home."

Mark pierced me with one final look. "It was my pleasure."

I locked the door behind Mark and turned to face the music. From the look on Billy's face, he was beginning to hear traces of the tune.

He took me by the hand and led me to the living room. I sat on the sofa, tucking my legs under me, and hugged a red chenille throw pillow to my chest. If only it were shaped like an "A" it would be perfect.

Billy sat next to me, for once not immediately pulling me into an embrace.

"The spook seemed a little tense. You gonna tell me what's going on?" he asked. His voice was low, almost hesitant.

I finally looked him, really *at* him. What I saw there upset me more than anything so far. Fear. He was afraid of what I was going to tell him. He thought—

"No! It's not like that . . . Billy, I never would have . . . you *know* you're the one—"

I thought I saw a tiny amount of relief in his eyes. Would he understand? Would *I,* in his place? The one thing I knew, as cowardly as I was feeling at the moment, was that I *had* to tell him what had happened. I couldn't compound my wrong by lying about it.

So, I started at the beginning. Took him with me through the wedding and the reception, explaining, as dispassionately as I could, my thought processes, trying to make him understand how I could possibly think he would do such a thing. I, of course, didn't go into detail about my encounter with Mark, other than that it had happened—that would be cruel, not to mention incredibly stupid.

I finished up my painfully long soliloquy with, "And then, when you came in"—I hurriedly wiped the tears from my face with a corner of the pillow—"and I realized what I had done . . ." I couldn't go on, not without sobbing, and I wasn't going to lay that on him.

He'd held himself still and granite-faced the whole time I was talking. "Thank you for telling me," he said at last, in a quiet monotone.

I was starting to panic. He looked so stunned, so emotionally . . . not there. I had to—"Billy, I love—"

"*Stop.*" His voice was harsh. "Do *not* tell me you love me. Not now."

I drew back, shrinking into myself like he'd backhanded me. "I—I—am so very sorry." I was crying openly, unable to hold it in anymore. "You have every right to be mad—"

"Oh, I'm mad." His eyes frosted over, but he wasn't looking at me. He was looking toward the front door.

"It wasn't his fault," I said quickly. Probably too quickly. But, God, I would hate myself even more if what I'd done caused a rift between Billy and Mark.

"Don't be stupid, Ciel. Of course it was," he said, voice rock hard.

"No, I told you—he thought I was mad at you, that I was questioning my relationship with you. I—stupidly, I know—*let* him think that, but only because I thought he was *you.* I was trying to goad you into telling me it was you, to make you come clean. It was part of the game I idiotically thought we were playing."

"Ciel, none of that matters. What matters is he betrayed me. Even if everything you say is true—and, don't worry, knowing how your mind works, I believe your story—even so, he should have, at the very least, *waited.*"

My sobs were coming faster and harder. He finally gathered me in his arms, holding my head close to his heart, stroking my hair, not saying anything.

When I still didn't stop, he lifted my chin and kissed me, not at all gently. Fiercely. Possessively. I responded—I couldn't not respond to Billy, it seemed—and it made me feel all the more shame. I pulled away.

"I . . . I need a shower," I said.

A look of bleak understanding fell over his face, followed by stony determination. He stood, and pulled me along with him, not stopping until we were in my upstairs bathroom.

"What are you doing?" I asked, though it was becoming more obvious by the second.

He yanked open the shower curtain and turned on the water. The spray was still cold when he lifted me and put me under it. I stood there as he kicked off his shoes, sputtering as the water hit my face. He stepped in and reached for my robe. Stopped himself.

"May I?" he said, with a forced calmness.

I nodded, standing there like a mannequin.

He pulled the robe off me and dropped it on the floor next to the tub. I was trying very hard not to shake, but the water was taking a god-awful time to warm up. I wanted so badly for this night never to have happened.

Billy found my bottle of body wash and squirted way more than I usually used onto his hand. He started with my back, working his way down until he got to my feet, then turned me around and continued, methodically replacing the aroma of Mark with the scent of cucumber melon bath gel. He saved the center of me for last, and by the time he got there I wasn't shivering anymore. Not from the cold, anyway.

I held on to his biceps to keep from toppling over as he let the now warm water cascade over me, washing away the last bit of foamy gel.

"Your clothes . . . got wet," I said inanely, my voice small.

He pulled the black henley over his head and dropped it, sopping, on top of my robe. His jeans took more effort, but they, too, eventually came to rest on the wet pile.

Naked, he took my hands in his and looked into my eyes, hard. "I should have told you I wouldn't be at the wedding—that part was my fault. But I have to know—did you really think he was me?"

"I did, Billy. I swear I did. I never would have—"

He pulled me into his arms. "Shhh. It'll be okay."

Chapter 16

Billy was gone from the guest bed when I woke up, giving me a moment of panic until I heard him in the kitchen. I went to my room for something to put on and was surprised to see the bed stripped down to the mattress. Sheets, pillowcases, and bedspread were nowhere to be seen. Ditto my dress, underwear, and bra.

I checked the bathroom. The pile of sodden clothing was also missing.

I dressed hastily in a T-shirt and a pair of yoga pants and went downstairs to find Billy at the stove, scrambling eggs. His eyes were guarded, but otherwise he seemed to be his usual cheerful morning self.

I thought we'd maybe weathered the storm. We'd slept in my guest room. Well, kind of slept. Mostly, we'd put a great deal of effort into proving we couldn't get enough of each other. He'd seemed determined to wipe any trace of Mark from my consciousness, and

I was equally determined to prove he had nothing to worry about on that score.

Heck, I had more than enough worry for the both of us.

"Hi," I said.

"Cuz," he said with a tiny bow of his head. "How many pieces of bacon would you like?"

"Two," I answered automatically, not really giving a damn about bacon. I wandered closer to the stove and leaned back against the counter. "So, I notice my bedspread and sheets are gone . . ."

He shrugged and kept pushing the eggs around the pan. "I threw them away. Don't worry, I'll buy you some more. Bra and underwear, too. I don't expect you want me to replace the dress."

Okay. I could understand his actions. "No, I don't need another dress like that one."

He scraped the fluffy yellow eggs (they looked much better than when I cooked them) onto two plates and added strips of bacon. Not looking at me, he carried our food to the dining table. I followed him with forks.

"Juice?" he said as I sat, sounding like a waiter.

I let out a breath through puffed cheeks. "You're still mad."

"No, I'm not." He sat, started to take a bite, then pushed his plate aside. "Okay, I am. Damn it, Ciel, you should have *known.*"

"How? How could I know for sure? You're a damn good adaptor—when you're wearing someone else's aura, *nobody* can tell it's you unless you allow it. I assumed you were going for complete realism."

He looked at me wryly. "That's just it. How could you think I'd be *Mark*?"

"Why wouldn't you? We all cover for each other. You know how seriously Mark takes his job—I assumed if one of you had to stay and finish the assignment, naturally it would be him."

"I wasn't asking that, and you know it. I meant how could you think I'd be Mark for *you*?"

"Geez, Billy, it's not as if you haven't offered. I mean, the other day you were ready to sweep me off my feet as Jackson Gunn!"

"Yeah, and *that* would have been fine. I knew it wouldn't mean anything to you. Hell, I'll be happy to wear Hugh Jackman for you, or Daniel Craig, or that guy you like on the *Vampire Diaries*—"

"Ian Somerhalder? Don't bother. You look enough like him as it is," I said, trying desperately to lighten the moment.

He lifted one corner of his mouth. Halfway there?

"The point is, I know you don't feel anything beyond a passing lust for any of them. If I were going to pretend to be Mark for you—and that's a damn big 'if,' because, trust me, I'm not that big an idiot. Anyone else, fine—but let's say, for the sake of argument, that I lost my freaking mind and did it. Do you honestly think I wouldn't have thrown in something to crack your impression that he's perfect?"

He seemed to be loosening up, now that he was letting it out. When he saw I wasn't going to argue with him, the barest hint of humor appeared in his eyes.

"Hell, I would have given him Limburger breath, if I thought it would kill your crush. At the least. And probably a really tiny dick."

That surprised a laugh out of me. I clamped my mouth shut, but the giggles kept coming.

Billy reached across the table and took my hand, his eyes finally forgiving me. "*Now,* Ciel. Tell me when you're laughing. I couldn't stand to hear it when you were crying."

My heart full, I declared it openly to him for the first time. "I love you."

His face relaxed, the tension he'd been holding at bay gone. "Told you so," he said with a wink. "Eat your eggs before they get cold."

Billy left me to my own devices after breakfast. He had a client of his own to meet with back in Manhattan.

As he walked out the door he said, "Limburger."

"What?" I said, perplexed. "You want me to get you some cheese?"

He shook his head. "That's our new safe word. If you ever need to know it's me, ask if I want some cheese. I'll say 'Limburger'—that's how you'll know for sure."

"Okay. Limburger." I supposed it was better than "tiny dick."

I was hoping the drive would give his anger toward Mark a chance to cool, but I hadn't brought it up again, not wanting to strain our fragile rapprochement. When he came back, we were going to put our heads together and figure out the best way to deal with the Jackson Gunn situation.

The first thing I did after he left was reach for my phone. I doubted Billy would appreciate it, but I had to explain things to Mark. I wasn't looking forward to it a bit either, but confession was apparently good for the soul. Besides, in the immortal words of my dad, if you make a mess, you clean it up yourself.

Mark didn't answer, so I left a message to call me when he got a chance, hoping my voice hadn't cracked as much as I feared it did, frankly grateful for the reprieve. I still wasn't sure what I was going to say to him.

I showered again, put on clean clothes, and dug out fresh sheets for both beds, wishing it were as simple to tidy up my conscience. That was when I noticed the small, still-damp velvet case on my nightstand, and my heart tried to exit my body through my mouth. Was *that* Billy's surprise? Surely he hadn't intended to . . .

But no. What it was clamped around my heart more than any ring could have. It was a small brooch, made of diamonds and white gold, shaped like an open parachute. The folded note in the case read: *Congratulations on facing your fears. Stick with me, Ciel—I'll never let you fall.*

He must have had it made after my first ride in his plane. I felt the tears prickle again. Aw, crap. Why'd he have to be so thoughtful? And how could I have been so *stupid*? Had I wanted to have my cake and eat it too so badly that my brain had come up with the perfect scenario to achieve it without guilt? Man, I *sucked* at being a girlfriend.

I tucked the beautiful pin away in my top dresser drawer. It was too fancy for jeans and a sweatshirt, and besides, I didn't deserve to wear it. Not yet. But I was determined to fix that.

At loose ends, I decided to walk to the grocery store. It was a hike, and I didn't need all that much, but it was something to do. I had to keep busy.

Mark was at the door, about to ring the bell, when I opened it to leave.

"Is he gone?" he said, his face giving away nothing.

I tried to remain as calm—outwardly, anyway—as he seemed. Nothing was going to slow my heart down, but he didn't have to know that. "Yes. He has a client to see in New York."

He nodded once. "May I come in? Or would you rather talk in the park?"

The patch of green across from my condo wasn't big, but it did have a bench and a statue, so maybe it qualified for that designation.

"It's nice out," I said, pleased my voice didn't shake. Not being in the place where I'd thrown myself at him might be best, all things considered.

The bench was empty, so we sat, not looking at each other. There was a squirrel scolding us from the other side of the statue, apparently irritated that we'd dared invade its territory.

"So," I finally said, "about last night . . ."

"Ciel, before you start, you need to know something." He turned to me. Even smiled a little, maybe trying to reassure me. "I don't play games. I wouldn't have taken you to bed if I didn't intend for there to be something between us. I'm not a fling kind of guy. Even if I were, I wouldn't do that to you."

This was going to be worse than I thought.

"Mark, I have to tell you—"

"That you feel bad about Billy? I understand. You think I don't feel like shit about it myself? He's my friend." Mark ran a hand through his short hair, obviously frustrated at the situation.

"No, I wasn't going to say that, exactly. I mean, I do, but . . ." I trailed off, looking away, hoping for an infusion of courage.

"Look at me, Howdy." I did. His eyes were still gentle, but his voice was firm. "If you're going to try to tell me you were only using me because you were mad at Billy, that it didn't mean anything to you—don't. I know better. You're not that kind of person. Last night, in that bed with me, you were where you wanted to be, and it wasn't with Billy."

"Mark, last night I thought I *was* with Billy," I blurted.

"What?"

Okay, guess he *hadn't* figured it out.

I went through the whole painful explanation again, watching his face. He kept his anger hidden behind a passive mask, but I could feel it emanating from him. I went so far as to explain how I thought I'd detected a certain animosity toward Nils, and how that made me sure it was Billy, since I knew he—Mark—had liked Nils.

"Nils is fine. I didn't like the way he was looking at you," Mark said bluntly.

Oh. Well, I wasn't about to go there, so I finished by pleading stupidity about the Billy mix-up, and begging his forgiveness.

His jaw was set, his mouth hard. "Has Billy done it before—been me with you?" he asked, watching me intently, like some sort of human lie detector.

"No! Never. I only thought . . . because he knows I still react to you"—I was blushing furiously, I could feel it—"that he might have . . . you know, to get you out of my system or something—never mind that. It was a stupid assumption on my part, and he would *never* use your aura that way—trust me, if I didn't realize it before, I do now."

A whole slew of emotions had skittered through his eyes during my clumsy explanation, ending with shock. "You told him? He knows you slept with me?"

I nodded. "I wasn't going to lie. Not to either of you."

"Jesus. He must hate my guts."

"He's . . . not very happy with you at the moment, no. But I told him it wasn't your fault. He'll understand . . . eventually. If it's any consolation, he was pretty mad at me, too."

"Well, that makes two of us," he said under his breath, looking at an old lady curbing her dog across the street.

I leaned toward him and spoke rapidly, anxious to salvage what I could of our friendship. To make sure he didn't hate me. "I don't blame you for being mad—I know this whole mess is my fault, and I'm going to do everything I can to fix it. If I hadn't had that stupid crush on you for all those years . . . Look, I'm sorry. I'll find a way to make things right between you and Billy again, I swear. I won't bother you ever again. I won't melt when you're near me, I won't make moon eyes at you. Hell, I won't even smile at you."

He looked at me with rueful resignation. "You don't understand. That's not going to fix this. I *want* you."

I sucked in a breath too fast.

He shook his head, with the least happy smile I'd ever seen on anyone. "Wipe that horrified look off your face, Howdy. I'm not going to abscond with you."

"But . . ."

His eyes weren't hard, but they were far from gentle. More . . . determined. "But nothing. When you get tired of Billy or . . ." He didn't say it, but I knew he was thinking, *when Billy gets tired of you.* "When you guys part company, we'll talk."

"That's crazy, Mark. You'd never . . . listen, you and I both know your job is everything to you. It comes first, always has. Always will."

" 'Always' is a long time, Howdy. Maybe Tom and Laura got me thinking. Maybe you *can* have both. Laura seems to think so, anyway."

I slumped against the back of the bench, feeling strangely empty. "If you'd told me that three months ago, I would have thought I'd died and gone to heaven."

"And now?" he said, the guarded-but-hopeful look in his eyes jabbing my heart.

"Now it"—*hurts, damn it all to fucking hell!*—"doesn't matter anymore," I said, on the verge of tears yet again. I didn't let them fall. God, I really had screwed things up royally.

He nodded, stiff, mouth grim, and stood to leave.

I rose, wanting to reach for him, gripping my own arms instead. "Before you go—I know this isn't a good time to bring this up, but if you're leaving, I don't know when else to ask—I mean, about Jackson Gunn and the Conrads—"

"Not my mess. Billy hooked you up with the job. Billy can take care of it."

It was my turn to stiffen. "I see."

"No, you don't," he said harshly, then relented. "Howdy, I'm not trying to punish you. Do you really think Billy wants me working on it with him? With *you*?"

My shoulders sagged. "I suppose not."

For a second, I thought he might give me his usual kiss on the top of my head, but he didn't. "I'll be out of the country for the foreseeable future. Thomas will know how to contact me. In the meantime," he added before walking away, "think about what you were feeling in that bed with me last night, and who you were feeling it for. Because, for me, that was *real*."

I sat there for a long time after he left, until even the squirrels stopped being wary of me. One scampered up onto the other end of the bench and cocked its head quizzically at me. I thought I saw sympathy in its big eyes, but maybe it was just trying to figure out if I had any nuts.

All right, so my personal life was fucked up. When had it ever not been? I should be used to dealing with it.

What I needed was a plan. The best I could come up with was to push Mark totally out of my head. He said he was going to be gone. Fine. That was good. If I didn't have to worry about running into him unexpectedly, my immediate problem was solved. I could concentrate on getting it right with Billy. Billy deserved that much from me.

Next on my agenda would be a full-on assault on the Jackson Gunn problem. Finding out who really killed Angelica would keep my mind busy. With any luck, too busy to dwell on Mark's parting words. Because I was pretty sure thinking about them too closely would only lead to more trouble.

I stood, took a deep breath, and headed back to my condo. I had to pack for a funeral.

Chapter 17

The Golden Acres Funeral Home was a fair distance from Tinsel-Town, but that didn't stop the masses from showing up to gawk. *Hollywood royalty in pain—now, that's entertainment,* I thought wryly.

Jack had overnighted me the key to his Hollywood condo, his cell phone, and a cashier's check large enough to make me fervently hope my conscience wouldn't make me return it if it turned out he was a killer.

He was laying low in his Las Vegas home, which apparently he'd been unable to bring himself to leave since his face-the-press moment after Angelica's death. When I'd expressed my reservations, he'd sworn no one would know he was there. He'd given every member of his staff a week off and plane tickets to Hawaii as a reward for their dedication during his time of crisis, and he planned to keep the blinds closed and not answer his landline. I wasn't entirely comfortable not having a client under the supervision of my own employees while I was on a job, but frankly I was relieved he wouldn't be going back to the ranch as long as there were any doubts about him.

Angelica's service, being so well attended, had spilled out onto a freshly mown lawn that seemed to stretch for miles in every direction, with grass so perfect I had to check twice to make sure it wasn't fake. It smelled real enough, but in the land of virtual reality on steroids, who could be sure?

I scanned the crowd. Billy was out there somewhere, posing as the limo driver the studio had sent for Jackson, keeping a watchful eye on things. When I'd told him about thc job (in our new spirit of openness and communication), he'd said he'd meet me here, and that we could brainstorm our next move after the funeral. "I might be able to pick up some useful information amidst all the condolences. Gossip is currency in La-La Land, and I'm great at eavesdropping," had been his reasoning.

There were multiple large tents to provide shade, not to mention cover from the news helicopters flying back and forth overhead, their background drone adding to the general irritation of the day. I couldn't help but notice that a hefty percentage of the celebrities present, before retiring beneath the privacy tents, made sure the cameras in the choppers had ample opportunity to capture their presence.

The studio limo had had a well-stocked bar, which might have taken the edge off the hour-long drive if I were the kind to drink at eight o'clock in the morning. Luckily, there was coffee, provided by Jack's assistant, the one Billy's goth girl had filled in for on the snake set. Frannie. She seemed even younger than she had when I first saw her, and was obviously trying to hide it with her uber-adult black suit and her long brown hair pulled back into a severe bun. No makeup to speak of, but she was pretty enough that she didn't need it. She looked a bit on the heavy side under the bulky blazer, but that was only because she was ultracurvy.

Frannie was proving to be a capable aide, keeping herself planted between me and everyone else, quietly but firmly explaining that while I appreciated their sympathy, I simply wasn't ready to talk yet. I was going to tell Jack to give her a raise.

The one person she didn't keep away from me was Joseph Conrad. As he approached, Frannie quietly explained that the funeral director had told her Mrs. Conrad had had a small breakdown that morning, and wouldn't be in attendance.

"Jack," Joe said, reaching for me with open arms.

Fine. I can be a hugger. I opened my own arms. "Joe."

Instead of the manly bear hug I was expecting, he grasped me by both shoulders, stood on tiptoe, and tilted his head up so that his lips were close to my ear, and whispered, harshly, "You lose, you son of bitch."

I stiffened. He let go of me and took his seat on the front row of the elegantly upholstered folding chairs that had been set up for the service. The tent was tall enough to allow for an unobstructed view of the beautiful wooded hills in the distance, and there I focused, hoping everyone would take my shock for grief, until Frannie led me to my own chair. It was uncomfortably close to Joe's. What the hell had he meant?

He stared resolutely ahead, his eyes fixed on the ornate urn that held Angelica's ashes. I tried to listen to the eulogy given by one of her female colleagues from Conrad Fine Foods, but the pretty words couldn't penetrate the thoughts spinning in my head.

Was Joe referring to the stock certificates? Had getting them been his "win"? Did the real Jackson suspect as much, and was that why he'd wanted me to tail the Conrads? For now, there was no way to know. My more immediate problem was figuring out the right way to play this. Staring, somber-eyed, I was in character for the moment, but after the service—what then? Should I acknowledge Joe's statement or not?

After the eulogist was finished speaking, Joe rose and went to say his short piece. It sounded wooden to my ear, like a father trying his best to display no emotion at all lest he lose it entirely. He never once looked at me. When he was done, he went to stand on the far side of his daughter's urn.

I stood when Frannie touched my elbow, noticing for the first time that she'd sat herself next to me. My handler for the day. No one seemed to think it odd. She handed me a piece of paper and whispered, "I typed up what you wanted to say about Angelica. I know you said you wouldn't need a script, but just in case the emotion of the day . . ." She gave a tiny shrug.

Crap. Jack hadn't told me I'd have to speak. Guess he considered that covered by his blanket "don't worry, my assistant will take care of everything" statement. I clutched the paper like a lifeline and made my way to the front, walking slowly. The few steps didn't take nearly as long as I would have liked. Once positioned, I bowed my head, on the surface appearing to compose myself, but really frantically reading over the words on the paper I'd laid on the podium.

I cleared my throat. "Angelica was—"

A sudden breeze caught the corner of the paper and sent it floating into the air. *Shit!* I lunged for it, hoping like hell to catch it before it blew completely away.

A second later, the urn exploded. Sharp pieces of expensive pottery flew through the air, with puffs of Angelica rising like a cloud around them. Two, maybe three, seconds of utter silence, and then pandemonium struck, people running in all directions, either for the shelter of the main building or their cars.

I stood tall (in retrospect, perhaps not the smartest move) to scan the crowd. Because, unless I was very much mistaken, someone had just tried to shoot me—and I wanted to know who.

My eyes jumped first to Joe Conrad. He was staring at me, the look on his face somewhere between surprise and anger. Trouble was, I couldn't tell if he was angry because someone had shot his daughter's urn or if he was mad that the shot had missed me. Or perhaps even wondering if the bullet had been meant for him, seeing as how the urn was between the two of us.

Fueled by the adrenaline of near death, I stepped toward him, intending to find out if he was somehow behind it, if this had something to do with his strange comment to me earlier. Before I could reach him, I was tackled from behind.

I rolled, prepared to use Jack's strength to beat the hell out of whoever had it in for him. Stopped with my fist centimeters from Frannie's face.

"Jack, stay down, for God's sake," she said, breathing hard, trying her best to shield me with her body.

And then she did the oddest thing. She burst into tears and kissed me, full on the mouth. When she finally detached herself, I saw my driver—Billy—standing over her, scanning the crowd. He did not look happy.

The police left the funeral home after searching the grounds, and everyone in attendance, including some extremely put out actors and studio honchos who thought they were above being patted down by law enforcement. The officers compiled a comprehensive list of everyone's names and addresses (and, boy, some of the stars were even more unhappy at having to show ID than they were at being groped—how dare the cops not recognize them!), and gave orders for all to make themselves available for further questioning as necessary.

Their interviews with me and Joe were more extensive, naturally, considering not only our relationship to Angelica, but also that one of us might have been the intended target of the urn shooter. They questioned us separately, so I had no idea what they were asking Joe.

It took some fast talking to convince the police I didn't need to be taken into protective custody, that I would have plenty of private security between here and my house back in Vegas, where I would be returning as soon as I saw that what was left of Angelica's ashes were safely interred. Eventually they listened. I gave them Jack's private cell phone number and assured them they could reach me at my Vegas home number starting later that night.

After the police were through, Frannie took charge of me, and I let her. I figured Jack, in his grief and shock, would be more than willing to have his assistant handle the details.

The ride back to Jack's condo was awkward, more so because Billy kept grinning at Frannie's attempts to scoot closer to me. His mood had improved greatly after I found a private moment to assure him I wouldn't be filling in for Jackson again after this. If someone was out to kill my client, Billy wanted to make sure it was my *client* who got killed and not me. Me, I'd just as soon it was neither one of us.

Not having any idea of the true nature of Jack's relationship with Frannie, I wasn't sure how to act around her. Did she suffer from unrequited love for her employer? Did he know it, or was he oblivious to it? Or was he having an affair with her, too? I mean, hey, if he cheated with Lily-Ann, why not Frannie?

I finally decided my safest course of action was to plead exhaustion, close my eyes, and pretend to be asleep for the long ride back to town. Convincing Frannie it was safe to leave me alone at the condo was trickier. She apologized for kissing me, tears in her big brown eyes, saying she knew how inappropriate it was to do that at my wife's funeral, but she'd been so afraid for me, and she hoped I wasn't mad at her.

Which didn't clue me in about her relationship with Jack, because even if Jack were boinking her on a regular basis, surely he'd consider kissing him anywhere in public, much less his wife's freaking funeral, to be a lapse in propriety. Thank God we'd been blocked from the helicopter news cameras by the tent when it had happened.

To keep Frannie from setting up outside the condo as a self-appointed bodyguard, I promised we'd go to dinner, just the two of us, as soon as I was up to resuming my commitment to the movie. When she still hadn't seemed inclined to leave, I gave her a mission: to redecorate my Fifth Wheel trailer. Knowing from my file on Jack that Angelica had been the one to decorate it originally, I told Frannie I'd never be able to bear going into it again—the reminder would be too painful.

Frannie was ecstatic. Admitted she never thought it suited my true personality anyway, swore she'd turn it into a completely different place as soon as humanly possible, so I'd be able to come back to the set without fear.

If Jack had a problem with that, so be it. I had a problem with being shot at.

Billy winked at me after he ushered her back into the car, so I knew I'd be seeing him later. As soon as they were gone I'd tried calling Jack, who of course didn't answer. *Damn it.* I'd thought he'd know it was me if he saw the call was from his own cell phone, but it looked like he was taking my admonition not to answer the phone for *anyone* way too seriously.

Either that or he wasn't there. Which got me thinking in a whole other unpleasant direction.

I was still waiting for Billy (currently stuck running redecorating errands with Frannie, according to the text he'd sent) when Jack finally called, a good five hours from the time of the shooting. Time enough to drive back to Vegas, if one were inclined to believe he was somehow involved. But why would he do something like that? It didn't make any sense.

He claimed he'd been afraid to answer my calls at first, after seeing the news of the attempt on "his" life (it was splashed all over television almost immediately, with lots of aerial footage of panicked A-list celebrities, via those handy choppers). Apologies poured out of him for putting me in that kind of danger, that if he'd known something like that would happen . . . yadda yadda BS yadda. Frankly, his smooth tongue was starting to wear thin.

"Hold on, Jack. The police aren't sure the attempt was on *your* life. For all we know, someone was aiming at your father-in-law. Or even the urn itself."

"Why would anyone shoot an urn full of ashes?" Jack said.

"You got me," I said. "But why not Joe? Maybe someone is out to get the Conrad family."

There was a pause, filled with breathing. "Yeah . . . yeah, I suppose you're right. They do have a lot of enemies. Corporate ones, I mean. But surely no one would go this far."

"Listen, Jack, Joe said something odd to me before the service. 'You lose, you son of a bitch.' What did he mean by that?" I wished I could be looking him in the eye as he answered—reading somebody is so much harder over the phone.

"You must've misheard. There's no reason for him to have said that."

Had his voice sounded tighter? More stressed? Difficult to say.

"No, I'm certain I heard him right. He enunciated each word very clearly," I said. "Jack? Are you there?" The breathing began again. I was starting to worry he might have asthma. "Does this have anything to do with why you wanted me to follow the Conrads?"

"*No.* I don't know what the fuck he meant by that. Listen, has anyone checked on Lily-Ann? I hate to bring it up, but she probably hates her father worse than anybody."

"She's wearing a tracking anklet, Jack"—had he not known that?—"so she's the one person we can be sure wasn't the shooter today."

"Those things aren't infallible. They can be tampered with."

"Right. I'll check on it," I said. As soon as I finished up our conversation, I texted Billy, telling him not to worry if I wasn't there when he got back.

The winding cement path leading to the front door of Nigel Overholt's large house in the Hollywood Hills was so artfully landscaped that one hardly noticed its primary purpose was wheelchair access. Abundant flowers, decorative grasses, and multitiered shrubbery had made the necessarily long walk to get up the hill a pleasant one.

I'd told Jack everything I'd said to the police at the funeral home, so he wouldn't appear to contradict himself if asked the same questions again. Said he'd better start answering his home line again, in case it was them, and to expect his cell phone by special messenger sometime that evening.

Now it was time for a little chat with Lily-Ann. I wanted to meet her face-to-face and decide for myself if I thought she was capable of murder.

She turned out to be a pleasant surprise. When she wasn't screaming at TV cameras she came across as a genuinely nice person. Her long brown hair was pulled back from her heart-shaped face, making her look even more waifish in those big black-framed glasses. A long T-shirt, a short denim vest, and a chunky necklace confirmed her dedication to hipster fashion. The only thing out of place was the tracking anklet—it's tough to hide one of those under leggings.

Nigel had left us, for the moment, in what was one of several tastefully decorated rooms on the first floor of his magnificent Laurel Canyon home. The big picture window offered a spectacular view of the iconic Hollywood sign, not something I was expecting, considering his accident. When he'd noticed where I was looking, he'd shrugged and said it was a good reminder of the difference between a calculated risk and pure stupidity. Seemed like a healthy attitude about mistakes to me. Once again, I was impressed with the man.

Lily-Ann and I were seated on a tan camelback sofa, waiting for Nigel to return with refreshments.

"I hear I have you to thank for my bail," Lily-Ann said. "I'm a little cloudy on the why, though."

"Not me, exactly. A friend of mine." At least, I hoped Mark still considered himself my friend. "As for why . . . well, I'm a sucker for a good cause, I guess. You and I have that in common. I admire your work for animals."

She cocked her head. There were still questions in her eyes, but I could tell she wasn't going to question the gift. "Thank you. And thank your friend for me, too. I'd do it personally, but"—she glanced at her ankle—"I'm a little tied up here."

A sense of humor—good. Lily-Ann and I were going to get along fine. "No thanks are necessary," I said.

"No? Well, pardon my bluntness, but if you're not here to feast on my gratitude, why did you come?"

Yeah, I liked her.

"As long as we're being blunt," I said, "I'm here to find out if there's any way possible you could be the one who shot your sister's urn."

Her eyes widened for a moment, then narrowed as her mouth twisted into a smirk. She shook her ankle. "Um, gee, I hate to disappoint you, but as I said . . ."

"Ms. Conrad—"

"Call me Lily."

"Lily. I phrased that badly. What I mean is, I'm here to rule you out in the attempt on either Jackson's or your father's life, whichever it was."

"Is that what that goddamned fucking asshole is claiming now?" Lily's voice inched toward her post-arrest TV level. "That not only did I kill my sister, but I somehow managed to slip my leash and try to kill him or my father, too? He's *such* a dick. Trust me, if I'd been there with a gun, I *would* have shot him."

Nigel rolled in with a drinks tray connected to the side of his chair. "Did I miss something? Do share."

"Don't worry, Nige. I'm not divulging case strategy. I was merely confirming Jack's status as celebrity asshole of the year for Ciel."

Nigel shrugged and handed us each a glass of electric yellow liquid over ice.

"Jack's personality is neither here nor there. He has an alibi, and

I've yet to come across a trace of evidence that he may have hired a killer. And now, with this incident at the funeral, it appears even less likely he could have been responsible for Angelica's murder. It looks like we'll have to rethink our strategy."

"Tell me something, Lily," I said, not bothering to explain Jack's earlier claims that she couldn't have killed her sister, because now who knew if he'd even been sincere? He'd certainly shifted the blame back to her fast enough in our last phone conversation. "If Jack *didn't* have an alibi, would you think he killed your sister? Would he be capable of that?"

She huffed an unamused laugh. "In a heartbeat. In fact, the only thing that might make me doubt he's involved is that I don't think he'd hire someone else to do it—I'm sure he'd have wanted that pleasure for himself."

"Pleasure?" I said.

"Oh, yeah," Lily said. "Jack is charming when he wants to be. But when he doesn't . . ." She shrugged. "He can be cold. Cruel. When I broke it off with him, he kicked one of my foster dogs across the room, just because it was trying to get between us. To protect me. And the look on Jack's face when that little mutt yelped in pain—it was sick. Twisted. I was so stupid about him."

Nigel interrupted. "Let me take a moment here to remind Ciel that this is all off the record."

"Don't worry—I'm not about spill any beans you don't want spilled. I'm only trying to compile the complete picture in my head, so I'll know if . . . the information . . . I have will prove useful for you."

I could sense his ears perking. "Why not tell me what you know? That would be the simplest way to find out," he said.

"Afraid there's nothing simple about it, Nigel. But first—Lily, why should I believe you had no wish to harm your sister? Even setting aside your affair with her husband"—she had the decency to look ashamed—"Angelica was in lockstep with your parents, helping run the company whose practices go against everything you believe in so passionately."

There was a lot to admire about Lily—her compassion for animals, and her courage in standing up for her beliefs at great cost to herself, financially at least. But being disinherited had to rankle. The question was, did she resent her sister's choosing to remain loyal to their parents enough to kill her?

Lily looked at Nigel before answering my question. Guess she found the okay in his eyes, because she continued. "It's true my sister and I don't—didn't—agree on much with regard to the family business, but she did have a certain amount of sympathy for what our parents called my foolish regard for food animals. Only, she maintained she'd be able to do more to ensure their humane treatment in the long run by playing the good daughter, and eventually inheriting, than I could hope to accomplish with my 'basically useless' demonstrations."

I nodded and took a sip of my drink. Bleah.

Lily sipped hers, too, and made a face. "Seriously, Nigel? Not even a shot of vodka to make this more palatable? And I'm not just talking about your crappy healthy water either."

"Sorry. Vitamin 'V' is not on the menu here," he said, drinking his with seeming enjoyment. No accounting for taste.

Lily gave me a what're-we-gonna-do shrug and went on, sounding calm, though her trembling hands told me another story. "The prosecutor is trying to twist Angelica's toeing of the parental line into some big rift between us. He's claiming that's my motive for killing her, which couldn't be further from the truth. As much as I enjoy shooting my mouth off on the picket line, I'm fully aware that Angelica's plan was more practical. See, I thought we could have it both ways—I could have the pleasure of gumming up the works of my parents' chicken-killing empire now, while knowing Angelica would stick it to them posthumously, once she gained control. But I never once considered they might outlive her."

"Okay, I might buy that, but I can see where a jury could find it difficult to swallow. Even if your affair with Jackson doesn't become public knowledge, you have motive," I said. "You were also at the house in Vegas the night Angelica was killed—that's opportunity. Did you know where they kept their guns?"

She nodded. "My prints were even inside the gun closet—Angelica and I used to go to the range together, back when impressing Jack was important to her. How's that for suck-tastic luck?"

"And there you have means," Nigel said.

Despite that, I didn't believe she'd done it. Of course, it helped now that I knew she'd been within sight of either Nigel or his aide all morning—they'd been watching television coverage of the funeral. There was no way she could have been the one to fire that shot, even if she had figured out a way to disable her anklet.

"They haven't found the murder weapon yet," I said. "That has to be some help."

Nigel looked at me sharply. "That's not general knowledge."

"Oh?" I said. He hadn't asked a question, so I didn't rush in to explain how I knew.

"It doesn't matter, though," he continued. "They're going on the assumption that Lily was able to get rid of it somehow, maybe by handing it off to one of her fellow warriors against animal cruelty."

"Which is totally unjustified!" she said, the crusading light flashing in her eyes. "Those fascist assholes have no right to go after my friends."

"Be that as it may, they are. It's not an unexpected tactic, and not an avenue they can afford to ignore. They're pressuring us by pressuring them, and there's not a damn thing we can do about it."

"But they're digging into things that aren't remotely connected to the case, things in their personal lives. It's not right," Lily-Ann said.

"No, but it's legal," Nigel said, keeping his cool. He reminded me so much of Thomas.

"Yeah, and I don't know how much longer I can take it. Fuck it all. Maybe I should take the plea deal," she said, her bravado deserting her.

"You can't do that!" I said.

Nigel looked as if he'd heard it before. "Unless you're telling me you killed your sister, and you want me to shop around for the best place for you to serve out a life sentence, I suggest you stop talking like that."

She rose and crossed to the window, looking as if she'd like nothing better than to open it and run. "Why should I? Hell, maybe I did do it. Maybe I snapped and went all Rambo on my own sister."

Her outburst washed over Nigel like raindrops on a duck, but I was worried by the look I'd seen in her eye. She might be holding it together with her combo of righteous indignation and a smart mouth, but she was scared. And possibly close to breaking.

I went to stand next to her, careful not to crowd her. "Listen," I said softly, "if it helps any, I believe you didn't kill your sister."

She whirled on me. "Who the hell are you to say that? You don't know me. You didn't know my sister, and you don't know my fucking family! If you did, you'd know Conrads are capable of anything."

Okay. Not one to react well to someone being "nice" to her. Yeah, a jury would just *love* her. But her outburst did trigger an idea.

"Even your mother?" I asked. When Lily stared at me blankly, I added, "She wasn't at the funeral. Does she know one end of a gun from another?"

Lily looked appalled at the thought. "Well, yes—she and my father used to take us skeet shooting all the time when we were kids—but there's no way . . . she couldn't . . . you're not implying she killed Angelica, are you? Even a Conrad wouldn't . . ." She looked at Nigel, whose eyes lit at the new possibility.

"I admit, it doesn't seem likely, but if she doesn't have a credible alibi for the time of Angelica's death we could use it to plant reasonable doubt in the minds of the jury," he said.

"No," Lily said, voice low, face set. "You don't know her. She can be a bitch, but she's not a murderer."

"Okay," I said, impatient with her refusal to consider an avenue that might help her own cause. "You're right. I don't know her, or if she had any reason to want your sister dead. But I do know your brother-in-law. And I know for a fact it is at least possible that *he's* the fucking asshole who shot Angelica. Him, personally."

"What?" Lily said, stunned.

Nigel looked at me steadily. "I think you better explain that, Ciel."

Oops. Probably shouldn't have gone quite that far. But if it kept Lily from making a premature—and really ill-advised—confession, so be it. I took a breath. "I will. But first, why was Angelica divorcing Jackson? It wasn't just his cheating, was it?"

Lily twisted her mouth into a wry smile. "No. She was very understanding of the cheating, as long as he was discreet. She once told me screwing starlets and fans was like masturbation for him—distasteful, but understandable in a man who oozed as much testosterone as he did. She used to joke that at least it kept the sheets at home clean."

Ouch. Yeah, sounds like a man with size issues, I thought. *Always trying to prove his virility.* "But she didn't feel that way when it was you, did she?" I said.

Lily's face registered a flash of naked pain. "No. She didn't. That was when she brought out every piece of ammo she'd saved up over the years. She didn't just want to divorce him. She wanted to destroy him. All because of my stupidity." Lily took a deep breath. "He knew she could do it, too. There was something in her file that scared the hell out of him."

"Did she tell you what it was?" I asked.

"She never said—she was mad at me, too, remember. But from the way Jack acted after he found out what she had on him, I know it was something big."

"Do you have any idea where she might have kept that file?" I asked. If I could get my hands on it . . .

"If I had to guess, it's hidden somewhere in Jack's home office. That's where she used to hide his birthday presents. She said it was the last place he'd think to look. I know she kept the file on a thumb drive—she showed me that much—so she could have slipped it anywhere."

"Okay, let's forget about Jack's alibi for a minute," I said. "That file sounds like a damn good motive for murder for him."

Nigel nodded. "Yes, he has motive. You can even make an argument for means, since he does own quite a few guns of the caliber in question, and is proficient with them. But the opportunity . . . that one's hard to argue, seeing as how dozens of witnesses were working with him—in another state—at the time of the murder."

"And besides, somebody tried to kill *him* at the funeral," Lily said.

"Or possibly your father," I added for the sake of keeping the facts straight.

"Or my father," she conceded. "But you can't tell me Jackson would have set up something so risky for himself. According to the news, that bullet missed him by inches. Maybe I was wrong about him. Maybe he *didn't* have Angelica killed."

"About that . . ." I said. Damn, I hoped I wasn't going to regret this. I'd done enough regrettable things recently—I didn't need to add to the list. "Look, before I go any further, I'm going to have to ask that this stay between the three of us. In fact, I shouldn't say anything at all, not before I have you sign one of my nondisclosure agreements. Would you be willing to do that?"

Nigel was looking wary. "If you give me time to read it carefully, and I find nothing egregious about it, I suppose so."

Lily-Ann inclined her head toward Nigel. "If he says it's okay to sign, I'll sign."

"Great! I don't think you'll find anything confusing about it. Thomas drew it up for me himself, and he's pretty clear cut. Do you have a computer and a printer I can borrow? I can access it online."

Nigel finished paging through my standard contract. He was a fast reader, but I could tell he hadn't skipped a line of it.

"So," he said, "as I understand it, in exchange for your services, we agree not to disclose anything about how you go about performing said services, or anything we learn, advertently or inadvertently, about you or your associates during the course of your performing said services. Is that about it?"

"That covers it nicely. Of course, for our purposes here today, my 'services' entail telling you certain information I'm privy to, and demonstrating how I came to be privy to it. Also, you'll notice I nulled out the portion of the contract that deals with my fee. I'm not charging you anything, of course."

He studied my face, considering God knew what. Coming to a decision, he signed with a flourish. Lily-Ann followed suit with her copy of the contract, which she'd given only a cursory glance. Guess she trusted Nigel.

I collected both contracts and checked the signatures, to make sure they hadn't signed "Mickey Mouse" or "Donald Duck." Not that it would matter much if they had. Thomas had creative ways of dealing with clients who willfully broke a contract, no matter how cute they got with their signatures.

Satisfied, I folded the documents and stuffed them into my purse. This was the tricky part with all new clients. (If I was honest, it was also kind of fun.) Deep down, they were always sure the person who had referred them to me was mistaken. They never really believed it until they saw it for themselves. Some of them even fainted. And those were the ones who'd heard about aura adaptors through the grapevine before they approached me. Nigel and Lily-Ann were getting it cold.

"Okay," I said. "The reason we can't rule out Jack just because there was a probable attempt on his life is because that wasn't the real Jack."

Nigel looked skeptical in the I'm-listening-politely-but-I'm-not-buying-it way lawyers have. (Thomas was a master at that look.) "What? Are you saying Jack sent some sort of stunt double to his wife's funeral? Does he have a twin brother we don't know about?"

"Not exactly a stunt double, no. Or a twin. More like . . . me."

"What are you talking about?" Lily-Ann said.

"I'm saying I was standing in for Jackson at the funeral, just as I was when Angelica was shot. It's my job."

They both stared at me, saying nothing. I took that as an indication to continue.

"It was while I was pretending to be Jackson on the set that he left my client hideaway—a guest ranch in Arizona—for several hours. In other words, there was, at the least, a window of opportunity for him to kill your sister, and to hide what could be the murder weapon in my barn for later retrieval."

Lily spoke first, sounding like a kid who'd been offered an ice cream cone, only to have it snatched away at the last second. "Nigel, she's crazy. Get her out of here."

Nigel ignored her. "You found the gun in your barn? I was told the police didn't have it."

"Uh . . . well, they don't. Not last time I checked, anyway. I'll explain that part later," I said, loosening my belt and kicking off my shoes.

I called up Jackson's aura and waited for their reaction.

Lily jumped up and backed away from me, almost tripping over a small table in her rush. "What the fuck?" she said, looking decidedly pale. I hoped she wasn't a fainter, because it was a marble floor. Guess that worked better than carpet with Nigel's wheelchair.

Nigel stared, processing. Finally he asked, "What are you?"

I dropped the aura and refastened my belt. Left my shoes off, though, because, hey, barefoot is always better than wearing shoes.

"I'm an aura adaptor. So is Thomas, by the way."

"There are more of you? Are you . . . human?" This from Lily, who was keeping her distance.

"Completely and totally human," I said, doing a slow spin so they could see I was still me from all angles. Then I went into my spiel about how we had a genetic quirk that allowed us to project the aura of anyone whose energy we touched, yadda yadda yadda. I had to go over it with all my clients, after which I typically reminded them of the contract they had signed and pointed out, ever so politely, that my legal shark brother would divest them of all their worldly possessions if they ever divulged what I had shown them.

I somehow didn't think I would need to state that to Nigel, who was no longer looking shocked, only highly curious.

"You say you can become anyone?" he said.

"Not become. I'm always still me on the inside. All I can do is project their aura. In other words, take on their physical appearance."

"Can you do me?" he asked.

"Sure," I said, and loosened my belt again. "Give me your hand."

He extended his arm, I took some energy, and voilà! I was him. Only I was still standing, and could walk around.

"But you're not paralyzed," he said.

"Nope. I took care not to project your injured spine and I left some muscle tone in my legs."

"You can pick and choose parts?" Lily said, gradually becoming less fearful and more fascinated.

"Yeah. Though usually it's easier to project the whole package. Requires less concentration, and less effort to keep it up. It doesn't make much difference for short adaptions, though."

I had, of course, been speaking in Nigel's voice, and had unconsciously mimicked the rhythms of his speech. I tend to do that automatically—Mom says I have a good ear. Nigel couldn't quit staring at me.

Finally, he gave himself a shake (only his upper body and head moved) and said, "Could you stop, please? It's . . . rather disconcerting to talk to myself."

I dropped his aura at once.

"So, do you see what I mean about Jackson now? I don't know

for sure he's the guilty one, but I sure as heck know he *could* be. That's something, right?"

Hope sparked in Lily-Ann's eyes for the first time since I'd arrived. Nigel squashed it with a brutal truth.

"But judging from the impressive stack of papers your brother drafted, and we signed, knowing how it's possible isn't going to do us a bit of good in court, is it?"

"Not in court, no. But I swear I will find a way to help you. I won't let an innocent person go to prison. You have to believe that."

Chapter 18

Billy and I picked up food at the In-N-Out drive-thru and checked into a hotel, where we proceeded to stuff our faces with their legendary Animal Style burgers (the grilled onions were fabulous) and Animal Style fries (topped with cheese, secret sauce, and more grilled onions) from the not-so-secret menu as we discussed our findings. He hadn't gathered much of any use, either from the funeral guests or from his shopping spree with Frannie.

I'd left Nigel and Lily-Ann, both still somewhat agog from my revelation, with a promise to get back to them soon. I told them to stay the course, that I was meeting with a trusted friend who was helping me work on a plan to find out who the real killer was.

Yeah, "plan" might have been an overstatement. We were still at the bouncing-around-one-ridiculous-idea-after-another stage, hoping something would fall into place. But I didn't want Lily-Ann to worry. I had faith Billy would come up with something—he was a master at getting out of trouble.

The first thing I told Billy was that I'd had to tell Nigel and Lily-Ann about adaptors. Not nearly as uptight about revealing our ability as Mark was, he shrugged it off. All he asked was if I'd made them sign the nondisclosure agreement.

"Duh. Of course I did," I said, around a mouthful of fries.

"Shouldn't be a problem, then. Thomas's contracts are the best muzzles I know."

"Yeah, me too. Of course, Mark will probably jump down my—" I stopped myself. "Sorry. I wasn't thinking."

He shrugged it off with no more than a slight clenching of his jaw. "It's okay. It would be stupid to pretend he doesn't exist. So, have you talked to him since . . . ?"

He courteously left off "he screwed your brains out," but it reverberated in my head anyway. "Yeah," I said. "I, um, explained the circumstances to him."

"And how was that received?" Billy asked wryly.

"Not well. He was . . . understandably . . . angry with me."

He nodded. "He texted me to cancel the job we had scheduled. Said he could handle it alone."

"Are you still mad at him?" I asked after I got up the courage.

"Fuck yeah." He expelled an exasperated breath "No. Not really. If I'm honest with myself, I probably would have done the exact same thing in his position. Doesn't mean I'm not glad he'll be gone for a while."

"Billy, I can't tell you how sorry I—"

"It's done, cuz. Let's try to forget it." He took a huge bite of his burger, without dribbling any of it down his chin.

Okay, I was cool with forgetting. I could do that. I looked at the array of wadded up mustard- and ketchup-stained napkins on my side of the small table.

"I still don't understand how you can eat something this messy without spilling any of it," I said, more than willing to change the subject.

He lifted a fry and let the cheese and onions drip into his mouth before finishing it off. "Practice. Loads and loads of practice."

I shook my head. "Even with an adaptor metabolism, by all rights you should be three hundred pounds."

"Maybe I am," he said, waggling his eyebrows.

"Nah. You enjoy being comfortable too much. I would have caught you by now."

"Comfortable" was adaptor code for being yourself. It was possible to hold a secondary aura for extended periods, but it did require more energy, so most adaptors liked to relax in their own forms. Even me; otherwise, I'd maintain an extra four inches of height indefinitely.

"True," he said. "Anyway, you eat almost as much as I do, and you're still a shrimp."

The fact is, you'll rarely see an obese aura adaptor. Apparently projecting other people's auras burns a lot of calories.

"Yeah? Well, you're a big doofus," I said, and threw a particularly dirty napkin at him, which he caught handily and lobbed back at me.

I batted it out of the way and was rearming myself when he picked me up and tossed me on the bed.

"What do you think you're doing?" I suppressed a huge grin, because I knew exactly what he was doing.

He landed on the bed next to me. "Now that I've topped off your tank, I'm taking you for a spin."

"Oh, boy, a joy ride!" I said.

Turned out his choice of metaphor was apt—my head *was* spinning within seconds after he started kissing me. And no onion breath at all. One of the nicer perks of being an adaptor.

This, I thought while I was still capable of thinking at all. *This* was why I couldn't let go of Billy. This playfulness. This teasing. This *fun.* Laughter was as essential for me as food and water, and he provided it better than anyone else I knew.

But it wasn't only the laughter. "Billy," I said hesitantly, later, as I lay cradled to his chest during a lull in our activities, "I found the parachute. It's beautiful. Thank you."

I felt him shrug beneath my cheek. "It made me think of you. I was hoping it would make you think of me."

"It will. It's perfect—I love it." I lifted my head and looked at his face. Curls, damp with sweat from our exertions, spilled onto his forehead. "You know, you've never said it to me either. Not seriously."

The humor in his eyes was instantly replaced by something deeper. "I love you, Ciel. I always will."

Guards. Jackson had hired guards. Every door, every ground-floor window, and even some guy on the roof dressed in workman's gear who might have been hired to fix the terra-cotta tile, but I wouldn't put money on it, because he was scanning the grounds a lot more than he was working.

Either our Jack was terribly worried someone was out to kill him, too, or else he hadn't found Angelica's file yet, and didn't want anyone to beat him to it.

"Shit," I said.

Billy nodded. "Agreed. I can't see a good way in."

We'd hopped into Billy's rental car first thing that morning (thank God his Mooney was being serviced) and resumed brainstorming on our way to Vegas. The only concrete part of our plan so far was "find the file." Anything else we did would depend on what was in it. Trouble was, Jackson seemed to be avoiding my calls. I'd tried his landline and his cell phone (which the messenger I'd hired had assured me had been delivered at precisely three minutes before ten the night before) several times each. Shunted to voice mail every time.

"I suppose we could just knock on the door and ask to speak with him. One of us could keep him busy while the other searched," I said.

Billy shook his head slowly. "That might work if we knew where it was—if he let us in to begin with—but I think those guards are a good indicator of Jack's level of paranoia. I doubt there'd be the opportunity for a lengthy search. Also, we know he has guns. And, if he is our culprit, obviously isn't afraid to use them should we get caught."

I gave him a sideways look. "I thought you were the king of risk takers."

He draped an arm over my shoulders and gave me a squeeze. "Not where you're concerned."

I thought about arguing with him. Saw how firmly his mouth was set, thought ahead to the likely outcome, and didn't waste my breath. My mind tumbled crazy ideas around. Skidded to a stop at one that was insanely simple.

"Hey," I said, "what if I could walk right past the guard and search the whole house without ever being seen?"

"And you would do this how, precisely?"

"Easy. I'd be invisible."

A few months earlier, while working on a solution to a particularly tricky aura-adapting glitch Molly had been dealing with, James (my nonadaptor scientist brother) had come up with a formula that had had an interesting side effect. It had suppressed his primary aura—the only aura he was capable of projecting. As a result, he'd disappeared. But only visually. He'd been as solid as ever if you happened to bump into him.

Billy hadn't seen it, but I'd told him all about it afterward.

"I thought that only happened to James because he's not an adaptor. Besides, didn't you tell me it made him sick?"

"He was a little washed out—so to speak—but not until it was wearing off. He was perfectly fine while he was invisible, and he recovered quickly enough. As for it working on an adaptor . . . well, we won't know until we try, huh?"

Billy still looked skeptical. "It might be worth a shot, but only if I'm the one doing it."

"Oh, geez. Are you getting all macho on me again? It doesn't make sense for you to do it. I've studied Jackson's house"—the plans were in his dossier—"so I know it better than you do."

"I doubt that. Remember, I was going to do the snake job until I passed it along to you. I met with him at his house, so I've been inside it, which is more than you can say. Plus, I have infinitely more experience than you when it comes to moving stealthily through houses where I don't belong."

I quirked my mouth. "No doubt. Never mind. We'll discuss it later. It might be moot, anyway, if James's magic potion doesn't work on adaptors."

He tugged my hair. "Dibs on testing it."

"No. Absolutely not. I can't let you risk it." James's face was set.

We were at his lab, James having refused point-blank to simply send the damn potion via the fastest possible courier. One thing I'll say, flying was getting easier for me, if not more pleasant. I hadn't even needed any medicinal gin. Instead, Billy had spent most of the flight giving me hand massages. He claimed the acupressure would help with my anxiety. Maybe it had, but it was more likely the naughty suggestions he kept whispering in my ear that had distracted me.

I cocked my head and asked Billy, who'd been trying, along with me, to make James see reason, "Do I look that sour when I get all stubborn about something?"

"No, you look positively adorable when you get stubborn. Cuter than a speckled setter pup."

I growled at him.

"See, *that's* when you look sour," he said with a wink.

James shook his head at our banter. "Amusing. The answer is still no."

I tugged the sleeve of his white lab coat. "Come on, James, I explained why we need it. If we test it out—"

"And by 'we,' she means *me,* if that's your concern. No sisters will be harmed while conducting the test," Billy said.

I didn't object, figuring James would be more amenable to risking Billy's skin than mine. Like all my brothers, he was on the protective side. Besides, I figured if it worked on Billy, it would work on me, too. I'd save the argument about who was going into Gunn's house until we got back to Vegas.

"I can see why you didn't want to send it to us"—not really; I was humoring him—"but this will be under your supervision. Come on, James. If it didn't kill you, it's not going to kill Billy."

"We don't even know if it will work on an adaptor. It might only inhibit your ability to project secondary auras. Like with Molly, for instance—"

"You only gave her a tiny fraction of the dose that worked on you, didn't you?" I asked.

"Well, yes," James conceded. "That was why it took longer to suppress her unwanted secondary aura—"

"So, just give me the same dose you took," Billy said.

"And what if that size dose damages your adapting ability permanently? Do you really want to risk that?" James said.

Billy raised an eyebrow. "You're asking *me* about taking a risk? Bring it on."

"As a scientist, it's my responsibility—"

"To jump on it when the opportunity for scientific advancement presents itself," Billy said.

"Wait a second, Billy. James, what are the odds of the formula screwing up Billy for good? Give me numbers." Because I sure didn't want Billy hurt just to get the file. If need be, we'd come up with another plan.

James took a deep breath and held it for a second. I could almost see his brain whirring behind his eyes.

"All right," he said at last. "I admit the statistical probability of permanent impairment is low. But it does exist, and I can't in good conscience allow—"

"Do it for Mother Science," Billy said.

"For science!" I echoed.

James was weakening. I could see it on his face. "—you to go forward—"

"Who knows when you'll get another willing volunteer?" Billy interjected.

James's shoulders drooped. ". . . without knowing what you might be getting yourself into," he finally said.

Another victory for Mother Science.

"It's going to feel a bit odd at first—" James said.

Billy knocked back the small beaker of neon-green fluid like a shot of tequila, grimacing after he swallowed.

"—and it tastes vile," James finished.

Billy nodded, coughing. "No argument there."

"How long will it take?" I asked, watching Billy intently, trying not to hyperventilate. If anything bad happened to him, my conscience would hound me into hell. I'd have to retire from life, move into a convent, and spend the rest of my days trying to atone. After I, you know, converted to Catholicism.

"It didn't take long for me," James said. "I started fading within minutes . . . Ah. And there you go."

Fading was the right word for it. Billy became progressively more transparent—at a fairly rapid rate—until he was gone. I instinctively reached out to him, reassuring myself that the empty jeans and shirt still contained him.

He took my hand and squeezed. His other sleeve rose, bent at the elbow, to face height. He was looking at his hand. Or rather, not looking at it. "Whoa," he said. "This is freaking *awesome.*"

"You might change your opinion when you're coming out of it," James said.

"Eh. I've had my share of hangovers. I can deal with it," Billy said.

I couldn't seem to let go of him. It was so weird to see my seemingly empty hand, fingers curved, skin pressed flat against Billy's see-through palm.

"Do you feel all right?" I asked. "No ill effects?"

"None at all. Other than a leftover bad taste in my mouth from the concoction, I feel great. Surely you can add something to the next batch to make it taste better, James."

"Flavor isn't high on my agenda with this stuff. Now, if you don't mind, I'd like to run a few tests. Could you try to display one of your secondary auras, please?"

There was a pause, and Ian Somerhalder appeared in Billy's

clothes. He gave me a wicked wink (which I ignored) and said, "Well, I guess this is your answer—" Ian disappeared.

James, scribbling furiously on a notepad, nodded. "Interesting. Try another," he said.

Billy dutifully cycled through about half a dozen more, ending with Kate Middleton. He did like to collect royalty. Each one, in turn, popped out of existence after a few seconds, as the effect of James's magic elixir grew stronger.

More scribbling by James. "Try your primary aura again."

The clothes were empty in an instant.

"Now a secondary one," James ordered. The clothes remained empty this time.

"Okay, then," James said. "Secondary auras are suppressed, too. Now, we wait."

James got a call from Auntie Mo, reminding him he'd promised to visit Molly's school that afternoon to talk up careers in science to her class.

"Of course I'll be there, Mo. Wouldn't miss it for the world," he said into his phone. As soon as he disconnected, he said, "Damn. I'd forgotten all about that."

"I hear absentmindedness is part of the job description," I teased.

"Ha-ha. Very funny." He turned to Billy. "I'll be an hour and a half, tops. If you start to reappear before then, lie down on the sofa in the alcove. You might feel light-headed—or even pass out—during the transition, as your body metabolizes the last of the stuff out of your system, but you should be fine once it's gone. If your breathing becomes difficult, call me at once. Ciel, there's an oxygen canister in the supply closet. Oh, and Billy—you might want to lose the clothes for now. They look damn freaky walking around empty."

"What are you doing?" I asked Billy after James left.

"Following orders." I could hear the grin in his voice.

His shirt floated up, swayed in the air for a few seconds, and dropped to floor. Shoes and socks were next, followed by pants. The metal button undid itself as I stared. The zipper descended, slowly. *Very* slowly. It was a strangely erotic sight.

"You're doing that on purpose, aren't you?" I said, mesmerized in spite of myself. Who knew *not* seeing nakedness could be titillating?

The zipper was all the way down, the top of his boxer briefs showing. I could see the outline of what was beneath.

Uh-oh. "I don't know if this is such a good idea . . ."

The pants dropped, underwear with them, and slid across the floor, kicked aside.

"Billy? Where are you? Say something, damn it!"

I felt his breath on the back of my neck. "I'm right here."

I spun around and grasped his arms. "We are in my brother's lab!"

"With over an hour to kill." He pulled me closer, and I felt warm lips on my neck. If I closed my eyes, it didn't feel weird at all.

"But"—I made a tiny sound in my throat—"what if he comes back? What if he forgot something? He's always forgetting things."

He let me go and stepped away. I was surprised at how disappointed I felt. I mean, I'd never been made love to by an invisible man before. Then I saw the clothing rise up from the floor and float over to the supply closet, where they fell to the floor.

"Coming, cuz?" Billy's disembodied voice called out.

"What about my claustrophobia?" I said. Even the promise of

mind-blowing sex with an invisible Billy couldn't quite squelch my anxiety.

A few seconds later I felt lips near my ear. "We'll leave the door open if you want," he said, and tugged on my hand.

"But—"

"We can close it if we hear James."

When I didn't follow him, he picked me up, kissing me deeply as he walked across the room. As good as his word, he left the door open a crack. I still didn't like the walls so close around me, but the sight of my shirt unbuttoning itself distracted me. Ditto my bra unhooking itself. I kicked off my own shoes. Invisible hands rid me of my jeans and underwear.

I reached out to Billy, trying to keep track of where he was by sense of touch. He took my hands and said, "Uh-uh. I want you to hold on to this shelf"—he lifted my arms over my head and laced my fingers through the thick wire rack of lab supplies—"and, whatever you do, don't let go."

"Okay," I said. *This could be interesting,* I thought, and waited.

And waited. "Billy? Are you still there?" I said, starting to feel a little ridiculous.

Just as I was about to let go of the shelf, I felt a wet heat below my left collar bone. I jutted forward reflexively. And then it was gone. Another pause. My right thigh was next, a kiss, and a swipe of his tongue. Then it too was gone.

More kisses followed, randomly, on my arms, my calves, my neck, my stomach. I never knew where the next one would be, having no visual clues whatsoever. When his tongue dipped into my belly button, I giggled and nearly let go of the shelf.

"Ah-ah-ah," he said. "I told you to hold on."

His tongue swept over the tip of of my right breast. I bit my bottom lip. He did the same to the left. That one disappeared briefly when his lips sealed around it—apparently, anything completely inside Billy became a part of him, and was equally camouflaged. I bit my lip harder, but couldn't keep the moan from escaping.

His mouth abandoned my breast and left a long, wet trail downward. I closed my eyes, concentrating fully on staying upright. I clutched the shelf more tightly, grateful it was bolted onto the wall, because I was pretty sure it was holding all of my weight.

"Billy . . . I can't . . . I need—" My voice was ragged.

He was standing in an instant, pressed fully against me. I could feel his foot between mine, pushing my legs apart. "Hold on to me," he whispered, his own voice pretty damn raggedy, too. I let go of the shelf and gripped his shoulders, almost laughing when I saw my arms extended over the nothingness in front of me.

Hands grasped my butt and lifted me. I wrapped my legs around hard-muscled thighs, and gasped as he entered me. When he started raising and lowering me, my first thought was, *Damn, he's strong.* My second thought was, if anybody were secretly filming us, it would be the weirdest sex tape ever.

And then I couldn't seem to think anymore at all.

When my senses returned, I was on the floor, stretched out atop an invisible Billy mattress. He was lying on the cold tile floor, sparing me the chill.

"That was . . ." I swallowed, trying to slow my heartbeat.

"Yeah, it was," Billy's voice agreed. I could feel his heart pounding in sync with my own.

"You know what?" I said. "I think you may have discovered the cure for claustrophobia."

Chapter 19

Back in Vegas, several three-ounce bottles of James's magic potion (disguised as mouthwash) secreted in our carry-ons, Billy and I rented the biggest available car with tinted rear windows.

The tinted windows would be important when it came time to drink up and disappear. Much as I hated to hand over the reins, I was forced to admit that it made more sense for Billy to be the designated burglar. Not only did he have (as he took great pains to explain to me) vastly more experience than I did in the field, but we also already knew the formula worked on him.

He hadn't had much in the way of side effects from his test drive of the potion. He'd been a little weak and woozy as his primary aura reemerged, the same way James had been when he'd initially tested the substance on himself, but Billy had recovered more quickly. James thought that was probably due to the adaptor metabolism being faster than a nonadaptor's. He'd also dutifully warned us that repeated usage may result in a different outcome. Billy had shrugged it off, of course. He'd weighed the risks, decided the odds were in his favor, and didn't dwell on the negative possibilities. In other words, exactly how he approached life in general.

My job was to distract the guards at the front of the house for the thirty or so seconds Billy figured he'd need to get in the front door. He'd found out, through some contacts of dubious character at the home security company monitoring Gunn's alarm system, what kind of lock he'd be dealing with, and was happy to learn it wasn't top of the line. Guess Gunn figured his guards were enough of a deterrent to any would-be infiltrators.

Once Billy was in, I was to wait forty-five minutes, then distract the guards again, so he could get out. It didn't seem like enough time to thoroughly search such a large house, but Billy assured me he was up to the task. He'd learned to be fast and methodical when riffling through other people's belongings.

"This time it'll be a piece of cake, because I won't have to worry about being seen," Billy said as I drove us to Gunn's exclusive neighborhood. His eyes were shining, excitement buzzing off him.

"But what if Jack is in his office?" I said.

"It wouldn't be any fun if there were no risk involved," Billy said.

"Just going in is risky enough. What if you start to reappear before you find it?" Back at James's lab, it had taken a little over an hour for Billy's primary aura to return, but who knew for sure whether the results would prove consistent?

He gave my hair a tug. "It'll be okay, cuz."

I took a deep breath. "All right, then," I said, unable to think of another reason to stall. "Let's get this thing over with."

"Bottoms up," Billy said, lifting the bottle, his dimples betraying exactly how much fun he was having.

Once Billy was naked (i.e., invisible), I opened the back door and let him out. I'd parked down the road, between two other gated estates, so no one would know exactly which house the car was visiting. Billy would scale the fence (tall, but not impossibly so) and make his way to the front door while I gathered together my supplies: a small, fluffy dog, a long leash, and a cane.

We'd thought long and hard about what I could do that would pull the guards away from their posts without making them call the police for backup, and had finally decided to go with appealing to their humanitarian instincts. The sidewalk in front of the fence was visible, barely, from the front of the house. What strong man would be able to resist running to the aid of a poor little old lady who'd taken a fall while walking her dog?

Or, if they were not inclined to be helpful for humanitarianism's sake, fear of a lawsuit might be enough to motivate them.

Toddling along with my cane, projecting the aura of one of my favorite great-aunts, I used a doggy treat to coax Mr. Snuggles (a Pomeranian pup borrowed from a showgirl friend of Billy's) into circling my legs a few times with the leash. As I "fell," I let loose a piercing scream and tossed the treat through the fence. Mr. Snuggles dove after it, yapping his tiny head off.

"Help!" I shrieked at the top of my lungs. And then, yes, I said it: "I've fallen and I can't get up!"

All three guards came running. One picked up Mr. Snuggles and unhooked his leash while another started unwinding it from around my legs.

"Are you all right, ma'am?"

"I don't know what happened. Mr. Snuggles"—I saw no reason to change his name—"has never done anything like that before."

"Joe, call an ambulance—"

"No!" I said, looking past them. I saw the front door open enough for a person to slip through, and then close again. "I'm fine, really I am." I got to my feet with impressive agility for such an old lady, and walked a few steps. "See? Perfectly all right."

"If you're sure . . ." the guard who'd been at the door said.

"Oh, quite. If you'll hand me my precious Mr. Snuggles, we'll be on our way. So sorry to disturb you. I feel awful about keeping you from your work."

Yeah, right. Big fat lie. Surely God would make allowances.

The men, evidently realizing they'd left the whole front of the house unprotected, let me go on my way, one of them gently admonishing me to keep the leash shorter in the future. After I was certain they were back at their posts, I slipped into the car, hunched down so I couldn't be seen, and dropped Aunt Audrey's aura. When I saw her at Christmas, I'd have to be sure to tell her about her adventure.

Precisely forty-five minutes later (most of which I spent playing solitaire on my phone), I moved the car directly in front of Gunn's house. Leaving the engine running and the back door open, I trotted to the farthest edge of the estate and threw a flash-bang grenade as far as I could with the athlete's aura I had obtained from Billy. All the guards went running toward the explosion. I hied my ass to the car and waited.

I heard an *oomph* as Billy hit the backseat.

"You in?" I said.

"Go!"

I stomped on the accelerator as the door slammed. Once we were off the street Billy told me to slow down, that I'd attract more attention by speeding. The adrenaline coursing through me made it difficult, but I managed to ease my foot off the pedal.

"So," I said. "Couldn't find it?"

"Oh, I found it, all right," he said.

"Really? I didn't notice anything floating through the air before you got to the car. Where is it?"

"Trust me, cuz, you don't want to know."

Yikes.

Billy was visible once more when he emerged from our hotel bathroom after his shower. He had a short cylindrical tube and a look of relief on his face.

"Don't worry. I washed it thoroughly," he said.

"Ew. Did you know you'd have to do that?" I asked, now supremely grateful he'd insisted on handling that aspect of the job.

"A floating flash drive might make somebody nervous," he said.

"Couldn't you have carried it in your mouth?"

The look he gave me was priceless. "Damn. Never occurred to me." He shrugged it off. "Just as well. What with the running and hopping fences, I might have choked on it, anyway."

"So, where'd you find the tube?" I asked.

He shrugged. "Took it in with me. 'Always prepared,' that's my motto." He unscrewed the top and poured the small flash drive onto the table. "Okay, let's take a look at this thing and see what our bad boy has been up to."

I plugged the drive into a USB port on my laptop and started clicking. We read rapidly, sitting side-by-side on the bed, stopping a few times to give each other we-did-*not*-just-see-that looks.

"Whoa," I said when we were done. "Jack sure gets around."

"That he does," Billy said. I wasn't sure I liked how impressed he sounded. When he saw my eyes roll, he added, "What? You have to admire his stamina, if not his dimensions. And Angelica's foresight. Including those video clips was genius—words might fade in Hollywood, but, oh, how images linger."

"No shit," I said, rubbing my eyes. "If Jack thought Angelica would make these public . . ."

Billy nodded. "The trouble is, the same could be said for Lily-Ann. We know for a fact that *she* knew about this file. And all we have is her word that Jack knew about it. I can't see where this is going to help her at all, no matter how innocent your gut thinks she is."

My cell phone buzzed. "Crap. It's Nigel. I have to tell him."

I explained that our efforts hadn't been exactly helpful to his client, but told him not to worry, we were hatching another plan. "I can't get more specific on the phone, but . . . tell you what, we're headed back to L.A. We'll talk then."

"I hope your new plan is speedy," Nigel said, "because someone—maybe Gunn, maybe the Conrads—is putting a lot of pressure on the court to revoke Lily's bond, claiming she's unstable and an extreme flight risk."

"But why? They know she couldn't have been the shooter at the funeral—shouldn't that help her cause?" I said.

"I'm afraid not. They're now speculating that she's working in collusion with someone. The district attorney would like to see her behind bars in order to cut off any unsupervised contact with her supposed confederates."

"But *you're* supervising her."

"For some reason, I get the idea they don't trust defense lawyers," he said wryly.

"Okay, never mind. Don't worry, I'm sure our new idea will work brilliantly. Tell Lily to hang in there," I said, my voice only slightly reedy.

I hung up. "We need a new idea," I said to Billy. "The faster the better."

"I heard. Nigel's voice carries."

I started to pace. My mind works better when I'm moving. "We have to get Jackson out of that house and figure out some way to trip him up, make him admit he's guilty."

"You're sure he is?"

I thought back to what I'd seen on the video: Jackson Gunn, in his Fifth Wheel trailer with a much younger, but still recognizable, version of Frannie, who, according to Angelica's detailed notes, happened to be the daughter of J. J. Brookfield, one of Hollywood's most powerful producers. She'd been sitting on Jack's lap, naked and bouncing, oohing and aahing about his "gun." If Frannie was of age at the time, it wasn't by much. Maybe not quite the full Polanski, but close enough. And I was pretty sure if her daddy saw the video, Jackson would never work in movies again. Hell, if she *had* been underage, he might even be thrown in jail.

I stopped pacing. "You saw the same thing I saw."

"You mean the 'Roman' hands? True. I also saw our dear Mr. Gunn expressing somewhat more than a filial affection for his mother-in-law. Nicely preserved woman by the way—"

I cut Billy a dirty look. He laughed and continued speaking. "I'm just pointing out that the file could easily incriminate more than one person. Elizabeth Conrad, if she knows about its existence, might have her own objections to it being made public. And then, of course, there's Lily-Ann—I know, I know. Your gut. I'm only trying to point out how things would look to a jury."

"*Gah.* Damn it, Billy, I have to find out for sure who did it. I *have* to. We need to get him out of that house so I can talk to him face-to-face. Did you see any sign of him while you were in there?"

Billy's eyes followed me as he lounged on the bed. "He wandered between the kitchen and the bar, both of which seemed to be well stocked. Looks to me like Jack is set to camp out inside until Lily-Ann is safely tried and convicted. Hmm . . . I suppose we could always set the house on fire."

If he hadn't winked I might have thought he was serious. Heck, even with the wink, I wasn't sure he didn't mean it.

"*Think,* Billy. You have the most devious mind of anyone I know—"

He inclined his head in a regal bow. "Thenk yew. I do try," he said, with a shade of QEII in his delivery.

Which reminded me—he did have a lot of celebrity auras in his repertoire. Including a bunch of Hollywood types. I knew for a fact he had a perfect Meryl Streep.

I wonder . . .

"Hey, maybe we could . . ." I proceeded to outline a sketchy plan, throwing out ideas as soon as they popped into my head, ending with, "What do you think?"

He'd sat up, smile growing, as I spoke. It was an eye-crinkling double-dimpler by the time I finished. "And you say *I* have a devious mind?"

I grinned at his obvious approval.

"You know, cuz, I think we could make it work."

"You really think it's doable?" I asked.

"It would take some finesse to set up—don't worry, finesse is a specialty of mine—and we'd have to call in some reinforcements, but yeah. I think we might get him to follow his ego out the door."

Chapter 20

Billy took off to work some of his finessing magic with his Hollywood contacts while I went to fill in the blanks for Nigel and Lily-Ann. I planned to wave the flag a bit, and encourage them to hang in there until we could implement the world's craziest plan. Not that I'd necessarily pitch it as "world's craziest." No point in piling on the worry.

Nigel met me at the door himself, as dapper as always in his suit and tie. But the look on his handsome face was grim. The first words out of his mouth were, "Lily's gone."

"What? But she can't be—they'll revoke her bail for sure if she runs," I said.

"I tried to explain to her that I had other avenues to hold the court at bay for at least a little while longer, but she panicked. She cut her anklet half an hour ago, and left without a cell phone. I have no way to contact her."

Shit. "How long to we have before somebody comes to check on her?"

"I've already had a call from the monitoring agency, which I let the machine answer. They've probably already reported the breach. The police are overworked and understaffed—we might have an hour or two, or they might show up any minute. Tough to say."

Damn it. Stupid move, Lily-Ann. "You're not going to report her yourself?" I knew, as an officer of the court, he could get in serious trouble for not faithfully upholding his duties, possibly even lose his license to practice law.

"I'll have to if she's not back before the police get here," he said. "I know she's innocent, but I don't see a way around it."

But he hadn't done it yet—that meant he was good at heart. I could work with that.

"Look, we need to buy some time for Lily to come to her senses," I said. "Here's what we're going to do . . ."

When the police officer got there, he found me (aka Lily-Ann) stretched out on the sofa with an ice pack on my horribly swollen ankle. Nigel had called to report her unfortunate "accident," explaining that he'd had to cut the tracking anklet to keep it from cutting off the circulation to her foot.

I had, naturally, captured some of her energy when I'd met her. I tend to do that automatically when I shake someone's hand—it's a reflex.

"Sorry to be a bother," I said, faking a wince as the officer lifted the ice bag to examine my ankle.

Nigel, his wheelchair in its standing position, said, "It was entirely my fault. I'm afraid my cat is fond of getting underfoot. Lily-Ann, I apologize again."

"Don't worry about it, Nigel. At least it's not broken," I said.

"Are you sure about that?" the officer said. "It looks pretty bad to me. Maybe I should escort you to the ER."

"That won't be necessary," Nigel said smoothly. "My doctor came at once and examined Miss Conrad's ankle. That's why I missed the first call from the monitoring agency."

"A doctor who makes house calls?" the officer said.

"Yes. She left before you arrived. I keep a concierge doctor on retainer. A man in my position"—he didn't gesture toward his wheelchair, but it was obvious he wasn't referring to his financial status—"can't afford to take chances."

The officer didn't question it further, but even if he decided to, it would be okay, because the good doctor had in fact examined me, taking an X-ray with a portable machine before pronouncing my injury not at all serious. I hadn't puffed the ankle up quite as much for her at I did for the cop, not wanting to risk her suggesting a hospital visit. She'd left me with crutches to use if I felt the need, and orders to keep it elevated as much as possible for the next few days.

The officer hooked a new monitor to my other ankle, tested it, and was on his way. I'd taken care to project that ankle to be as thick as I could reasonably get away with (with a silent apology to Lily-Ann for giving her cankles), so I had no difficulty slipping the monitor off when I projected the smallest foot in my repertoire.

"Nigel, do you know the tracking radius on these things?"

"Not precisely, but it's fairly small. They have to be able to tell if you leave the house." His chair was in its sitting position, giving him a lap for his cat, a beautiful applehead Siamese.

Hmm. "Is that an indoor cat?" I asked.

"Yes, of course. There are coyotes in these hills. Why?"

I slipped the monitor over the cat's head. Other than an annoyed flick of its ears, it seemed not to object. "Do you mind?" I asked.

"I don't if Isis doesn't," he said.

"Do the police conduct random home visits?"

"They claim to, but in actuality they're so short-staffed they rarely come out unless they lose contact, as happened today."

"Great. Any idea where a panicked Lily-Ann might run?"

"I've been considering that. The best I can do is give you a list of animal rescue shelters where she volunteers. Those are the only people I know she trusts."

The list Nigel had given me was lengthy. I'd never be able to hit them all, not even if I enlisted Billy's help, which I didn't want to do because he had enough on his plate already handling the logistics for Plan B.

I narrowed the list by eliminating the larger, municipally operated shelters, figuring Lily would avoid anything too "official." Then I went online and looked up the location of the closest private shelters. She was on foot, after all. At least, I hoped she was avoiding public transportation, because it sure wouldn't be good if she were to be recognized out in the community while she was supposedly under house arrest. Practically everyone had a cell phone with a camera, most of which automatically recorded the date, time, and location of a picture.

There was a small shelter about three miles from Nigel's house. I found Lily in the back, spraying out cages, her hair tucked under a big knit hat. Her eyes always looked big behind her glasses, but they widened even more when she saw me.

"I'm not going back," she said, and pointed the nozzle of her sprayer at me, poised to squirt if I made a false move.

I raised my hands. "Whoa. Don't shoot. I'm not here for that."

She lowered the hose. "Are the cops looking for me?"

"Nope. As far as they know, you're right where they left you. I took the liberty of temping as you when they came to replace the anklet Nigel was forced to cut off you when you tripped over his cat and sprained your ankle."

She looked confused. I raised one eyebrow and waited for her to connect the dots.

"Oh!" she said finally. "Uh . . . thank you."

I lowered my arms, but didn't step closer. She didn't look as if she'd appreciate me invading her space.

"Look, Lily, I know how scary this must be for you, but taking off isn't going to help your cause in the long run. Billy—the friend I told you was helping me? He's my boyfriend, another adaptor—anyway, he and I are going to get you out of this mess, I promise. We're working on a plan to smoke out the real killer, whether it's Jackson or someone else."

She looked skeptical. "What's the plan?"

"It's kind of complicated. I'll explain it when we get the final details hammered out," I said.

"Yeah, and what if it doesn't work? I have friends who can get me out of the country—they'll be here in a few hours. This might be my only shot at avoiding prison."

"Is that how you want to live? Forever hiding, always looking over your shoulder, while your sister's killer goes free?"

"Of course not! But the law listens to money, and my parents and Jackson have that. And I refuse to go to prison for a crime I didn't commit. I *can't* go back to Nigel's and just wait for them to come take me away. I won't. I'm sorry about the bail your friend posted for me. I didn't ask for it, but I'll try to find a way to pay back the money someday."

Her eyes were getting wilder, her voice higher pitched. If I didn't handle this carefully, she'd bolt again.

I considered my options. "Okay. You don't have to go back to Nigel's. Isis is wearing your tracker, so we're good there for now."

"Isis?"

"Yeah. It was all I could think to do on short notice—I couldn't keep wearing it myself indefinitely. She'll move around enough to keep the monitoring agents from getting suspicious."

Lily smiled. "She's a good cat."

"But you cannot, under any circumstances, be seen in public, because that would be it for you. Your face is very well known from all the TV coverage, and if a cop sees you, you'll be hauled in and held until your trial."

She nodded. "I'll find someplace to hide. There's a storage room here I can use for now. My friends will bring me food. I don't have to go out at all."

Yeah, and what's the difference between that and jail? I thought. "I have a better idea," I said.

"Miss Lily-Ann, I sure am happy to make your acquaintance," Dave said after we got Lily settled. "You're welcome here at the Circle C. Do you ride? Because we have a few fine mounts who sure could use some exercise."

Lily smiled, visibly relaxing. "I do. I'm pretty good with a shovel, too, if you need any help around the barn. I like to earn my keep."

"Darlin', I can already see we're going to get along."

The Circle C was the best place I could think of to stash Lily. Dave and Rosa would be happy to look after her, and Cody—more cautious than ever since the gun-in-the-stall incident—would keep her safe. He'd see to it that she didn't get away from us again, but without making her feel like a prisoner, I was sure.

There'd been more than enough room for all three of us in the Mooney, and Billy had been thrilled to have an excuse to fly. (Me, I was just happy when I didn't barf. The anxiety center of my brain was probably getting numb to altitude.)

Rosa was more guarded than Dave. She knew who Lily was from all the recent TV coverage. "You're not one of those vegans, are you? Because I can make you food without meat, but I don't think I can cook without lard and cheese."

Lily smiled. "I eat meat as long as it's organic and free-range. And I do prefer my dairy products to be hormone-free, but I'm okay with a 'don't ask, don't tell' policy in a situation like this."

"That's fine, then. I like free-range, too—happy chickens taste better," Rosa said, content enough herself now that her cooking routine wouldn't be disrupted.

I dug up some of the shirts and nightgowns I kept at the ranch and gave them to Lily to use while she was there. "I think my jeans would be too short, but I can see if Cody has an extra pair you can borrow—he's skinny enough, and you can always roll them up. And if you tell Rosa your sizes, she'll go into town and pick you up some things."

She blushed when I mentioned Cody's jeans. They'd been sneaking peeks at each other ever since we'd landed.

"Thanks. I can't tell you how much I appreciate this," she said.

"You don't have to," I said. "All you have to do is keep a low profile and do what Cody tells you to—he's here to keep you safe." *And to make sure you don't take off again.* But no need to bog her down with the details. "Billy and I will take care of the rest."

Chapter 21

Billy stayed in L.A. to continue his finessing magic while I headed back east on a recruiting mission. One of us had to be on call to play Lily-Ann at Nigel's house, should it prove necessary. If the local police paid an unexpected visit, Nigel would say Lily was in the restroom, indisposed with an awful intestinal bug, giving Billy time to hie his ankle over there to fill in for the fugitive.

My first stop: the parental homestead. I could pay a filial visit and avoid the cost of a hotel at the same time.

It was the middle of the day, so I didn't bother to knock. Mom was probably on a job, making up for the time she missed while planning and executing the blitz wedding. If Dad was home, he was bound to be in his basement man-cave. I had a key—Mom mails a new one to me regularly, in case I'm as careless with them as she's under the impression I am with my cell phones—so I let myself in.

I left my carry-on in the front hall and made a beeline for the kitchen. With any luck, Dad would have weeded out most of Mom's more unfortunate culinary creations from the refrigerator, and I'd find one of her masterpieces. (Mom didn't have any middle ground when it came to cooking.)

Rounding the bend from the dining room I ran into Buffy the Vampire Slayer. Literally.

"Ciel! What are you doing home?" Buffy said, hastily lowering the wooden spoon she'd been holding like a spike at plunging angle.

"Um, visiting?" I said, backing away from her. I was pretty sure Sarah Michelle Gellar didn't know me.

"Buffy, you won't get away from me this time," a male voice called out from the living room in a distinctive British accent.

Spike ran in and grabbed Buffy from behind, bending his head down to nibble her neck. "Got you!" he shouted triumphantly.

Mom dropped the Buffy aura. "Patrick, stop. Ciel's home."

The hot, bleached-blond vampire spun his head around. "Oh, hi, honey. Nice to see you."

"Mom? Dad?" *Ew.* Was this what they did when my brothers and I weren't around?

Mom tugged on Dad's sleeve. He dropped the Spike aura.

"Thanks a lot, you guys. Way to ruin one of my favorite childhood shows," I said, giving each of them a hug now that I could bring myself to touch them.

"You're old enough to realize your parents have a sex life," Mom said.

"Hush, Ro. Don't listen to her, sweetie-pie. We were playing tag, nothing else," Dad said with a flirtatious wink at Mom. *Ack.*

Mom grinned, and it was kind of on the wicked side. "Right. Tag. We'll see how well you like playing tag later, buster."

I stuck my fingers in my ears. "La-la-la . . . I can't hear you! Can we please go back to pretending I'm too young to understand this stuff?"

"Knock next time, and you won't be traumatized. Now, come to the kitchen and let me fix you something to eat. Where's Billy? I thought you were with him."

I followed, crossing my fingers that there was no leftover calamari casserole lurking in the fridge. "He has a job out west." True enough. "Why? You want me to go stay at his place?"

Frankly, the idea that my parents might not be thrilled to see me had never occurred to me. And here I'd thought I'd been doing them a big favor by deciding to stay with them while I was in town. Kind of gave me a twinge in my solar plexus.

"Don't be silly, dear. You know we love it when you visit. Now, sit at my desk"—Mom's command center was set up in one corner of the kitchen—"and open the computer. The photographer sent the wedding pictures—they're absolutely stunning! You look so cute . . ." She raved about all the pictures while she pulled something from the pantry.

Please, God, not the canned calamari. I swear I'll stop using bad words forever if it's not the calamari . . .

The pictures were good. Laura was radiant. Thomas was as relaxed and handsome as I'd ever seen him. Even the ones of me in the banana dress didn't look too heinous. I peered more closely at the screen. Maybe the photographer had Photoshopped them.

And Mark . . .

My breath caught in my throat at the picture of us dancing together. No mistaking the enraptured look on my face there. And Mark's face was as every bit as adoring. Jesus, I hoped Billy never saw this picture.

How could I not have known? I mentally berated myself. It had to have been the cider. Mark had warned me it might knock me on my ass. Little had I known how prophetic his words would turn out to be.

". . . and that Molly," Mom went on. "Can you believe her performance? She's positively *gifted.* And I'm the one who gave her that Rock Band drum set. You remember? I must have known instinctively which instrument would call out to her. Of course, your brother deserves a lot of the credit. He's been giving her music lessons, you know . . ."

"Yeah, Mom. She's amazing," I said, and kept clicking through the pictures. There were a few of me with Nils—we looked like we were have a good time, but nothing more.

In a way, that was too bad. If I'd had the same look on my face in every picture of me dancing with a guy, well then, the look wouldn't mean anything. It would just be my dancing-with-a-nice-looking-guy look. I kept clicking until I came to a picture of me dancing with Thomas.

"Oh, that's a wonderful one of you and your brother. You both look so happy," Mom said, breezing by on her way back to the refrigerator.

"Yeah, it's a good one," I agreed. Certainly no look of exquisite longing on my face there.

Mom whizzed by again, carton of heavy cream and a bottle of maple syrup in hand. That could be very good or very bad, depending entirely on the other ingredients in whatever she was making. She put them on the counter and came to stand behind me.

"Oh, stop there—go back one. Who was that tall blond man dancing with Sinead? A friend of Laura's, right? She introduced me, but then one of your father's cousins called me away before I could really talk to him."

"His name is Nils," I said. "I think Laura met him when she was on an assignment in Sweden."

"So good looking! He's Swedish, isn't he? Is he single? How old is he, anyway? Too old for Sinead, I'm guessing. Liam would have a heart attack." She went to the counter and pulled the stand mixer out from the appliance garage.

I was almost through the proofs, and hadn't seen any other incriminating photos of me with Mark. If I could delete the one of us dancing, then maybe—

"Remind me to call Mo later and tell her to take a gander at that Viking." Damn. Auntie Mo had a set of proofs, too. "She's going to be so disappointed she didn't get a chance to dance with him. I know *I* am."

"He was a little clumsy," I said absently.

Billy was sure to look through all the pictures, to see what he missed. When he saw . . . No. I was probably overreacting.

"That's probably because of the height difference. If you'd worn heels, like I told you . . ."

The blender drowned out the rest of her sentence, thank goodness. I clicked to *the* picture.

Geez fucking Louise. It was every bit as bad as I'd thought. I tried to think back to the reception. When I was dancing with Mark, had I been *certain* it was Billy? Because that could explain the look on my face.

Of course, it didn't explain the look on *Mark's*.

"Oh, that's another good one," Mom said, pausing again to look over my shoulder at the screen. "Mark is such a nice-looking man. So hard and rugged, but when he smiles, ooh-la-la! You know, we should try to find him a nice girl. Maybe now that Thomas is married, Mark will see it's not so bad. Hmm. Jenny Harrison is still single . . ."

"Mom, Jenny Harrison has seven cats. That's why she's still single. Besides, she's forty-two years old."

"It's such an archaic concept that the man has to be older, don't you think?"

"She sews outfits for her cats!"

Mom shrugged. "Okay, how about Susan Westin? I don't think she has any cats."

"She gets seasick. Mark lives on a sailboat. You do the math."

"Tara Dickerson?"

"Too crunchy. She hasn't shaved her armpits since she was fifteen and found those Joan Baez records in her mom's closet."

I was still staring at the picture.

"Tough to let go, dear?" Mom said quietly.

"No!" I said. "I mean, I love Billy. He's so right for me. We're right for each other. I just don't understand why I still . . ."

"Go all tingly when Mark walks in the room?"

I slumped. Mom hugged me, leaning down and resting her head on my shoulder. "Honey, it's normal. I mean, look at the guy. I've had a few Mrs. Robinson thoughts about him myself."

"Mom!"

She patted my head. "Oh, sweetie. You are so sheltered. I really should have reined in your brothers when you were growing up, but it was so darn cute how they watched out for you."

I twisted around and looked up at her. "So I'm not terrible?"

"Of course not. And it will all work out. Give it a little time. Now, come here and peel the shrimp for the maple cream casserole while I get the spinach noodles started."

I looked skyward with a stifled a groan. *You can't hold me to it, Big Guy. Shrimp, calamari . . . close enough.*

I had to act fast. I'd ask the favor I'd come here to ask, and then I'd flee.

First off, I explained the Jackson Gunn dilemma. Mom was appalled that one of her favorite actors might do such a thing. Dad wasn't surprised, but he was upset that I'd worked in such close contact with a possible murderer. When I told them what I needed them to do, they looked a little dubious.

"Sweetie, you know we're always here for you, but isn't this whole criminal justice thing more up Thomas's alley?" Mom said.

"Oh, I'm going to hit him up, too. But a conventional legal approach won't work in this case—we have to be sneakier than that."

"Is Mark going to help?" Dad asked. "I would think his background would prove useful."

I looked at Mom, flushing. "No. He's out of the country."

Mom patted my hand. She was actually starting to look kind of excited at the prospect of spending some time in Hollywood. "Is Billy asking Mo and Liam? Because I can do that for you."

"That's where I'm heading next. Sorry I can't stay for dinner. You understand—"

"Don't be silly. I said I'd talk to them for you—you know they'll be happy to help. Now, sit down and let's eat. This is going to be so much fun!"

"I've helped you with your job before. You *owe* me," I said, suppressing a shrimp-maple belch.

"But I'm not an actor. I'm a *musician,*" he said.

I'd ducked out after dinner to meet Brian at the club where his band played. We were sitting in the bar, sipping beers between sets.

"Bri, you're an adaptor," I said quietly. "Adaptors are all actors—we have to be. Anyway, we mostly just need warm bodies who can project Hollywood stars. You don't have to say anything. If it helps, you can think of yourself as a prop."

"I don't have any movie star auras."

"Don't worry, Billy has a ton of them."

"But the band—"

"Can get by without you for a night or two. They do it all the time when you're busy chasing a new girl," I pointed out.

He gave me a look (only slightly stoned), but couldn't deny it.

I upped the pressure. "James and Devon are going to help."

I'd stopped by James's place on the way to the club. Devon had been there. James hadn't been especially eager to sign on, but Devon had talked him into it. Since he had given up chasing his own Hollywood dream to stay with my brother, I suppose James had thought it was the least he could do.

"*And* Mom and Dad. Come on, Bri, if *Mom* will do it . . ."

Brian sprawled in his chair. "You're not going to let this go, are you?"

"Nope."

"All right. I'll do it," he said at last.

I jumped up and hugged him. "Thanks, Bri. I'll call you and let you know when to come."

Two brothers down, one to go.

"Ciel, I'm on my *honeymoon*."

"No, you're not. You're back home. How was sailing, by the way? Laura's a great sailor, isn't she? Did you have fun on Mark's boat?"

"Fine, yes, and yes. And we may be home, but Laura and I are busy getting her settled into my place. *Our* place."

"But Laura wants to help," I said.

His eyebrows threatened to meet in the middle over his nose. "You already talked to Laura about this?"

"Well, yeah. I caught her out front, on her way to the gym. I wanted to make sure it was okay with her before I dragged you away. But it was her idea to come along and help, too. Come on,

Thomas. We need you. Heck, if you won't do it for me, do it for your old buddy Nigel."

He expelled a breath through his nose, and I knew I had him.

Next up: Nils. Billy might not be crazy about the Swede, but he was reliable and he was strong. Plus, since he was in the secret security biz, I figured he knew how to keep his mouth shut. Best of all, he was *big*.

After that, a quick call to enlist Sinead and Siobhan (I didn't expect any resistance from them—they'd jump at any opportunity to miss a few days of school) and I would be done.

Chapter 22

"Holy crap!" My voice echoed through the cavernous building. "The lights . . . the scenery . . . the props. How did you do it?"

I knew Billy had rented a warehouse, but to turn it into a soundstage in such a short time bordered on miraculous. Outside, there'd been a small sign reading "Property of Angling Entertainment. Trespassers will be Blacklisted."

When I'd asked Billy if it would be a problem that Jack hadn't heard of it, he'd assured me that production companies in Hollywood popped up and down faster than the critter heads in Whac-A-Mole. Jack wouldn't think anything of a new one approaching him as long as he knew the names behind it. Which we'd see to, of course.

"You ain't seen nothin' yet," Billy said. He squeezed my hand and pulled me over to the director's chair.

The name on it was impressively well known. There wasn't an actor in Hollywood who wouldn't sell his soul to work with him.

"Are you sure that's not a stretch? I mean, will Jack buy it?"

"If you're after a big fish, you have to use a big hook," he said.

"Have you approached him yet?"

"I have a meeting set up with him this evening. *Very* hush-hush."

The plan was simple enough, if not easy: offer Jackson Gunn the chance to star in the epic sci-fi movie of the decade. I knew from talk around the snake set that he was hungry for something "big" and "fresh," especially if he could stretch his acting chops by adding a certain nerdy intelligence to his typical kick-ass type of character.

Billy held out his hands in the classic directorial framing gesture. "Picture it. *Star Wars, Star Trek, Avalon, Raiders of the Lost Ark,* and *Alien* all rolled into one megablockbuster starring Jackson Gunn."

"God, he'll eat it up. But did you figure out how to keep his people out of it? If his agent gets wind of it, she'll be poking her nose around, trying to find out more about the project, won't she?"

"Yeah, I thought about that. I think the best way to play it is to tell Jack that the financing is wobbly. That I want him to come in to shoot some sample footage, that I need something to take to the money people to show them he's on board before they'll commit."

"And if he hesitates, that's when we bring in the names? You have all the right auras?"

"Got 'em. When's everyone coming out?"

"Tomorrow. Did you get hold of a costume? Because I found somebody big enough to wear it."

"Who?"

"Nils. He wants to repay us for the help we gave him with the neo-Vikings. Apparently, that operation turned out to be a good career move for him."

"Nils? You're dragging him over from Sweden?"

"Um, he was already here. He came to the wedding—you know he's a good friend of Laura's."

Billy looked at me closely. "How is old Nils, anyway? Still drooling over you?"

I rolled my eyes. (What? Sometimes it can't be helped.) Yes, I might have experienced a brief, very minor, attraction to Nils when I'd first met him, but it was over almost as soon as it started, and it had been *before* anything romantic had started with Billy. I can't stress that last part enough.

"He's fine. No drooling. From either one of us," I said.

Billy tugged my hair. "Remember—Limburger."

Laura flew out early, ahead of Thomas, who had some clients he had to see before he could tear himself away from D.C.

"Must be a pain to be married to somebody with such a strong work ethic," I teased her, sipping a ten-dollar can of soda from the minifridge.

I'd taken a break from my film-setup duties to meet her at the hotel. Once she was settled, she'd come back to the set with me and help out where she could. We were in her room—the penthouse suite. (Thomas had insisted, claiming they were technically still honeymooning.)

She laughed. "I wouldn't say that. Besides, the busier he is with his work, the less he can complain about mine."

I was dying to ask her if she'd heard from Mark, but didn't dare, for fear I'd blurt out everything that had happened after her wedding. I didn't want to put a smudge on her memory of the day.

"So, when are *you* going back to work?"

"Harvey has something lined up for me next week. A simple courier job. I should be insulted, but I know he has the best intentions, annoying as those are. After this job, though, he and I will be having a *talk.* Billy can't keep subbing for me forever."

"Is Thomas . . . um, okay with all that?" I asked, tentatively, because her job had once caused a major rift between them.

"Well, sugar, just between you and me, your brother can be kind of a chauvinist. But he's such an adorable oinker that I'm willing to work with him on that particular character flaw."

"Good luck with that," I said, laughing.

She cocked her head. "What about you? Are you and Billy okay? I was sorry he couldn't make it to the wedding. My fault, I guess, since he was subbing for me yet again."

"We're good," I said, meaning it sincerely.

"Ciel . . . do you have any idea why Mark left the country so suddenly?" she said, watching me intently. Damn spook instincts.

I swallowed. "Some emergency job, maybe?"

"I don't think so. He usually keeps me up to speed on anything related to work."

"Have you talked to him?" I asked.

"Yes. Once. He called after we brought his boat back to the marina."

"Um, how did he sound?"

I *know.* How could she not find that question odd? But I was worried about him.

"That was the funny thing. He sounded kind of . . . wistful. Not at all like himself."

I took a sip of my soda, and tried to sound casual. "Well, his best friend just married his work partner. Maybe he's feeling kind of left out."

"Maybe, but I think it's more than that. Hey, did you tell him about this job? He'll usually drop anything that's not of national importance to help you."

"I didn't ask him," I said, looking away from her. "I mean, this is my mess, mine and Billy's. Why should Mark have to clean it up for us?" When she still looked skeptical, I added, "It's different with you—you're family now. You have to help."

She nodded thoughtfully, but didn't push it.

I wanted to spill everything. It would be such a relief to talk to a girlfriend about it, someone who might be able to help me sort it all out in my head. Someone to act as confessor. But I couldn't expect her to keep it from Thomas, and telling Thomas would *not* be a good idea at all. I couldn't put that on Laura.

Billy, in the guise of the well-known director, had met with Jackson at a hole-in-the-wall dive fifty miles outside Hollywood while Laura and I were talking. When we met him at the impromptu soundstage, he looked supremely satisfied.

"Hook, line, sinker," he said when he saw us. "Hell, he swallowed the whole pole. Wait . . . did that sound dirty? I meant it to sound dirty."

Laura giggled. "You succeeded. And thank you again for doing my job for me. I'm sorry you couldn't be at the wedding." She gave him a quick hug.

"Me, too," he said. "But if one of us had to miss it, I'll bet Thomas is glad it was me and not you."

I laughed along with Laura, though I doubted I'd ever find anything about that day particularly funny.

"Okay, what's next?" I asked. "Everyone else will be here by ten p.m. at the latest, so we can get an early start tomorrow. What can we do now?"

"Laura, I seem to recall you're a whiz with electronics. I got hold of some cameras I'd like you to double-check for me . . ." Billy started to lead her to the center of the building.

"And me?" I asked.

He dimpled. "Would you hit me if I asked you make coffee?"

My phone buzzed before I could make a suitable fist. It was Nigel.

"Tell me the cops aren't there," I said, visions of being hauled off to jail in Lily's stead dancing through my head.

"Not quite that bad," he said. "Her parents are on the way over."

"What do *they* want? I thought they disowned her."

"They want to talk to their only remaining child. They're hopeful this 'whole sordid affair,' as her mother so eloquently phrased it, can be put behind them. They seem certain I'll be able to spin some sort of self-defense plea. I get the idea that they want to bring her back into the Conrad fold."

"I'll be there as soon as I can."

I arrived only minutes before the Conrads, running to Lily-Ann's room, Isis in hand, as they pulled into Nigel's long, circular driveway. While they made their meandering way up the curved walk, I changed hastily into Lily's aura and clothing, shrinking my foot enough to get the anklet on, in case either one of them had an eye for detail.

I hadn't spent much time around Lily-Ann, and didn't have a dossier to work from, as I did with my clients, so this was going to be tricky. I could only hope that between her being alienated from her family, and the general stress that being arrested for murder could be expected to put on a person, her parents might not notice anything too "off" about me.

I got my breathing under control before I met them in the living room. I decided to forgo the embrace—Lily didn't strike me as a hypocrite—but I wasn't sure what she called her parents. Mom and Dad? Mommy and Pops? No way.

I avoided Elizabeth's eyes because I couldn't look at her without remembering the video in Angelica's file. Had she wanted a "taste" of what Angelica had, like Jackson had claimed about Lily? More importantly, had she liked what she'd sampled enough to kill her own daughter? Or had she just been another woman taken in by Jackson's wiles?

Of course, it was also possible she somehow knew Jackson killed her daughter, and had tried to kill him at the funeral in retaliation. Was that the real reason she'd been absent from the service? Seemed an odd thing for a mother to sleep with her daughter's husband and then kill said husband, but stranger things have happened. Or maybe she'd been aiming for her own husband. Now that Jackson was free, had she been trying to free herself?

Still too damn many questions.

"Mother. Father," I finally said, figuring the formality wouldn't be unusual under the awkward circumstances.

Hope lit Mrs. Conrad's eyes. "It's nice to hear you call us that again, darling," she said.

Mr. Conrad *hmphed.* "Better than 'Joseph,' I suppose."

Oooh. So, that was how it was. I couldn't imagine calling my own parents by their first names. I guess Lily didn't put quite the same stock in the filial relationship as I did. I shrugged, and didn't try to explain, because, really, what could I say?

"What are you doing here?" I asked bluntly, because the little time I *had* spent with Lily had shown me that part of her nature.

They didn't look shocked, so I supposed they were used to it.

Mrs. Conrad spoke first. "Lily . . . darling . . . your father and

I want you to know . . . well, even though you've been . . . estranged . . . from the family, we don't believe you . . . I mean, your own sister . . ."

"You don't believe I shot my sister in the back? Huh. Gee, thanks for the vote of confidence."

Joe bristled. "Don't you speak to your mother that way, young lady. We're here to help you."

"Your altruism is commendable," I said. "Oh, wait. You don't really do altruism, do you? Not unless there's something in it for you."

"If you shut up that smart mouth of yours for a minute, you'll see there's something in it for you, too," Daddy Dearest said.

And here come the true colors, I thought. I looked at him as coldly as I imagined Lily-Ann would have. Didn't faze him. Must be used to that, too.

"The way I read it, right now Nigel here has maybe a forty percent shot at getting you acquitted. But those odds could go up—or down—significantly, depending on how your mother and I choose to testify about Angelica."

What? They were actually using their murdered daughter as a bargaining chip?

"Care to tell me what you mean by that?" I said.

"Yes, I'm curious, too," Nigel said sardonically. "Do tell me how you can help my case."

Mr. Conrad jerked his chin downward in a single, satisfied nod. "Angelica, for all that she chose to marry a celebrity, went to great lengths to keep herself out of the public eye"—he looked at me, disapproval written on every line of his face—"as was appropriate for her position in our company." Apparently, Daddy Dearest really objected to Lily's tendency to step up on her soapbox in front of any willing camera. "If it were to come to light that she were prone to irrational outbursts, violence even, in her own home, against family members . . . well, a jury might find that to be a mitigating circumstance for someone who might have been taken off guard and simply defending herself."

While he was talking, my whodunnit gears were still spinning. What if Joe had gotten wind of Angelica's impending release of the file? That could certainly be considered entering the public eye in a spectacular way. Joe could have decided to talk to her about it, and the conversation might have flared into violence if it hadn't gone to his liking.

"Was Angelica prone to such outbursts?" Nigel said. His face and tone were neutral.

"Possibly," Conrad said, and shrugged. "Or perhaps she was simply a good-hearted woman, a philanthropist in her own right, trying to reach out to the black sheep of the family. The black sheep who ultimately lashed out against her in a fit of wacko animal-rights rage. Context is everything, isn't it?"

Whoa. This was one seriously fucked-up family. "Let me get this straight. You're saying—presumably—that if I'm willing to toe the company line, you'll testify that Angelica basically got what she deserved?"

Lily's mother fiddled with the pendant at her neck. "It *could* have happened that way. If you say it did, then we'll back you up in court. Maybe we wouldn't even have to have a trial. We could all go back to the way it was, and those horrible people would stop following us around with their cameras."

"But we couldn't *all* go back to the way it was, could we, Mother? I mean, Angelica is dead"—she had the humanity to wince, which is more than I could say for her husband—"and I'd have to give up everything I believe in."

"Naturally, some reciprocity would be expected," Conrad said.

"You would be welcomed back into the family. You could even, one day, after you're mature enough to handle the responsibility, take over where Angelica left off. I brought these as a show of good faith."

He handed me a small stack of papers I'd last seen in the French bistro in D.C. I shuffled through them, saw they were what I'd suspected—stock certificates. A great many shares of Conrad Fine Foods, in fact, issued on the date of Angelica's birth. And, apparently, all legally signed over to Joseph and Elizabeth Conrad a few weeks before Angelica's death. Yeah, right.

"You want to give these to me?" I asked.

"Yes. We'll sign them over right now. Nigel can be witness," Joe said.

I cocked Lily's head, putting a considering look on her face. "And what, exactly, would keep me from taking the stock, and then, after my acquittal, picking up where *I* left off? Double jeopardy being what it is and all. Just curious," I said.

Conrad's eyes narrowed to slits. "I'm sure Nigel here could draw up some papers that would prevent that from happening."

Nigel remained neutral, neither confirming nor denying that he could.

"And if I were to tell both of you to fuck off?" Again, I could see the language coming from their youngest daughter's mouth didn't surprise them.

Conrad snatched the certificates from me and took his wife by the elbow. "Come along, Elizabeth. We have an appointment with the district attorney. I expect it's time we admitted we knew all along about the antipathy between our daughters. I'm sure he'll be sympathetic to our reluctance to do so before, not wanting to lose both of them. And then there's the press to consider. We can't keep avoiding their questions forever."

Assholes. They'd do it, too.

I looked at Nigel, searching for some clue as to what Lily might say under the circumstances. My gut told me she wouldn't give in to their blackmail-bribery mashup, but if she really thought her life—or at least her freedom—were on the line, who knew?

Nigel shrugged, almost imperceptibly. He didn't know either.

"Wait," I said. I had to stall somehow. "I'll . . . consider it."

"Darling, that's wonderful. It will be fine, you'll see," Elizabeth said. She tried to come to me, but Conrad held tightly to her arm.

"Overholt, you have until the end of business hours tomorrow to bring me the appropriate papers, signed by my daughter. After that, we'll *reconsider* transferring the stock. Good day."

Chapter 23

I raced to the soundstage as fast as my economy rental car and traffic would allow. Which was to say, I was in no danger of getting a speeding ticket. Billy and Laura were hard at work writing. Luckily, we didn't need a whole script.

I filled them in on what had taken place with Lily-Ann's dear old mom and dad, explaining our new deadline, and ending with, "Can you believe it? I will never complain about my family again."

"Best not swear to that," Billy said.

Laura smiled. "There's nothing to complain about with your family."

"Your family, too, now," I said. "Give it time—you'll see."

Billy grinned. "Gee, cuz, that lasted, what? Two seconds?"

"Okay, okay. I know how good I have it. So, what's going on here?"

"I showed Laura the Harilla costume. She thinks it'll fit Nils fine."

Harilla was the name we'd coined for the anthropoid half-hare, half-gorilla who was the antagonist opposite the swashbuckling anthropologist-slash-alien-hunter hero character in our phony production. Broad of chest and long of ear, all the costume needed was the right man to fill it. Nils was large, muscular, and trained in taking down baddies—exactly what we needed if a big guy like Jackson Gunn reacted poorly to our plan.

The costume? Billy found it on eBay, and since time was of the essence . . . yeah. At first we thought it might be too ridiculous, but then we figured it was exactly what we needed. Even a badass bunny costume is still a bunny, and bound to make Nils seem less intimidating to a skittish Jackson. Also, it was a darn handy place to hide a few weapons.

"Are you sure Nils knows what he's in for?" Billy asked. "Maybe I should do it."

"You're the director—we can't spare you. If you're not comfortable with Nils, then I'll do it," I said.

"You're not trained in hand-to-hand combat. Besides, what if we have another 'being Lily' emergency call from Nigel while we're shooting?" he said.

Good point. "It's settled, then. And don't worry—I explained it all to Nils clearly. Laura said he's a professional. I'm sure he can handle it."

"Nils won't let us down," Laura confirmed.

"I sure hope not," I said, "because if we don't get a decent vid by the end of the day tomorrow, Lily-Ann is screwed."

We were still at the soundstage at midnight. Our intrepid gang of volunteers was with us, all of them either absorbing their assigned auras from Billy and trying on their costumes, or, in the case of the nonadaptors, getting the particulars of their jobs from Laura.

Devon was in heaven. He loved being included at family gatherings, and being on a movie set—even a fake one—was gravy. James was, at best, resigned. The two of them had been drafted as the camera crew, since they couldn't become the "name" actors we were using to entice Jackson into accepting his role. James would also be standing by with emergency medical equipment, in case Jackson went batshit crazy on us. James wasn't a doctor, but he had lots of first aid experience. Labs weren't the safest places in the world to work.

Brian was going to be Charlie Day, one of the actors from *It's Always Sunny in Philadelphia,* looking to rack up more big-screen credits. It was one of Bri's favorite shows, so he could easily play the role.

Auntie Mo would be Rene Russo (she had a fondness for redheads) and Mom would be Sigourney Weaver (she loved to wear tall auras, which probably explained her modeling agency). Dad and Uncle Liam decided on James Marsters (Dad already having his aura at hand from the Spike character) and Liam Neeson (Uncle Liam apparently not wanting to learn a new first name).

Sinead and Siobhan were bickering over who was going to be Scarlett Johansson and who was going to be Zoe Saldana, each actress supposedly reading for one of the leads. I ignored them as best I could.

Molly was staying with friends in Manhattan, and, according to Auntie Mo, she wasn't at all happy about it. But Uncle Liam and Auntie Mo had put their collective foot down at the prospect of Molly being in close proximity to a suspected killer, especially when they'd be too busy to look after her properly.

When Hugh Jackman tapped me on the shoulder, I nearly dropped my clipboard.

"You don't happen to have any cheese, do you?" I asked, in case Billy was testing me.

He looked genuinely puzzled. "What are you talking about, Ciel? Billy said you had my script. Laura wants to run lines with me. I still don't know why you need so many of us. Seems like you and Billy, and maybe Sinead and Siobhan—they actually *want* to be here—could have handled it. How many human props do you really need?"

Ah. Thomas. I scanned the room, finally locating Billy. He was looking at me with a wicked glint in his eye. I casually flipped him the bird while pretending to scratch my forehead.

"Thomas, I told you how paranoid Jackson has been acting—we have to go all out to make this shoot look *authentic*. Now, stop whining. And remember, the script isn't set in stone—it's just a guideline to give you an idea of the situation. Feel free to improvise, as long as you stay in character."

"I'll be lucky if Laura ever lets me break this character again," he said gloomily.

"Aw. Poor baby. Honeymoon over?" I teased. "Don't worry, Laura told me how much she likes jumping your bones. About made me throw up my mimosa, she was so gushy about loving you."

Thomas grabbed the bound pages I held out, ignoring me, but I thought I saw a tiny smile on the Hugh mouth as he walked away.

Rene and Sigourney approached me next. "Honey, which one of us is going to read with the killer?" Mom asked. "Mo thinks it should be Rene, but I'm thinking Sigourney is more kick-ass."

"Actually," I said, "neither of you will be working with him directly—hey, Nils, come here a second, will you?—because if he tries something crazy, I want Nils close at hand."

Nils strode over, in full costume, looking every bit the badass

Harilla until the last few yards, when he switched to hopping. He was wiggling his highly realistic prosthetic nose when he reached us. I cracked up.

"I know it's difficult, considering the material, but I hope you're going to play it straight tomorrow. Jackson has to believe this is real or we'll spook him."

Mom and Auntie Mo were eyeing Nils up and down.

"Oh, I have no doubt Mr. Gunn will take him seriously," Auntie Mo said, giving him a perfect Rene Russo closed-lip smile.

"Heaven knows *I* will," Mom said. It appeared she'd shaved a few years off Ms. Weaver as Harilla was hopping over.

Nils gave them a courtly bow, the awe apparent in his eyes. I'd explained to him about adaptors, but he was still getting used to the idea. Mark was probably going to be pissed off at me for telling him, but I considered this "need to know."

I finished checking his costume, declared it perfect, and told him he could change into his street clothes.

Billy called everyone over to the director's area. He replaced his aura with an older, balding—but still boyishly handsome—façade. The remaining hair was red, as was the short beard.

"Okay, this is who I'll be tomorrow. I'm afraid, for this to work, you'll all have to treat me like I'm the boss. Mommo, Dad—I know that will be hard for you, but try." The grin hadn't changed much since the owner of the aura was a child actor.

"Sure thing, Opie," Uncle Liam said while Dad started whistling the theme from the old Andy Griffith show.

Auntie Mo linked her arm through Uncle Liam's. "Don't you mean Richie?" she said, referring to the teenager from *Happy Days.* "Careful, dear, you're showing your age."

"Hate to tell you, Mom, but 'Richie' shows your age, too," Siobhan said, and then ducked as her mother took a swing at her.

After the chuckles died down, Billy said, "Meet back here by six"—the collective groan almost drowned him out—"yes, that's a.m. It's going to be a long day, but think of the reward. By which I mean a warm spot in your heart at seeing justice served, because no one's getting paid for this. Now, go grab a few hours of shut-eye."

"Wait," Sinead said. "Ciel, who are you going to be? I want keep everyone straight."

"Well, mostly I'll be this lowly set gopher"—I displayed a slightly overweight young man—"but when the time is right, you can expect . . ."

I pulled up another aura, to the collective gasp of everyone except Billy.

Chapter 24

Jackson Gunn pulled his white Jag XJ convertible into the parking lot outside the warehouse. I'd been afraid he wouldn't buy that our big-name director would be associated with a brand-new production company, but Billy had explained to him that Big Name wanted to keep his new idea under wraps until it was a done deal, and could be released with all the appropriate fanfare. Jackson didn't seem to think there was anything odd about that.

"He's here," I said into my walkie-talkie.

"Okay, people," Billy hollered. "It's a go. Places!"

I melted into the background, wearing my nondescript gopher aura, biding my time. Nobody notices the chubby boy with the mousy brown hair and peach fuzz who's passing around coffee.

Laura, in her guise as production assistant, met Gunn at the door, gushing about how thrilled she was to finally meet him. He accepted her effusive praise of every movie he'd ever been in (boy, she must've stayed up late studying his IMDb page) with a modesty

I was sure he didn't feel, all the while casting wary glances around the warehouse. He definitely had his guard up.

Billy, dressed in jeans and a plaid flannel shirt on top of Ron Howard's aura, appeared to be in the middle of an important conversation with Liam Neeson. When he "noticed" Gunn, he glanced at his watch as if time had gotten away from him, and excused himself from Liam, who wandered over to an impromptu waiting area, made up of a sofa and several comfortable chairs, where Spike—I mean, James Marsters—Charlie Day, and Hugh Jackman were already sitting, reading over their pages. There was a fruit basket and an open box of doughnuts on a nearby table, with thermal carafes of coffee and tea, as well as an assortment of canned drinks on ice.

"Jackson," Billy said, reaching for Gunn's hand. "Glad you could make it. We'll try not to take up too much of your time."

"Happy to be here. Anxious to learn more about your secret project," Gunn said with the smile that had women in movie theaters everywhere sliding off their seats. "So, Liam, huh? And Hugh Jackman?" He wasn't concerned about Marsters or Day. Guess he only saw tall guys as his competition.

So far, so good. He seemed to be buying the setup.

Billy-Ron shrugged. "You know how it is. We can have favorites," he said, strongly implying that Jackson was his, "but the bean counters want options. They think it keeps the talent costs down."

The two of them wandered over to the set together, still chatting. I followed, two coffees in hand, and plastered an appropriately starstruck look on my face when Jackson turned to take one. He barely acknowledged my existence. Billy-Ron nodded and thanked me when he took his, as nice and unassuming as I'd always imagined the real Mr. Howard must be.

The set was dominated by an incredibly realistic replica of a moai—a thirteen-foot-tall monolithic statue of a head. Even close up, the carved and painted Styrofoam looked like ancient stone.

"This is what I see as the key scene. The script isn't finished yet, and this set is, of course, improvised, but this will be the heart of the film, where our hero"—Billy-Ron nodded slightly toward Jackson, as if to say the role was his for the asking—"discovers the real truth about Easter Island—that the giant statues of heads were put there by aliens. Now the aliens have returned, and they are not friendly."

Easter Island was the title we'd given our imaginary movie. Yes, I know. The bunny allusion. At least it was more serious than Billy's first suggestion—*Keister Island.* Though I had to admit that allusion was pretty funny, too, Jackson being the giant ass he was.

Enter Nils, on cue, in full costume, moving with purpose. When he stopped beside us, there was menace in his crystal-blue eyes, and his nose definitely wasn't twitching.

Gunn backed up a step. He was tall, but Nils was taller, especially with the lifts in his fake-fur-covered footwear. "I see what you mean. I have to admit, when you mentioned the rabbit monster at our meeting I was skeptical. Any other director and I wouldn't be here. Well, maybe Spielberg." He chuckled.

"Yeah," Billy-Ron said. "It sounded goofy to me, too, at first. But that's the beauty of the script. It sucks you in with the whimsy of the idea—I mean, who could be afraid of a bunny rabbit, right?—and then it gradually overwhelms you with the horror. Of course, for the real movie we'll be enhancing everything with CGI."

Jackson nodded. "I can see it. Kind of a departure for you, isn't it?"

"Hey, I've done aliens before. This might be a little darker than *Cocoon,* sure. But you gotta keep growing, right?"

At an unobtrusive signal from Billy, I stepped away and texted

Mom. A minute later, the door opened again. In walked Sigourney Weaver, accompanied by Rene Russo, chatting and pretending they'd run into each other in the parking lot. I ran to greet them.

Behind me, Billy-Ron was saying, "Excuse me for a second, Jack. Can't keep the ladies waiting."

"Of course not," the actor said, pleased speculation at his possible cast-mates spreading over his face as Billy-Ron greeted the pair and pointed them toward the coffee station. When Scarlett Johansson and Zoe Saldana came in minutes later, the speculation grew. I hurried back to him, offering him more coffee, which he waved away.

"Quite the ambitious project," Gunn said, speaking directly to Nils for the first time.

Nils nodded. "I'm happy to be a part of it. If things work out, this might be my big break," he said, nailing that strange combo of humility and conceit often present in younger actors new to the Hollywood scene.

Jackson quirked a wry smile at him. "Yeah? And who'd you have to blow to get your shot?"

Without missing a beat, Nils said, "My agent."

I almost dropped the fresh supply of coffee I was carrying. Nils obviously read a lot of Hollywood tabloids.

Jackson laughed. "Your agent knows? Ron asked me to keep things quiet until the deal was firm."

"Your agent is more powerful than mine," Nils said with a shrug. "He doesn't have to listen when Mr. Howard tells him not to talk. Mine does."

Gunn nodded, apparently satisfied with the explanation. He gave Nils one last appraising look. I hoped like hell he wasn't smelling anything fishy. This whole thing would be a big waste of time and money if he bolted now. I started breathing again when he said, "Excuse me while I go say hi to the others."

The rest of the morning was spent gathering footage for "Ron" to take with him to the money people. Mostly small scenes, designed to see how well the actors interacted with each other. I wouldn't say any of their performances would win an Oscar, but they did okay. Heck, even Jackson, the only real professional in the bunch, fumbled some of his lines.

Billy, aware of our deadline to save Lily-Ann from her parents' threat, kept things moving at a good clip. When I'd conveyed the Conrads' offer to her, Lily had apparently refused it in very colorful terms. Put Rosa to shame, according to Dave. Needless to say, she wouldn't be signing any papers, so we were under more pressure than ever to make our plan work.

One by one, as Billy-Ron finished their "chemistry tests," he let the actors go, holding back Scarlett Johansson (pretty sure it was Sinead), Jackson, and Nils. Zoe Saldana retired to the waiting area. The rest of them went to a rented RV parked behind the warehouse. It was equipped with satellite TV and a bar, so they should be happy enough.

The big scene was set. Billy-Ron started to explain, in great detail, exactly what he wanted from each of them, then stopped himself and said, "You know what. Just wing it. I want the natural flow of emotions. Show me what you got."

James and Devon were in place with sixteen-millimeter shoulder-mounted digital cameras at the ready. Thirty-five millimeter might have been nice—if more expensive to rent—but since it was only supposed to be test footage, we figured it wouldn't matter. Ditto a third cameraman.

Harilla took his spot behind the moai. Jackson and Scarlett sat on a large rock near the huge head, waiting for their cue. Knowing one of his sisters would be playing Ms. Johansson, Billy had written the script to make her the lead's daughter instead of a love interest. Jackson had said something about not being quite old enough to be Scarlett's father, but shut up when she said, "That's why they call it acting."

"Okay, everyone, quiet on the set. And . . . action," Billy-Ron said.

I held up the clapper board, said "*Easter Island,* Gunn-Johansson, The Big Goodbye, take one," clapped it shut, and stepped out of the way.

"You have to go," Jackson said in a serious, paternal voice. "It's not safe here anymore."

Scarlett stood and walked a few steps away from him, stopping at the masking-tape X on the floor. "I can't. I won't leave you here alone. I couldn't live with myself if anything happened to you."

Not bad. Go, Sinead! I thought.

Jackson crossed to her and said, "You have to. *I* couldn't live with myself if you were hurt because I dragged you along to help with my stupid research."

"It's not stupid. And it's *my* research, too."

"Go to your mother. Tell her I'll come home as soon as—"

Harilla lumbered into the scene from off camera, intense light blue eyes blazing behind the facial prosthetics. Jackson pushed Scarlett behind him, blocking her from the gorilla-like gaze of the big-eared monster.

"*You!*" Jackson said.

Scarlett tried to push her "father" out of the way. "It's . . . it's *real?*"

As Nils stepped menacingly closer to the pair, something slithered out from beneath a fake shrub at the base of the statue. Several somethings, in fact. Big, squiggly somethings. Brian had successfully carried out the one duty he had other than being a background actor—releasing the wriggly reptiles hidden in the cage behind the bush.

Watching Jackson intently, I saw the precise second he became aware of the snakes. Without missing a beat, he shoved two of them aside with his foot, looked Harilla in the eye, and improvised, "Call off your pets." He then proceeded to execute the rest of the scene flawlessly until Billy yelled, "Cut!" Never even broke a sweat.

Afraid of snakes, my ass!

It was all I could do not march right over to him, drop the dorky aura I was wearing, and confront him. He'd *used* me. But Billy caught my eye and gave a small shake of his head.

Time for Phase Two.

"Take five, everyone," Billy-Ron said. "Somebody tell Zoe it's her turn with Jackson and the snakes."

Uncle Liam and Auntie Mo were hovering close, trying to pretend they weren't. Looking around, I saw that everyone had wandered back in under some pretext or another (mostly going for the doughnuts). The air of expectancy around the set was intensifying. I just hoped Jackson was too focused on his performance to notice.

When Billy-Ron said, "Action!" I read off the scene and clapped the board again. As soon as Jackson and Siobhan began, I slipped behind the moai. It took twenty seconds to lose the gopher clothes (I'd counted during practice sessions with Billy). Beneath them I was already wearing what I needed. Now all I had to do was switch auras and wait.

"Go to your mother," Jackson said, to Siobhan this time. "Tell her I'll come home as soon as—" That was my cue.

As entrances went, mine was impressive, if I did say so myself. The color fled Jackson's face as soon as he saw me, apparent even beneath his makeup. Sweat followed, popping out on his forehead like condensation on a cold drink.

There's the reaction that was missing with the snakes, I thought with satisfaction.

"Angelica?" he said, his breath coming in short gasps.

"You don't look happy to see me, Jack," I said, mimicking his dead wife's inflection based on the film footage of her from every TV news show I'd seen since her murder. "What's the matter, haven't you missed me?" I stepped toward him, arms extended for a hug, not giving him time to think.

He backed away and shook his head, opening and closing his eyes, looking as if he might topple over at any second. "That *can't* be you. I *killed* you! I fucking *shot* you seven times in the back!"

And there it was. The confession we needed.

I let out the breath I'd been holding. "Maybe you're not as good a shot as you think you are," I said, reaching into my pocket and pulling out a flash drive. "Still looking for this, by any chance?"

His eyes zeroed in on the small device in my hand, narrowing dangerously.

Wait for it . . .

He lunged at me, exposing his teeth in a twisted parody of his trademark smile, growling like an enraged wolf.

Cue Nils.

Harilla dove between Jackson and me, hitting the action star low in the gut, bringing him to the floor as I jumped out of the way. Maddened, Jackson grabbed Nils by his bunny ears, trying with all his strength to throw off the big Swede. Nils clung hard, rolling with him until they crashed into the base of the moai.

The giant statue came down hard, hitting the big rock and cracking in two. I might have worried about Nils being crushed, except, you know, Styrofoam.

"Now!" Nils shouted, and rolled onto his back, Jackson on top of him.

Laura stepped in, dodging the moai pieces, and plunged a syringe into Jackson's thigh. He struggled for a moment more. Came close to standing before his legs finally gave out and his eyes fluttered shut.

"Cut!" Billy yelled. "And that's a wrap."

Chapter 25

"What do we do with him now?" I asked.

Gunn was stretched out on the sofa in the waiting area, wrists neatly zip-tied together. He was still snoring, thanks to Laura's handy needle and the swiftly acting sedative James had provided. It had bought us a few hours to make sure Jack's "audition" was safely transferred from the cameras to a laptop Laura had supplied. We'd also taken the opportunity to add Angelica's footage of him with Frannie to the beginning.

Billy shrugged. "We let him sleep it off for about"—he looked at his watch—"another fifteen minutes. Then we wake him up and show him our masterpiece of filmmaking. Find out if he's ready to see reason."

Nils, happily out of the rabbit costume, said, "If that doesn't do the trick, you're on your own, because I'm not putting that damn thing on again. It's hot."

"Thanks again, Nils," I said. "You're a trooper. I can't tell you how much we appreciate your help. Isn't that right, Billy?" I said pointedly.

Billy, himself again, grinned. "Yeah, Nils. Way to take one for the team. We can give you a copy of your big scene if you want."

"If I ever decide to change my profession to actor I'll take you up on that," Nils said with his own good-natured grin.

Laura had already left, claiming all she wanted to do was get her husband to the hotel ASAP. She'd made several copies of the incriminating video, which showed me only from behind, so anybody who happened to see it would think Gunn was hallucinating.

Everyone else was gone, too, assured by Billy and Nils that Gunn was well in hand. By now, they would have picked up their luggage from the hotel, and might already be at the airport.

Mom and Auntie Mo had been reluctant to leave us with a crazed killer, but eventually had been convinced the trussed-up star didn't present much of a danger, especially with their new hero, Nils, there to guard him.

Jackson began to stir, whimpering in his drugged-out sleep.

"How are you going to explain seeing his dead wife to him?" Nils asked.

"He knows about adaptors already. It won't be that big a shock to him to find out she was me."

I'd gotten the energy secondhand from Billy, who'd met Angelica when he went to Jack's Las Vegas home to set up the job. He collected auras like some people collected comic books (guilty), and had shared it with me when we were hatching our plan. It had been kind of creepy when he'd called up her aura so he could transfer the energy to me, and even more so when I'd had to hold it the requisite several minutes to make sure it took, but it had obviously had the desired effect. It was the first time I'd projected the aura of a dead person, and I hoped I never had to repeat the experience.

We were lucky Jackson had been too stunned at seeing his dead wife to put two and two together about how it could be possible—that's what we'd been counting on, and it had worked like a dream.

"What the fuck?" Gunn's groggy voice came from the sofa across from us. He rubbed his face with his zip-tied hands.

"And there he is," Billy said, rising. "Nils, I'd like you to meet the internationally famous star of the silver screen, Jackson Gunn."

Nils nodded down at Jack.

"Jackson, may I introduce Nils—I believe he'd rather not divulge his last name—of the Swedish security police?"

Comprehension was slowly building in Jack's face as he looked from Nils to Billy, and finally to me. "You."

He could have meant either Billy or me. Maybe both. In any case, he didn't look pleased to see us.

"Ron Howard? The other actors?" he asked numbly. Apparently he couldn't focus on the worst part of his problem yet.

"All adaptors, I'm afraid," Billy said, sounding jolly.

"How many of you fuckers are there?"

"Enough," I said.

"So there's no movie?" he said, stuck on that.

"Oh, there's a movie, all right," Billy said. "Let's watch it, shall we?" He touched a key on the laptop we'd set up on the coffee table.

Jackson sat up and stared in horror at what played out on the screen in front of him. He reddened at the sight of the young Frannie bouncing up and down on his . . . lap . . . and paled when he saw his confession to "Angelica."

"Fine," Gunn said after it was over. "You got me. What do you want? Money? How much for the video?"

"Oh, we don't want money, Jack," I said. "All we want is your confession."

"You know I can't do that." He stood. Wobbled, and sat down again. "Not without giving away your part in all this."

"Come on, Jack. You know what you have to do."

It took a minute, but it finally dawned on him. "I can't confess I hired a hit man when I didn't!" he said.

"Too honorable to lie, Jack?" I said. "Pardon me if I find that difficult to swallow."

"Look, if this is about Lily-Ann, I can help there—I never meant for her to get caught up in it. I'll testify that Angelica was unstable, that she hated Lily-Ann. I'll swear in court that it had to be self-defense on Lily's part—I'll make sure she's acquitted."

"Ah. So it's not the lying you have a problem with," Billy said. "Not good enough, Jackson my man. Her name would still be ruined."

"I'll pay off my house staff—they'll say there was an intruder, that they didn't come forward before out of fear he'd come back and kill them, too." The desperation was growing on his face.

"It's already been established that none them were home that night. They were all seen elsewhere. You can't pay off everyone, Jack," Billy said.

Gunn's shoulders slumped. His face went slack, his eyes dull. "I'll be ruined. Either way, my career is over and I'm in jail for life." Then a spark ignited something in his eyes. He stood, steadier this time, and said, "But, God damn it, if I go down I can at least take you and your kind with me. Go ahead, show your fucking video to the world!"

Panic exploded through me. I hadn't for a second considered that he wouldn't do anything and everything to keep that video from going public.

Billy, remaining a hell of a lot calmer than I felt, said, "You're not thinking straight, Jack. You have access to the best lawyers in this country. You don't believe one of them—or hell, a whole team of them—could keep you from a life sentence? Maybe even get you acquitted? Hell, even if you got a few years, it would only be another line item for your résumé. It would add to your tough-guy street cred. Hollywood will forgive killing your wife—in whatever fit of passion you care to dream up—but once J. J. Brookfield sees you with his daughter, it's over. Was she even of age in that video, Jack?"

Gunn paled even more.

"No? I thought not. Yeah, I'd say that was a definite career-ender."

"That was all her, damn it! She threw herself at me. If Brookfield hadn't made me take her on as an intern—don't you understand? It was her fault!"

Billy shook his head sadly, keeping a pleasant expression on his face, but I could see the disgust in his eyes. "It always is, hey, Jack? And Lily-Ann? Was it her fault, too? How about Elizabeth? Surely one of them is your fault."

Gunn glared at Billy. You could see he wanted to argue. That he was scrambling for a way to salvage something, anything. And you could see when he realized his tantrum wasn't going to get him what he wanted.

"Overholt's the best," he said, considering the solution we'd offered him. "But there's no way he would take me on, not after defending Lily. It would make him look like a—"

"A what? A brilliant defense lawyer?" I said.

My phone buzzed. Speak of the devil.

"Why don't we ask him?" I said, and swiped my finger across the screen. If he wouldn't take Gunn's case himself, maybe he could recommend another lawyer. All we had to do was convince Gunn his confession was worth the risk of a little jail time.

"Hey, Nigel. What's up?"

"The police are on the way," he said.

From the look on Jackson's face, Nigel's voice had carried. Panic at its purest. He looked around, wild-eyed. Stood, and with a mighty grunt, yanked his arms apart, breaking the zip tie, leaving oozing bloody lines on both wrists. In a matter of seconds, he picked up the laptop, bashed Nils over the head with it, kicked the coffee table onto Billy's legs, and took off running.

Guess we should have zip-tied his ankles, too. Though judging by what I had just seen, it probably wouldn't have stopped him.

Billy pushed the table out of his way and ran after him, but Gunn had the advantage of longer legs and the fear-induced surge of adrenaline. He was out the door before Billy could change to an aura fast enough to catch him. Nils pushed himself up, rubbing his head, and tried to join the chase. Thought better of it, and sat on the couch, signaling me that he was okay.

I lifted the phone back to my ear. "I'm on my way. Tell them Lily has the runs, if you have to. That she's barfing. Anything gross enough to make them wait."

I hung up and went to check Nils for myself.

"You're going to have a lump," I said after running my hands lightly over his whole head. I know. My diagnostic skills are amazing. "But no indentations. And your pupils are even. I'm pretty sure that's a good sign."

Nils smiled and groaned at the same time. "Not the first time my head has taken a beating."

Billy came back, out of breath, minutes later, and dropped the long-legged distance runner he'd briefly become. "You okay?" he said to Nils.

"Fine, fine. Just a little dizzy."

Billy nodded, still breathing hard. "I probably could have caught him, but I wouldn't have been able to hold him. Couldn't risk changing to a stronger aura out in public."

"I have to go," I said. "The police are heading to Nigel's house. You guys figure out how to track down Gunn."

"But—" Billy said.

"They're probably only doing a check. I'll go make an appearance, and be back to help as soon as I can. Go! Catch Gunn."

Conrad hadn't waited until the end of the business day to talk to the DA. Or else his definition of "end" was different from ours. What I really suspected was that dear old Dad believed turning the screw when the pressure was already on was more likely to achieve his aim.

Billy was calling his Hollywood contacts, using every resource he had to hunt down Jackson. When your face was as well-known as Gunn's, there couldn't be that many places you could hide for long. I hoped.

I parked out of sight when I got to Nigel's, and snuck around to his back door, which he'd left unlocked for me. Isis was in Lily's room. Guess I was a little agitated, because she dove under the bed when she saw me. I changed as quickly as I could, remembering to make Lily's face paler than usual. Nigel was in his living room, holding the officers at bay by telling them I had a stomach bug, but they wouldn't wait forever.

"Here, kitty. Here, kitty, kitty . . . nice Isis," I said softly, forcing myself to stop freaking out.

I finally managed to calm down enough to convince the Siamese I wasn't there to attack her. She belly-crept toward me, mewing loudly. (Siamese are vocal cats.) When she was close enough, I whispered, "Sorry, cat, I don't have time for cajolery," grabbed her with both hands, and dragged her the rest of the way out.

Geez, you'd have thought I was pulling her claws out with pliers from the sound she made.

There was a heavy knocking on the bedroom door. "Lily-Ann? Are you all right?" Nigel said.

I pulled the tracking anklet off the cat, stifling my own vocalization as she sunk her teeth into my wrist. As I slipped it over my foot, I called out, "I'll be fine. Just give me a second."

I ran to the en suite bathroom, flushed the toilet, washed my wound, and pulled my sleeve down over it. I didn't have to try to make myself look shaky when I went to open the door. At the last second, I remembered to puff up my "bad" ankle.

The police were in front of Nigel. To protect him, I supposed, in case the "crazed killer" took it into her head to do away with her attorney. "I'm afraid you'll have to come with us, Ms. Conrad," the older one said. "The judge has revoked your bail."

Nigel looked totally pissed. "There was no reason for the judge to do that."

"Sorry," said the other officer. "Just following orders." She pulled my arms behind me and cuffed me.

Shit. "Nigel, tell my bro—tell Thomas what happened, okay? Not on the phone."

After I was processed, I was put in a holding cell.

It's not as if you haven't been there and done that before, I told myself, trying to squelch my ever-growing anxiety by remembering how benignly my last foray in a jail cell had played out.

Myself answered, *Yeah, but never as a girl.* (Myself is such a pessimist sometimes.) I'm as much of a feminist as anyone, but I couldn't deny it—I felt much more vulnerable as an incarcerated female. I'd have given anything to be able to project some brawn. The other three women in the cell with me looked as if they could bend me in half backward without breaking a sweat, and wouldn't mind doing it. Lily-Ann's frame wouldn't offer much resistance.

I was standing in the corner—had been for hours—because when the last one came in she basically, with one malevolent look, evicted me from the bench where I'd been sitting. The bitch didn't care that, for all she knew, my ankle was sprained. Sliding down to sit on the floor was getting more tempting by the minute. My legs were killing me.

I glanced down at the floor. *Gross.* Nope, not an option.

There are some times you're happier to see a cop than others. *This is one of those times,* I thought as a burly woman in the short-sleeved black uniform (with what looked like a Batman utility belt around her waist) came to get me.

Thank God. Maybe Billy had found Gunn, and made him confess. I wanted to ask the officer, but she didn't strike me as the informative sort. She led me to a room with a table and two chairs. One of the chairs had been moved aside to make room for the wheelchair.

"Hi, Nigel. Did you come to spring me?" I said.

"Not exactly."

He didn't say anything else until after I was seated and cuffed to the table, and the officer had left us. Supposedly, we had privacy.

"What's up?" I asked. "Did Billy find Jackson? Is Nils okay? Did you talk to Thomas?"

Nigel sighed. His face morphed briefly into my brother's.

"Thom—" I started, and covered it with a cough. Who knew how much privacy we really had? "Um, can we talk openly here or what?"

"I'm reasonably certain that's possible, yes. Within limits." He scanned the room. "I see no evidence of cameras, at any rate. There aren't supposed to be recording devices of any kind in use when a lawyer and client are talking. But there is that window in the door."

"Gotcha. So, back to my questions . . ."

"Nils is fine—he's on his way to Sweden. Duty calls. We're still working on finding Gunn. Billy is doing everything he can. I called Mark to see—"

Crap. "Why'd you do that? He's not even in the country."

"Because," he said so quietly I could barely hear him, "he has access to resources that we don't, not even Laura. He's on his way."

"I don't think it was necessary to disturb him," I whispered back.

"You're in jail. I happen to think that requires immediate attention. And"—he looked over his shoulder at the window in the door—"since my original plan doesn't appear to be feasible, I'm very glad Mark is coming."

I knew exactly what plan he was referring to, since I'd pulled it myself before. He'd intended to switch places with me—to become Lily so I could leave as Nigel. (My big brother didn't like the idea of me in jail. He seemed to think it was a scary place.) We didn't dare try it, though. With the window right there, the risk of discovery was too great.

"Does Billy know Mark's coming?" I asked.

"He's the one who suggested I call him. Billy is frantic to find Gunn. He wanted to come here instead of me, but I told him he's more valuable on the street—he knows Hollywood better than I do."

I stared down at the table, mainly to keep from meeting Thomas's eyes. Billy must have been really worried to ask for Mark's help. My mind started to race. What if they couldn't find Gunn? He had a hell of a lot of money—he could even leave the country.

Disappear for good. What the hell would I do then? Rot in jail as Lily-Ann and pray Nigel and Thomas, between the two of them, could get me acquitted? Would we have to work with Lily-Ann's despicable parents?

"I don't understand Jackson's running like that. He has to know we'll expose him. Why would he risk that?" I said.

"Billy said he took the laptop with him. Maybe he thinks he got away with the evidence."

"But Laura made copies."

"Yeah, but does he know? He might think there wasn't enough time for that."

I couldn't pace, so I drummed on the table with my fingers instead. *Think, Ciel. Where would Jackson go?*

"Tell Billy to check, um, my parents' house," I said. He'd know I meant the Conrads.

"You think Jackson would go after them, too? Would he hurt them?"

"No, I *think* he might ask for their help." I continued speaking softly.

"Why?"

"Because what he said he'd do to help, you know, *me* was too similar to what they said they'd do—claim Angelica was unstable and invited her own death. Seems odd that they'd come up with the same thing, doesn't it? I mean, unless she really was unstable. It might be a coincidence, but since we don't have much else to go on . . ."

He nodded. "It's worth investigating." He studied my face, as if he were trying to see beneath Lily's aura. "Are you okay in here? Be honest. There might be something I can do."

I thought about the other women in the holding cell. "Will they be moving me to a cell with a bunk, do you know?"

"Yes. They have to if you'll be here overnight. Are you . . . worried about that?"

I blew a puff of air out through loosely closed lips. "Me? Nah. I'll be fine."

"I'll do everything in my power to get you a private cell tonight. It may take a few hours. After that, if we haven't found Gunn by then, I'll try to get you moved to a pay-to-stay celebrity facility. You'd be in one already if it weren't for the judge—he's an asshole who happens to be unimpressed with the Conrad name."

I did my best to smile. Not sure how well it came out. "Who can blame him? 'My' parents are jerks. Anyway, don't worry about me. I can do a few more hours standing on my head."

Chapter 26

There was another woman in the holding cell when I was returned to it. She was circling the cell, scratching her arms. Smelled like she hadn't seen the inside of a shower in weeks. Even the hard-ass women who were there first kept casting her wary looks.

I tried to go back to my corner, but she blocked me. Raising my hands in an I-don't-want-any-trouble gesture, I walked to another corner, not bothering to limp. It wasn't like it was going to earn me any sympathy with this crowd. "Itchy" beat me to it. I nodded, and went to stand by the door.

Same thing. Apparently, this was a fun game. Anyplace I wanted to stand, she wanted to stand.

I looked to the other women, each in turn. They were watching with mild interest. One of them—an older woman with flat black hair, gray roots, and a tattoo on her neck—wore a half smile that might have been sympathetic, but she shook her head wearily, as if she'd played this game before and didn't want to get involved now.

"Look, just tell me where you want me to stand and I'll do it," I said to Itchy.

She pointed to the hall beyond the bars. "Out there."

I sighed. "Well, see, that's going to be a problem, because I don't have *the fucking key.*"

She smiled evilly, and not the fun kind of "evilly" like when I'm teasing Billy or one of my brothers. "I guess you do have a problem then, little Miss Rich Bitch."

Shit.

The first punch landed in my belly, doubling me over. Before I was able to suck in a breath, the second one caught me in the left eye, pushing me upright. The third one broke my nose. At least, I was pretty sure it did. It hurt like hell and bled like a son of a bitch.

Damn. I wondered if the real Lily-Ann had gone through anything like this when she was here. Her face had looked okay, but not all bruises show. I also wondered where the hell a guard was when you needed one.

Thinking about Lily, trying to protect her aura, I got my arms up and began blocking the blows. The other women started hollering out directions, telling me to hit back, and where I should aim my punches. I listened, taking their advice as well as I could. Eventually, I managed to kick my leg out sideways and trip Itchy. She hit the ground hard, and lay there, dazed.

One of the other women—the young one who looked like a grown-up version of your worst nightmare from the locker room in high school—jumped up from her bench and lifted my arm like a boxing referee. "And the winner is . . . hey, what's your name, honey?" she asked, smiling at me for the first time. I kind of wished she hadn't.

"Lily-Ann," I said, wiping the blood still dripping out of my nose on my sleeve.

"Lily-Ann! Hey, kid, you did good. But what gives? I thought all you rich bitches knew kung fu, and shit like that."

I laughed, touching my nose gingerly. "Guess I wasted my time on yoga."

Itchy and I were taken to the clinic, where our injuries were seen to by a nurse practitioner who probably hadn't been surprised by anything since sometime in the last millennium. She asked what happened. I glanced at Itchy (still glaring at me malevolently) and told the nurse I fell. The bored guard didn't contradict me.

The nurse nodded and smiled wryly. "Slippery floor in there."

After she set my nose and put a splint on it (not something I *ever* want to do again), she gave me two painkillers and what looked to be a set of orange scrubs with "L.A. County Jail" printed across the back of the shirt and down one leg of the pants.

Yeesh. And I'd thought yellow was bad. I'd hate to see what this color did to my primary aura.

Thomas, as good as his word, got me a private cell. It was small and cold, and a guard came by to check on me every thirty minutes or so, near as I could tell. There wasn't a clock in view.

The mattress was covered in green plastic and there was no pillow. One of the guards brought me a rough green blanket when he saw I was shivering. I thought that was nice of him, and sincerely hoped he wouldn't expect payment.

The stainless steel toilet and sink were right out in the open. Apparently, modesty was a privilege not permitted to prisoners. I very quickly learned to pee fast, right after the guard's rounds. Hadn't been caught so far.

There was a small, white desk—more of a deep shelf attached to the wall—and a round stool in front of it, also attached to the wall. No paper or pen on it, though. No books, no TV or radio, no entertainment of any kind.

So I had plenty of time to worry about what would happen when Billy and Mark saw each other again. Which wasn't a lot of fun, but at least it took my mind off how much my face hurt.

I was roused from my sleep way too early the next morning by a sardonically cheery female voice.

"Rise and shine, buttercup."

I opened my eyes. Make that "eye"—my left one appeared to be swollen shut. Lovely.

Since I'd been wearing Lily's aura when I was hit, the bruising and swelling would be showing up just fine. And since I was always me beneath a secondary aura's surface, I'd have to remember to adapt the injuries away if I didn't want them to show when I was myself again.

The new guard on duty was a slim, older black woman with super short salt-and-pepper hair. She winced when she saw my face, so I imagined I looked pretty impressive. Didn't know for sure, since the accommodations didn't include a mirror.

"Damn, buttercup. Who'd you piss off?"

"I fell," I said, pushing myself to a sitting position. I slipped my feet into the prison-issue sneakers.

"Right. I see you're a fast learner," she said, and looked at me thoughtfully. "You know, if somebody went after you, you can tell me. You're a 'keep away'—they won't put you back with anyone who might hurt you again."

I yawned, remembering halfway through to cover my mouth with my hand. "What's a 'keep away'?"

"If they put you in orange, it means you're to be kept away from the rest of the population, for either your protection or theirs. From the looks of you, I'm guessing it's for yours."

"Thanks," I said. "But let's keep it at 'I fell.'" I'd always heard snitches didn't fare well in prison.

She shook her head. "Whatever you say, buttercup. Your lawyer's here. If you don't trust me, maybe you can tell him."

Crap. If Thomas saw me like this . . .

Nothing I could do about it. If I'd been thinking, I would have adapted away the ravages before they bloomed, but now that I'd been seen it would be too obvious. Nobody heals that fast. I did reduce the "swelling" in my ankle, though. I was going to pretend that was all better, since nobody here would be likely to notice.

Nigel's face was usually hard to decipher—like most good lawyers, he was adept at bland neutrality of expression when he needed to be—but there was no mistaking the anger on it when he saw me. I smiled ruefully and shrugged, but didn't say anything until the guard left us alone.

"What happened?" he said, his voice tight.

"An unkempt woman objected to my presence in the holding cell. Don't worry—I won." I tried to wink, and realized I already was. Stupid shiner. But at least I could open it partway now, if I really tried.

"Are you all right? Have you been seen by a doctor?"

"Yes and yes. Only . . . how does my nose look? Can you tell if it's straight under this splint?" It should have been the least of my worries, I knew, but I'd really hate to have to spend the rest of my life adapting away a bent nose.

He swallowed, looking positively bleak. I'd been expecting the anger, but this looked like something more.

"Thomas?" I whispered.

He shook his head, once.

"Nigel?"

Another shake.

Uh-oh. "Limburger?" I said.

He nodded, clench-jawed.

"What are you doing here? Did you find Gunn? Did he confess?"

"Mark is following a new lead. He and Laura are working it."

"Mark is here?" Duh. Stupid question. He'd just said as much.

"He got on a company plane as soon as Thomas contacted him."

"Not that I don't appreciate your keeping me in the loop, but shouldn't you be out there helping them?" I said.

He pushed a small button on the inside arm of his chair, lifting himself to a standing position, and rolled over to the door. He looked out the window, both ways down the hall. Wheeled himself over to me, keeping his back to the window, took my hand.

"*No.*" I tried to pull my hand away.

Too late. He was already Lily-Ann, bruises, squinty eye and all. Wow, I really *did* look horrible. He already had Lily-Ann's aura, but he needed to add the swelling and bruising in the exact configuration I had. It would take a minute or so to set.

"Start unzipping, cuz. I'm sorry, but I'm gonna need that nose splint, too. Snap-snap!"

He held on to my hand as he undid the straps holding his knees to the chair.

"Billy, stop it. We don't have time for this."

"It's happening, cuz. And if you'll be so kind as to tell me who did that to you, I will see that they never try anything like it again. On anybody."

"You can't. I'm in a cell by myself, perfectly safe." I bent over and unzipped as much as I could without letting go of Billy. "Which is why this is unnecessary. And stupid. Stoo. *Pid.* Somebody could see us."

I leaned down and carefully untaped the splint from my nose, sucking in my breath as I pulled it free. The anger pouring out from Billy through Lily-Ann's eyes intensified.

"If you think I'm leaving you in a place where somebody beat the shit out of you, *you're* stupid." He let go of my hand. "There. I think I've got it." He continued disrobing, holding Lily-Ann's new facial features without difficulty. He'd always been a fast absorber.

Now that he didn't need to touch me, I popped into my tiniest aura, slipped my hands out of the cuffs, and finished stripping. "If they catch us—"

"Hurry the fuck up and they won't," he said, and put on my discarded clothing.

"Why in the hell does Nigel have to wear a suit every single freaking day?" I said, buttoning the dress shirt as fast as my fingers—well, Nigel's now—would move. "Hey, can you help me with this tie?"

"Sure, just a sec." He slipped the prison shoes on, then reached for the expensive blue silk dangling from my neck. "I can't believe you haven't learned to do this properly yet. You have three brothers, for God's sake."

I slapped his hand away. "Never mind, I'll do it myself. You get those cuffs on."

"Let me get you strapped into the chair first."

I yanked on black socks and slipped my feet into black wing tip loafers before I backed up to the chair. "You realize I have no idea how to drive this thing."

He finished stabilizing my legs and pointed to the controls on the arm of the chair. "This is up. This is down—yeah, go ahead and lower it. You'll feel more stable sitting. Think of this little lever as a joystick. Push it whichever way you want the chair to go."

"How did you get here? How do I get back?" I said as I grappled with the tie. Wasn't as good as Billy's knot had been, but it would do. "Where the hell is Nigel, anyway, and how's he getting around without his chair?"

"There's a black van with a driver parked in one of the handicapped spaces near the entrance. The driver will see you coming and take it from there. Nigel is at home, staying out of sight," Billy said as we settled ourselves into the proper places. Seconds later, the guard's face appeared at the window. His eyes flitted over us, and he left.

"That was cutting it close," I said, matching Nigel's inflection precisely. "If I hadn't already had Nigel's aura, we would have been caught."

"I knew you had it."

"How, huh? How could you be sure?" I was a little disgruntled at being rushed into the switch before I was convinced it was necessary.

"You told me after you showed Nigel and Lily how adaptors worked."

"Okay, well . . . it was still stupid. And dangerous. My God, Billy, what if Mark and Laura don't find Gunn? Or what if they do find him, and he still won't confess, huh? Are you going to sit in jail forever?"

He leaned forward. Tried to reach for me, but was held back by the handcuffs. "No. Only until Nigel and Thomas get Lily acquitted."

"And what if they don't? They're good, yes, but they're not infallible."

"In that case, I'm a lot better suited for prison life than you are.

In fact," he said with a cocky tilt of Lily's head that was painful to watch, "you never know, I might even enjoy life in a women's prison."

"Stop trying to make me laugh. It's not going to work this time."

"Fine, sourpuss. Then get out of here and go help the others get *me* out of here."

Chapter 27

Nigel was waiting for me in his study, with the curtains drawn. He sat in an older-model wheelchair, still motorized but not self-rising. He looked very glad to see me.

"Thanks for the use of your aura," I said.

"It was the least I could do. How's Ciel? Is she holding up okay?"

I dropped his aura and got myself out of his chair. "I'm fine, thanks."

I was, of course, keeping my injuries hidden. No reason for him to feel bad about something he'd had no control over.

"Where's Mr. Doyle?" he asked.

"Billy decided he was better suited to stay than I was." To forestall the questions I saw bubbling behind his eyes—lawyers are so inquisitive—I added, "So, can I help get you back to the cool wheels?"

He accepted the change of subject with grace. "No, I can manage."

He rolled the chair he was in until it faced the one I had vacated, and locked its brakes. Using only the strength of his arms, he levered himself up and over, moving his hands from the arms of one chair to the other, deftly twisting his body around, like a gymnast on the parallel bars, until he could lower himself into the new seat. He adjusted his legs and fastened the straps with quick and easy motions that spoke of years of practice.

"Wow—impressive!" I said, hoping I wasn't being rude.

He smiled, and maybe even blushed a tiny bit, though that might have been from the exertion. "Thanks. I work out."

"Well, unless you have any news for me, I guess I better go find my brother. I only came by to drop off your chair and let you know I didn't do anything too embarrassing while I was you." Unless, of course, you count almost running over a law clerk as I exited the building, but no need to bore him with the details.

"If you don't mind waiting a few minutes, Thomas will be here. I've asked him to be an official consultant on Lily-Ann's case. That way he won't have to use my aura to visit the jail. Not that I mind, but I realize it can be a pain to get around in this fine set of wheels"—he smiled that Clooney smile—"if you're not used to it. We're going to discuss the best way to proceed if Gunn can't be persuaded to do the right thing."

"Let's hope it won't come to that," I said. "Have you heard from Lily? Is she all right?"

"Actually, I got a cryptic text message last night from someone named Cody. Anyone you know?"

I'd given Dave as a contact at the ranch when I'd told Nigel where we'd stashed Lily-Ann. "Cody's my security-guard-slash-ranch-hand. What'd he say?"

" 'LA is fine. Hates pony.' LA is obviously Lily-Ann, but I'm not sure about the second part. From what I can tell, she loves all animals, so I think it might be code for something."

I rose from my spot on the sofa when Thomas entered the room with Laura. I'd changed out of Nigel's suit into some of Lily's clothes. Too long for me, and a little too hipster-ish, but otherwise fine.

"Hey, new sis!" I said. "How's the—" I stumbled over my words when I saw who else was with them. Mark.

Thomas gave me a big bear hug. I tried not to flinch when my face hit his shoulder. "Ciel? What are you doing here? We were supposed to meet Billy."

"Um, Billy insisted on trading places. Don't worry—we were careful."

I glanced at Mark. I'd added the last part so he wouldn't get mad at us for risking exposure. He kept his face carefully composed.

Thomas was immediately suspicious. "He had to know it wasn't safe to make a switch in that room, or else I would have done it myself. He was only supposed to check on you, and tell you the reinforcements had come. What made him change his mind?"

"Well, um . . ."

"Sugar, are you all right?" Laura said. "You're looking a little squinty. And your nose is bleeding."

Crap. I wiped my nose with my hand—it was only a few drops, thank goodness—and concentrated on opening my eye more.

Mark finally approached me. "Drop it, Howdy," he said quietly.

"I don't know what you—"

"Cut the crap and show us. Now." Mark again, more firmly.

I stopped the cover-up. Laura gasped. Thomas and Mark turned into twin thunderclouds.

"God damn it!" Thomas said.

Nigel, the sensible one, called his aide for ice. "You should have told me at once, Ciel. I'll contact my doctor immediately."

"No," I said. "I'm fine. Really. The nurse at the jail fixed me up."

"Your nose . . ." Laura said delicately.

"What? Am I still bleeding?"

"No. It's a little . . . off center," she said.

"Call your doctor, Nigel," Thomas ordered. After a look from Laura, he added, "Please. If you don't mind."

While we waited, I explained what happened in the holding cell after Thomas left the day before. I downplayed it, making Itchy sound less frightening than she had been, and more like a pathetic vagrant who'd gotten in a lucky punch.

"I don't think she was all there, if you know what I mean. Took me by surprise, is all. Once Billy got a gander at me, though, he was Lily-Ann before I could stop him, and I had to change fast so we wouldn't get caught. Frankly, I think he'd be more useful with you guys on the outside."

Mark had stared at my face the whole time I was talking. "He did the right thing."

Thomas concurred.

Laura looked at me curiously and asked, "You get in any punches?"

I grinned. "Yeah. I won. Kicked her legs right out from under her. It was kind of awesome."

She held her hand up for a high five, which I proudly gave her.

"Stop looking at me like that, Tom," Laura said. "Girls can kick ass, too."

"And get their asses kicked," he said.

"And get their asses kicked," she agreed. "Ciel, how would you feel about some serious ass-kicking lessons? From one sister to another."

"Hell yeah!" I said.

Thomas shook his head and sighed, but didn't raise any objections. Man, I was going to *love* having Laura in the family.

The doctor arrived before I had a chance to ask what was up on the Gunn front. She was every bit as friendly and efficient as she'd been when she'd examined my fake sprained ankle when I was being Lily-Ann. After a little probing, she said she thought it was uneven swelling that was making my nose look skewed.

"Have it checked by your own doctor in a week or two, when the swelling goes down. I'll apply a splint for now. Be careful not to run into any more doors," she said.

I looked at Nigel. He shrugged. Guess he thought telling her I'd been injured in a prison fight would have scared her.

"I'll do that," I said, and thanked her.

After she left, I started asking questions. "Anybody gonna give me an update? Have you found Gunn? Is he going to confess or what?"

"I've put men on watching the Conrads," Mark said. "I think you might be on to something about the connection there. We're monitoring all of their homes, and the office where Conrad does most of his company-related business. If Gunn tries to contact them, we'll know it."

"What if we show the Conrads the video? Surely they'd see it as a motive for him to hire a hit man. Maybe we could get them to help us," I said.

Mark nodded. "Might be worth a shot. Nigel, can you set up a meeting?"

"It would be my pleasure. Especially if I can be there to watch."

The collective horror on the faces of Mr. and Mrs. Conrad was a thing of beauty to behold. Not that I didn't pity them as the parents of a murdered child, but it was difficult not to feel a touch of schadenfreude, especially when the *schaden* boomerangs on people who've dealt out so much of it themselves.

We were in Nigel's media room. It had three rows of black leather recliners, four across, with built-in cup holders. A free space in the middle of the last row accommodated his wheelchair.

His top of the line, eighty-inch LED television—with extremely high resolution—was mounted to the back wall. Mark had asked Nigel not to dim the lights, so we all had a clear view of the Conrads' faces when the scene of their son-in-law with Frannie played out before them. Naturally, we stopped the video before the movie scene with Angelica—it would have been beyond cruel to let them think, even for a second, that their daughter might still be alive. Not that the camera angle showed her face, but her voice would be easily recognizable. That scene was for Jackson's eyes only, extra incentive for him to confess to hiring a hit man—the only way Billy and I had been able to think of that would see justice done without exposing adaptors to the world.

"Would you care to see it again?" Nigel asked politely when it was finished.

"No!" Elizabeth said, averting her eyes from the screen.

Joe's mouth was set in a straight line, lips pressed tightly together. We gave them a minute to absorb what they'd seen.

Mrs. Conrad was the first to realize the truly important implication. "Does this . . . does this mean Lily-Ann didn't do it?" she asked, still stunned.

Conrad, face still tight, said, "Don't jump to any conclusions, Elizabeth. All this proves is that Jackson Gunn is a filthy cheater"—Elizabeth blanched and gave me a fearful look—"with a lot to lose if this sordid piece of smut gets out. It doesn't mean Lily-Ann didn't do it."

"But, Joseph, this is exactly what Lily-Ann tried to tell us, and we wouldn't listen, and now my baby is in that horrible place, and the whole world thinks . . . We *have* to get her out." She turned to Nigel. "You have to get her out of that nasty jail *right this minute.*"

"I'm afraid that's not possible, Mrs. Conrad. As your husband says, nothing about this video *proves* Lily-Ann didn't do it. After what you and your husband told the district attorney, we're going to have to come forward with something concrete."

"But that was supposed to *help*! Tell him, Joseph. Tell him how being harder on her was going to make her see reason, so that when she was acquitted, she would sign the agreement, and we could keep her close, and she would never, ever have a chance to do anything so awful again"—her eyes were getting wilder the more she comprehended—"but, oh my God, if she didn't do it, then . . ."

She finally crumpled, sobbing quietly. Conrad remained still, not even reaching out a hand to comfort his wife.

"We can't go back to the DA and tell him we lied," Conrad said.

"Even though you did," I said.

"We had no way of knowing that. Lily-Ann has always been impulsive. We've had to employ tough love with her, it was the only way—"

"To control her?" Thomas said, his disgust plain. He was more circumspect with his clients, but these weren't his clients.

Joe glared at him. "Spare me any lectures on parenting. Just tell me what we can do to get this straightened out with a minimum of exposure in the press."

Mark stood. "That's where I come in."

"And who are you?" Joe said.

"I'm the guy who's going to make sure your son-in-law pays for killing your firstborn."

"*If* he did. I'm still not convinced that because he cheated, he necessarily hired someone to kill Angelica."

Some people just can't admit when they're wrong. "His whole career is at stake if Brookfield sees that video. He did it. I can't tell you everything about how we know, but trust me, we know. You'll help us find him?" I pressed.

He glanced at his wife, who still looked shell-shocked. "Yes. I'll do whatever you say."

"Good," Mark said. "First thing—do you know where your son-in-law is?"

"I do not."

"Have you spoken to your son-in-law in the past twenty-four hours?"

Conrad squirmed uncomfortably in his chair. Apparently, being the one questioned chafed. "I have."

"In person?" Mark said.

"On the phone."

"Did he call you or did you call him?" Mark was exhibiting great patience, I thought.

"He called my cell."

"So you have the number he called from?"

"I do."

"Mr. Conrad, this would be a lot more productive if I didn't have to pull the details from you one at a time," Mark said, sounding reasonable.

Argh. Great time to exhibit restraint during questioning, Mr. CIA Operative. Personally, I wanted to scream at the man, and Mark couldn't even raise his voice? Maybe threaten a little bodily harm?

I glanced at Elizabeth, who was looking pretty ghastly. Maybe Mark was trying not to upset her any more than necessary.

Conrad looked annoyed and pulled out his cell phone, scrolling through until he found the number, and gave it to Mark. Thomas jotted it down and left the room.

"That's not his usual number. I don't know where he was calling from."

"Thank you. We'll track it down," Mark said.

"Excuse me," Laura said. "Mrs. Conrad, are you all right? May I get you something to drink? Or perhaps I can show you where to powder your nose?"

Trust Laura to put it delicately. The woman looked like she was about to barf.

Nigel spoke up. "My aide will be happy to—"

Laura waved away his suggestion. "That's all right. I know where it is." She hooked her arm through Elizabeth's and helped her stand.

"Thank you," the still bewildered woman said, following Laura gladly.

Good ol' Joe looked like he'd hold her back if he could. The control freak probably didn't want her out of his sight.

"Now then, Mr. Conrad," Mark continued, "what did Jackson want from you?"

"Want? Why would he want anything? He's a millionaire in his own right, even if you don't count what he inherited from Angelica. That's why I didn't think he had any reason to get rid of her."

"Let me rephrase the question. What was the reason for his call?"

"He mentioned some of Angelica's possessions. Wondered if Elizabeth and I had them."

"Possessions?" Mark said.

"Nothing of any import."

Uh-huh. The stock certificates, maybe? Or possibly a few stray flash drives with Angelica's file on them?

"And what did you tell him?"

"That we'd look when we had the time." Joe was starting to sweat. "Really, it's nothing. Trinkets. That sort of thing."

Thomas returned, and shook his head at Mark's questioning glance. Guess the phone number had been a blind alley.

Mark nodded. "Okay, Mr. Conrad, here's what you're going to do. You're going to call Jackson's cell phone and leave a message—"

"What if he answers?" Joe interrupted.

"He won't. Leave a message telling him to call you back as soon as possible, that it's urgent."

"And when he does, you'll trace the call and find him?" Joe said.

"That's one possibility, yes. But I'm guessing he won't be on the phone long enough, so I want you to invite him to dinner at your place."

"What makes you think he'll come? He's a busy man," Joe said, looking uneasy at the prospect of face time with his son-in-law.

Mark looked at Thomas and Nigel. "We need to make sure he comes. Ideas?"

Thomas, after a brief pause, said, "Tell him Angelica had mailed a package to herself at the company address before she was killed, and that you think he, as her widower, should be the one to open it. I'm guessing wild bears couldn't keep him from coming for something like that."

"But there is no package," Joe said, looking downright dewy on top now.

"You have a problem with lying?" Thomas said, raising one sardonic brow.

"There will be a package," Mark said before Conrad could respond to Thomas. "We'll fake one up."

Conrad pulled out a handkerchief and dabbed his head. "When do you want him there?"

After the Conrads left, Laura filled us in on her interlude with Elizabeth.

"That woman is completely under her husband's thumb, and utterly terrified about something. No doubt that would be the possibility of her dalliance with her son-in-law coming to light."

"Will she be a help?" Mark asked.

"Oh, definitely. She'll jump on anything she thinks will save her from scandal."

"Great," I said. "Um, not to sound dense here, but what's up with the package?"

Mark smiled at Thomas. "If I'm not mistaken, your Machiavellian brother is hoping Jackson will think Angelica mailed the elusive flash drives to herself to keep Jackson from finding them. And possibly the stock certificates, if he's even noticed those are missing."

Thomas took a small bow. "With a little luck, Jackson will think he has the chance to clean up all his loose ends, and will jump on it."

"And we'll be there to get him tomorrow?" I said, slipping that "we" in as casually as I could. I didn't want to make a big deal of it, but no way were they leaving me out of this part of the operation.

Conrad was supposed to set up the dinner for the next evening at his Malibu home. He'd call Nigel with the details once he had Jackson nailed down to a time. If Jackson even called him back. I was still holding my breath on that one.

Mark looked at me and nodded. "Yeah, Howdy. We'll be there to get him."

He hadn't even looked at Thomas for permission to include me. I thought that was progress.

After we made our good-byes to Nigel, promising to keep him updated on breaking developments, I realized I didn't have a ride, so naturally I asked Thomas. When I told him where Billy and I had been staying, he looked somewhat pained. It was pretty far from his hotel, and he was no doubt anxious to salvage some remnant of his honeymoon with Laura.

"I'll drop her, Tom. It's on my way," Mark said.

Yikes. Things had seemed almost normal with him while we were talking to the Conrads, when we'd had Thomas, Laura, and Nigel as a buffer between us, but alone with him? Wasn't sure I was ready for that.

"Thanks, Mark." Laura winked at him. "I owe you."

"And I won't let you forget it either," Mark said, humor in his eyes.

Laura gave me a quick hug. "See ya later, sugar," she said, adding, in a whisper, "Don't look so nervous. He's not going to eat you."

Huh, I thought. *Shows how much you know.*

"Hop in, Howdy," Mark said once they were gone.

He was still acting like the old Mark, the pre-sleeping-with-me Mark, so maybe this would be okay. I mean, I was willing to pretend it never happened if that was the way he wanted it. I can be big that way.

"Is that a Rolls?" I asked, temporarily distracted. "You can rent those?"

He nodded. "A Wraith. And you can rent anything in Hollywood."

I whistled. "Nice. Maybe a tad excessive, but nice."

"I like to blend with my surroundings," he said, and opened the passenger-side door for me.

"You know, I've never driven a Rolls before . . ." I said.

He smiled—again, almost as if nothing had happened between us. "Sorry. I'm the only driver allowed by the rental agreement."

I slid into the passenger seat with a regretful sigh and a shrug, suppressing the thought that Billy wouldn't have let that stop him.

"Oh, well. I've never ridden in one either. I guess that's the next best thing."

The ultrasoft, ivory leather seat hugged me in luxury. It wouldn't do to get too used to this. Might make one decide to do anything for money, and that would conflict with my inner altruism.

We chatted about the car for most of the drive to my hotel—the paint job (black sides, silver-white hood and top), the bold grill, the classic Rolls hood ornament. Not that I knew all that much about cars—or even cared, other than recognizing a seriously cool ride when I see one—but I figured it was a safe topic of conversation. Mark seemed to agree.

When he parked at the hotel instead of letting me off I began to feel a little uneasy.

"You don't have to walk me to the door," I said. "It's a safe hotel."

"Yeah. Reasonable, too. That's why I'm staying here. I'd rather put money into cars."

Uh-oh. "When you said it was on your way . . ."

"Can't get any more 'on the way' than this," he said, keeping it friendly. Casual.

I twisted in my seat to face him. "Mark . . ." Oh, hell, what did I even want to say?

He met my eyes with the softer version of his. "Howdy, now isn't the time to discuss anything other than how we're going to get Jackson Gunn, and we've already done that. Let's just go to our separate rooms and get some rest before tomorrow."

I nodded in agreement, my relief safely outweighing a stubborn streak of disappointment.

Chapter 28

Well, I can cross seeing Billionaires' Beach off my bucket list, I thought. Not that spending time at the pricey Malibu locale was ever on it. I prefer my sun and sand less densely populated.

The houses were, for the most part, large and luxurious. But honestly—and I didn't think this was sour grapes—they were too close together, and the beach was on the narrow side. Killer view of the ocean from the Conrads' huge kitchen, though, which overlooked a long lap pool.

I was currently playing sous chef to Laura's cook. (Which meant I was basically doing nothing but waiting, since Laura wasn't dumb enough to let me actually help.) The real cook, along with the other servants, had been given the evening off to keep them out of the line of fire, should it come to that. None of us thought Jackson was going anywhere unprotected these days. He could even be legally armed—it wasn't tough for a celebrity to get a concealed-carry permit in California.

If Jackson got uncomfortable after he arrived, and tried to run this way, he'd wind up with Laura's foot in his face. I was actually kind of hoping that would be necessary. (Vindictive? Moi? Well . . . yeah. I didn't appreciate being anyone's alibi.)

I had to stay out of sight until later because Gunn would recognize me at once. I couldn't adapt to be one of the servants, for instance, because the Conrads didn't know about adaptors.

Mark was filling in for their usual butler, and would be on hand for any trouble at the front of the house. If Gunn questioned the Conrads about it, they would say the other guy had been poached by a family down the beach. Nothing unusual about that—rich people lured away their friends' servants all the time. Good help was hard to find, and all was fair when it came to keeping your household running smoothly.

Thomas and Nigel were hidden away in Joe's office, to be brought out later, in case Jackson needed more convincing that it was worth his while to plead guilty and hope for a relatively light sentence. Nigel was willing to take him on as a client because it would ultimately help Lily-Ann. "Of course, the notoriety doesn't hurt business either," he'd admitted, with his Clooney smile.

"He's here. Get ready." Mark's voice sounded oddly intimate in my ear. He'd fitted us all with tiny, almost invisible earpieces and microphones, so we could communicate throughout the evening. All we had to do was speak in a quiet voice, and the sensitive wireless mics we were all wearing beneath our collars would transmit to everyone in our group.

"Standing by," Laura said. It sounded weird to hear her both from across the kitchen island and in the receiver in my ear at the same time. She placed a few more hot and cheesy something-or-anothers on the tray next to the thick, crab-salad-stuffed cucumber slices.

Elizabeth came into the kitchen a few minutes later, looking pale and nervous. "I don't know if I can stand to look at him. And Joseph is more agitated than I've ever seen him. Worse, even, than when we found out about Angelica."

Laura glanced at me, telegraphing an alert with her expressive eyes.

I gave a tiny nod. "Mrs. Conrad, why don't you sit here with me for a few minutes while Laura takes the hors d'oeuvres out? Maybe we can have a drink of water, or tea, or—"

"I have a new pinot grigio—would you care to try it?" She crossed the kitchen to the wine fridge and grabbed a bottle. "I keep a corkscrew in that drawer right behind you—be a dear and get it, won't you? Oh, and the glasses are in the cupboard behind you."

"Um, sure," I said.

Laura left with the cheesy whatchamacallits, mouthing the words *be careful* as she left.

Never have I seen a bottle of wine opened and poured faster. She put a half-full glass in my hand, clinked hers to it, and drank. Relief settled over her face, relaxing it into its more familiar composure. Huh. So that was how she managed to stay so calm in front of the cameras.

"Cheers," I said, and sipped a microscopic amount. I wanted to keep my wits sharp.

"Do you like it? It's Italian, of course." She added a token splash to my glass, and refilled hers. "Funny, but I don't care for the California pinots—does that make me disloyal? Joseph says we should support the local wineries. I mean, since we live here. But he doesn't even drink wine unless he's forced, so what does he know?"

At least the color was coming back to her face.

"I think you should drink what you like," I said, trying to appear engaged, all the while straining to listen to the voices in my ear. They were indistinct. Apparently, the mics only picked up the wearer's voice clearly.

Definitely two men talking. Must be Joe and Jackson. But I thought I'd heard a woman's voice in the background, too. I assumed Laura could hear what they were discussing, and would find a way to relay any essential information.

Elizabeth was still yammering about the wine. ". . . drink red when he has to, but prefers whiskey. I say a light, crisp pinot is so much more refreshing . . ." She poured herself another refill.

"Excuse me, Mrs. Conrad, but hadn't you better go back?" I said. "I mean, Jackson might think it odd if you didn't at least say hi, right?"

The panic flared in her eyes, but not as strongly as before. She nodded and took another fortifying—not to mention extended—sip of her wine.

Laura returned as Elizabeth left. The tray was still full. Seemed no one was hungry.

"Well?" I said.

"Gunn is in place," she said. "Seated, with a drink. But he brought company—his assistant drove him here. He said his car is in the shop. I suspect his loyal minion has been helping him hide."

"He might not be lying about the car. He drives a Jag—I hear those things practically live in the shop. But, geez, he brought Frannie *here*? After what the Conrads saw in that vid—"

"Never mind that now," Mark said in our ears. "I have the library door covered. Looks like we're set."

"We're ready when you are," Thomas said from Conrad's office.

"Mrs. C is looking iffy," Laura said. "Might want to move it along."

"Ditto that," I said.

"No time like the present," Mark said.

"I don't think he's going to like this present . . ." I mumbled, picking up the small FedEx box we'd dummied up for the occasion. Everyone chuckled.

I stepped out of the kitchen, Laura behind me. Nigel and Thomas were leaving the office. Mark waited for us outside the library, where the Conrads were with Jackson and Frannie. The French doors didn't offer a lot of cover, so we stood to the side, out of view. Peeking, I saw the Conrads sitting in stony silence. Not that I could blame them. I mean, what *can* a good host and hostess say to the man who killed their daughter, much less to his barely legal sidepiece?

Mark, good butler that he was, went in ahead of us and announced, "Mr. Conrad, the package you requested . . ." He handed the box to Gunn, who held it for a moment before giving in to the temptation to open it. A spring-loaded flag with the word "SURPRISE!" popped out. Frannie jumped a good foot off the couch. Guess she was a little on edge.

Gunn looked accusingly at Joe, who was every bit as startled. "What the hell?"

That was my cue. I walked in, pointed my finger at Jackson like a gun, and said, "Hi, there, Jack. Gotcha."

He stood, shocked out of his gourd to see me.

Laura slipped around me, over to the window side of the room, so that exit was covered, too, though he'd have to be an idiot to jump through the glass onto the concrete drive below. The library was on the street side of the house.

"What's going on?" Gunn said, keeping his voice measured.

"Jack, you ran off so fast the other night that we didn't have time to tell you," I said. "We made copies of the video we showed you on the laptop you stole."

Nigel rolled in, Thomas at his side. "I hear you might be in need of a good defense attorney, Mr. Gunn. I'm here to offer my services," Nigel said.

Gunn turned on Conrad. "You set me up, you miserable son of a bitch."

Joe smiled, lips closed, a grim and ugly sight. "*You had my daughter killed.* All because of that piece of trash beside you. What's the matter? Both of my daughters, and my *wife,* not enough for you? Or just not *young* enough?" Guess good ol' Joe knew more than he'd been letting on. Elizabeth clutched her collar, like she suddenly couldn't get enough air. "You're lucky I'm letting the authorities handle this instead of doing it myself."

"Is that what the two of you tried at the funeral?" Jackson said, anger building. "What's the matter, Elizabeth, your aim a little off? Too much wine in the morning will do that, I hear. The real question is, which one of us were you aiming for?"

Elizabeth shrank into herself. She didn't admit anything, but she didn't deny it either.

Jackson stared at her, a nasty look on his face. "To think I felt sorry for you. What a waste of a fuck."

Frannie was looking at Jackson like a puppy who'd just been boot-kicked in the belly, the recipient of a hard lesson about loving the wrong man.

Joe glanced at his wife, disgust and pity fighting for the upper hand on his face. He spat out his next words to Gunn like it sickened him to say it. "Overholt has agreed to defend you. This doesn't have to ruin you. Or us." The Conrad name was everything to him. Above all else, he was desperate to keep the scandal from hitting the press.

Mark and Laura edged themselves closer to Gunn, who was looking wilder by the second. "If you think I'm going down alone for this, that I won't tell the world about Lily and Elizabeth, and those goddamned stock certificates you stole—"

Joe stepped on his words. "Calm down! I told you, *we can work this out.*"

Elizabeth was staring, lips parted, at her husband. "Joseph, what are you going to do? You can't let him—"

Gunn stood, his face turning vicious. "Yeah, I know about the stock. Who else could have taken it? Certainly not Goody Two-Shoes Lily—she wouldn't dirty her hands with Conrad money. But her sister's husband? Now, that was another story. She was happy to get down and dirty there."

I swung my head to gauge Joe's reaction to Gunn's accusation. Got tripped up by the look on Frannie's face—and the gun in her hand.

Shit! I lunged, trying to stop—

Too late. Three shots rang out in rapid succession. Within a second, I was on top of her. A fraction of an instant later, Mark was on top of both of us, hitting Frannie's gun hand against the marble-topped end table.

"He was going to marry *me*! He said so!" Frannie screamed.

The gun fell to the floor; Mark kicked it toward Nigel, lifting himself enough that I could squeeze out of the human sandwich. Nigel reached down for the gun.

Frannie's screams turned to quiet sobs. "He said he would marry me after . . . after . . . he *said.*"

Splotches grew, red and ugly, on Gunn's shirt. Laura had run to him, catching him before he went down. Thomas was beside them, helping her lower him to the floor.

Fuck! I couldn't believe she'd shot him. My stomach rolled. I fought back the heave.

Laura put her bare hand over the wound that was bleeding the most profusely. She grabbed one of Thomas's hands and placed it atop another wound. "Press here, firmly," she said. "And here." She put his other hand on the third wound.

"What do you need?" I asked, voice shaky, desperate to do something, anything, to keep me from throwing up or passing out.

"We could use some towels," Laura said, calm as you please. Spooks. Always keeping their cool in an emergency.

I ran as fast as I could to the powder room across from the library, snatched a pile of snowy white hand towels (monogrammed with a "C") from a basket beside the sink, and ran back. I gave one to Laura; she carefully lifted her hand, placed the towel over the gushing hole, and reapplied pressure. The towel was totally red in seconds.

Thomas's hands were a gory mess when he lifted them for the towels, even though the bleeding wasn't as profuse from the wounds he was covering. He was pale but composed. "Somebody call 911," he said calmly.

"I already have," Nigel said. Sure enough, he was putting his phone away.

Elizabeth appeared to be in shock. At least she wasn't screaming. I would have taken her for a screamer. Maybe the wine had helped.

Mark had pushed Frannie facedown onto the sofa and secured her hands behind her back with a zip tie. Did everyone but me carry those? At least *she* didn't look strong enough to break one.

"You . . . stupid . . . fool," Jackson said, barely above a whisper, eyes glassy. "I *would* have . . . married you."

Frannie tried desperately to push herself up, to wiggle her way toward Jack. "Oh, God," she said, still sobbing. "Jack, I didn't mean it. I'm sorry. I'm so sorry!"

Mark, knee planted in the center of her back, leaned down close to her ear. "You move and I'll have to break your arm," he said in a quiet tone that nonetheless carried a world of menace. She got very still. "Nigel, can you cover her?"

Nigel pointed the gun at Frannie's head. "Got it."

Once Mark seemed satisfied she was no longer a threat, he crossed to Jackson, and stood at his head. "Is he conscious?"

Laura gave a brief shake of her head.

"Good," Joe said quietly. "*Good.*"

The EMTs pronounced Jackson dead at the scene. Laura and Thomas had done everything they could to keep him alive, but one bullet had hit an artery.

The cops showed up not long after, took tons of pictures, collected evidence, and arrested Frannie. By the time the body was removed from the house to be taken to the morgue, a whole host of reporters and paparazzi were stationed along the perimeter of the property. Didn't take long for word to leak this close to Hollywood. Probably a reporter listening to a police scanner recognized the address.

Before the Conrads retired upstairs, I took a moment to tell them I knew about the forged stock certificates, implying I was some sort of private detective Jackson had hired to follow them in D.C. Maybe not precisely true, but close enough for horseshoes. Since I'm basically a nice person, I only let them panic for a minute or two before I told them it would remain our little secret as long as the certificates were transferred to Lily and they stayed off her back about the animals. They agreed readily enough, telling us to make ourselves at home for as long as we needed. We could see ourselves out.

As for the funeral shooting . . . well, Elizabeth hadn't admitted to it outright, and even if she'd been the shooter, it wasn't like she'd succeeded. Or maybe she had. Maybe she'd only ever intended to scare the shit out of Jackson. Besides, it was moot now. I'd tell Lily about it, and let her decide how to proceed. I suspected she'd let it go.

"Well, that was unexpected," I said to the others once the Conrads were gone.

We'd come equipped to videotape Jackson confessing to hiring Angelica's killer, figuring once he knew we had copies of the incriminating video of him with Frannie, he'd have no choice but to capitulate. Frannie had thrown us all a curveball.

"Looks like you have your work cut out for you, Nigel," Thomas said. "If you decide to take the case."

Nigel smiled. "Are you kidding? 'Loyal Assistant Shoots Celebrity Abuser'? Piece of cake. But there's the matter of Lily-Ann to finish up first."

"We can still provide you with a video of the confession, if you want," I said. "Right, guys? I can be Jackson"—ugh, another dead aura—"if somebody knows how to alter the time stamp so it looks like it was made before he died."

"Easy," Mark and Thomas said at the same time.

"Okay, then," I said, "let's get this thing done." *Before I throw up.*

Chapter 29

Within an hour, the video was mysteriously leaked to the press. Nigel had suggested it, saying it would make getting "Lily-Ann" released from jail that much faster, which none of us objected to in the slightest, least of all me. The press would eat it up.

When I thought closely about the ethics of everything we were doing, I had to admit to a twinge of conscience. But, really, whether it was technically ethical or not, it was *right* that Lily-Ann would be free, and without the taint of suspicion. Besides, I figured if what we were doing were truly bad, God would have zapped me with a thunderbolt by now.

We could only speculate as to why Gunn had done the job himself instead of hiring someone. Maybe he'd hated his wife that much. Or, as Mark thought likely, it could have been that he didn't want to leave a hired killer in the position to blackmail him. When the opportunity for the perfect alibi arose, he couldn't resist using it himself.

Laura had used an untraceable burner phone to record what appeared to be a secret video of Jackson hiring the killer (ably played by Mark, using an unrecognizable mixture of his oldest auras) in a secluded alley. Assuming Gunn's aura again had been distasteful in the extreme, but I'd held my nose and done it in one take. Nigel, when presenting it to the judge (who'd been pulled from a dinner party to view it), said it had been sent to him anonymously after Gunn had refused to capitulate to the killer's blackmail attempt. Hey, Mark's thought about what Gunn might have been trying to avoid by killing Angelica himself had been a good one—why not use it?

"Lily-Ann" was released from prison in the middle of the night, so there weren't as many paparazzi surrounding the place as there might have been. The few die-hards who showed up were charmed by Billy's self-effacing performance. He even managed to plug some of her favorite charities, claiming more empathy than ever for the poor, abused animals who wound up—through no fault of their own—in substandard kill shelters.

"Lily-Ann could take a lesson in public relations from you," I said when we were alone in the backmost seat of Nigel's luxurious van. Nigel was next to the driver, having wheeled his chair into the spot specially modified for it. Since the middle row of seats had been removed to accommodate Nigel's chair, we were far enough away to keep our conversation private, if we spoke low enough.

Fortunately, the Conrads would be hiding from the press in their Malibu mansion until the media frenzy abated. We told them Lily-Ann wanted a few days of much-needed recovery time. After that, it would be up to the real Lily-Ann to deal with her parents.

"I believe I'll leave the crusading to her from here on," Billy said, with a pained look on Lily-Ann's face. I wished it were safe for him to drop her aura, but he couldn't, not before we were back at Nigel's.

"Are you all right?" I asked. Softly, so Nigel and the driver wouldn't hear. "Nobody tried to . . . do anything . . . to you, did they?"

He reached out to touch my face, lightly tracing the eyebrow above my black eye, and my nose splint. "Jesus, Ciel, I . . . no, nobody did anything to me. I wish someone had tried," he added in a fierce whisper.

"Billy, I'm fine. Nigel's doctor checked me out, and it's not serious. I'm not even going to have a crooked nose when the swelling goes down," I said, hoping I was telling the truth.

"It never would have happened if I hadn't gotten you the stupid job. It's my fault," he said.

"That's the dumbest thing I've ever heard. You had no way of knowing—"

"That's just it. I *should* have known. If I weren't so reckless—"

"Stop that! You had a job lined up. I needed work. You offered it to me, and I jumped on it. That's all there was to it."

"You got hurt because of me. There's no getting around that, Ciel. Would you just let me fucking apologize?" he said, voice raised. "Sorry, Nigel," he added when I put my finger to my lips.

"Fine. Okay. Apology accepted," I said, bringing the volume level way down. "Can we move on? Because I've missed you. A *lot.*" I looked at him significantly.

He didn't say anything, only pulled me against him, tucking me under his arm and cradling my head gently beneath his chin. It might have been Lily-Ann's body I was snuggled up to, but it was Billy's heart I heard beneath my ear. That would have to do for the moment.

The driver dropped us at the back entrance to Nigel's house, where the van could pull closer to the door and the reporters were blocked by a tall stone wall and a sturdy gate. Nigel, pleading a long day, excused himself after he showed us to our adjoining rooms. Lawyers were so discreet. Billy changed at once into the clothes he'd left at Nigel's when he'd borrowed the lawyer's aura to visit me in jail. They'd been washed and folded.

"Shouldn't we wait until morning to get Lily-Ann?" I asked.

"The sooner, the better—I want to put this whole cluster-fuck behind us. And I'm going by myself."

"What? Why?" I said.

"A, because you hate flying and you've had to do too much of it lately—"

"But I'm getting better at it!" I interjected.

"And B, on the off chance that somebody official comes looking for Lily-Ann for any sort of follow-up, you need to be here to fill in." He was already walking toward the back door, the press being camped out in front of the house. "Call Dave and tell him I'm on my way."

"Wait. Aren't you forgetting something?" I asked.

He stopped and looked at me, his eyes not quite connecting with mine. I stood on tiptoe, pulled his head down to my level, and kissed him. He hesitated at first, then wrapped his arms around me and kissed me back with a passion that bordered on desperation. Finally, he tore his mouth from mine and set me away from him.

"I'll be back as soon as I can," he said.

My stomach clenched as I watched him leave. Something was very wrong.

I called Dave, told him Billy was on his way, and asked him to make sure Lily-Ann was ready to leave. Then I kicked off my shoes, brushed my teeth, lay down on top of the bed covers, and proceeded to not sleep.

What in the heck was up with Billy? It wasn't like him to pass up happy time in the boudoir, even if circumstances dictated a quickie. With him, quality never suffered when you added speed.

Had he been hurt in jail, and wasn't telling me? The idea of that made me feel sick to my stomach. Or was it me? I rushed to the full-length mirror in the bathroom. Maybe he'd been turned off? My splinted nose sure wasn't the sexiest thing going. The bruising around my eye still looked pretty gross, too. Maybe I should have adapted that away before I saw him. But Billy had always been the last person I couldn't be myself with, so I hadn't thought of it.

I finally gave up analyzing and lay back down. I must have drifted off eventually, because the next thing I knew, it was morning and voices were drifting through the bedroom door I'd purposely left open for Billy. They must have returned.

I made a quick pit stop, washed my hands and face, brushed my teeth and tidied my hair with the grooming implements thoughtfully left on the bathroom vanity, and ran downstairs.

Lily-Ann was in the kitchen with Nigel, Thomas, and Laura. Her face lit up as soon as she saw me, and fell when she saw the bruises and splint. "Thank you. Thank you so much for everything."

"I'm glad it worked out. But, hey, what's this about hating my pony?" I said.

She chuckled dryly. "You mean the demented creature who bit me when I tried to feed him?"

"Crap. Sorry about that. Eeyore's kind of an asshole sometimes. I hope it won't scar."

"Only a nip, and not in a place that's generally on display." She winked, but still looked concerned. "It's not nearly as bad as what you went through for me. I should be the sorry one," she said.

"Tell you what. Let's call it a draw," I said, keeping it light. She had worries enough of her own still to face without adding me to the mix.

Nigel, Thomas, and Laura had been sipping coffee throughout our exchange. "That smells wonderful," I said.

"Coming right up, sugar," Laura said, and started pouring.

I looked around the room. "Where's Billy?"

Laura glanced at Thomas before answering. "He's in Nigel's office talking to Mark."

"Great! Will we be having some sort of debriefing? Good idea. I'll be back for that coffee in two seconds," I said.

"Wait, Ciel—" Thomas said.

"Two seconds!" I hurried to the office, stopping outside the door to compose myself, and adapt away the visible bruising at least. The splint would have to stay.

I heard Billy's voice first. ". . . my area of expertise. I won't let you down."

"Are you sure about this? It's a long assignment. I can get someone else," Mark said.

"I'm sure." Billy's voice again. "I can start right away."

There was a pause, and I almost burst in to ask what the hell was going on. But then Mark's voice stopped me.

"And Ciel? Won't she have something to say about this?"

Damn straight she will! I thought, and again reached for the doorknob.

"Come on, Mark. You gonna make me say it? You were right about me. I'm a lousy boyfriend. Have you seen her? She was beaten up. In *jail.* Because of me and the stupid job I got her."

I did shove the door open then. "You planning to tell *me* before you take off on whatever asinine assignment Mark has for you?" I said. If I looked half as angry as I felt, they both would have run the other way.

Billy paled. Tried to rally with a smile, but it was a sick imitation of his usual merry expression. "Eavesdropping, cuz?"

"Yes. I was. Mark, will you excuse us?"

Mark left, making not a sound as he walked across the floor. He pulled the door closed behind him.

"Ciel, let me explain," Billy started.

"This wasn't your fault! How many *fucking* times do I have to tell you that before you'll believe me?"

"You get *hurt* around me." He yanked up my T-shirt sleeve and revealed the scar on my upper arm. "For Christ's sake, you were *shot* a few months ago. Working a job I got you—"

"That wasn't your fault either. If anything, that was my own stupidity, and you know it—"

He raised his voice, shouting now. "You were almost killed at the funeral—another client I hooked you up with. And you had the crap beaten out of you—in fucking *jail*—because of me."

"Well, guess what? I'm an adult and I get to make my own stupid decisions about which stupid jobs I take," I said, trying my best to sound more reasonable than exasperated.

But he wasn't listening. "This isn't a healthy relationship for you. And I mean that literally. If you were smart, you'd be running for your life," he said.

I pushed my sleeve down. "Well, I must be an idiot then, because I'm not running. I *love* you, damn it!"

"Then you *are* an idiot," he said, and left.

I was leaning against Nigel's desk, staring at the open office doorway, when Thomas came in. He looked supremely ill-equipped for the situation. Laura probably made him do it.

"Sis? You okay?" he said.

I tried to tell him I'd be fine, but my throat closed against a sob, and wouldn't let the words pass. I gave up and shook my head. He was in front of me in an instant, gathering me into his arms.

"Why does he have to be so *stupid*?" I asked.

"He's a man?" Thomas said.

"He thinks he's protecting me. From *him*. God, he's such an *idiot*," I said, punctuating the final word with a sideways slug to Thomas's shoulder. (What? He was strong. He could take it, and I needed to hit something, or else I might start throwing Nigel's valuable knickknacks against a wall.)

Thomas nodded and kept holding me, letting me rant on until I was out of steam and my mouth was too dry to speak anymore. After a few minutes of quiet, Laura came in with water. In a plastic bottle. (See? *Women* were smart.)

"Thirsty, sugar?"

I let go of Thomas (*that* shirt might never be the same) and nodded. She twisted off the cap and handed the bottle to me. I downed half of it in one go. Guess I was feeling dehydrated.

"Where's Mark?" I asked.

"He left right after Billy did," she said.

"Do you know anything about this assignment they were talking about?"

She shrugged. "You know Mark. Captain Need-To-Know."

Yeah, I knew. I also knew that Laura was Lieutenant Need-To-Know, so I didn't press her.

"Nigel and Lily-Ann? Did they hear everything, too?"

She smiled sympathetically. "It was kind of hard to miss, hon. Your voice does carry."

I quirked my mouth. "That's okay. If they already know, it'll spare me having to make any awkward explanations."

Rosa set a plate containing squares of hot, buttered corn bread and a big steaming bowl of the world's best chili in front of me at the large pine table. The chili was topped with sour cream, grated cheese, chopped green onions, and black olives. She'd already served Lily-Ann. Dave and Cody were in the kitchen filling their own bowls at the stove.

"I can't possibly eat this much," I said. Normally, I'd have no trouble downing it all and asking for seconds, but we'd had a huge breakfast less than three hours earlier. Also, my appetite had been a little off.

"Eat!" Rosa ordered. "You're getting skinny. You'll never grow bigger boobs if you don't pack in some calories. Look at Lily—she knows what's good for her."

Lily-Ann smiled around the spoon sticking out of her mouth. When I'd told Thomas and Laura that I was going to take a little time off from work to do some riding and give my face time to heal before heading back east, she'd asked if I wanted some company, seeing as how she wouldn't mind disappearing from public view for a while either. We'd been here for a week and had fallen into an eating-riding-reading-and-eating-some-more pattern.

After seeing all the furtive glances flying between Lily and Cody since we'd arrived, I had a feeling there was more to her desire to accompany me than escaping the paparazzi. She seemed happy—which she certainly deserved after everything she'd been through with her family—so I refrained from warning her about men, and how they'll lead you on before they rip your heart into tiny pieces and toss it into the desert for carrion eaters to feed on.

Okay, so maybe I was feeling a tad bitter.

Lily-Ann swallowed, wiped her mouth politely on the red bandana napkin, and said, "If I stay here much longer none of my clothes will fit."

"Don't worry," Rosa said. "I have plenty. You can borrow whatever you need."

I dutifully took a bite, for my boobs' sake if nothing else. "It's delicious, as always, Rosa. Thank you."

The gentlemen joined us, Dave sitting next to me, and Cody next to Lily-Ann. "Honey, don't you listen to Rosa. You are cute as a button just like you are. But try not to let anyone beat up on that adorable face any more, okay?"

I ran my finger down the bridge of my nose, happy to feel no lumps. The splint was no longer necessary during the day. Rosa's doctor friend from town had been out to look at it, and had said to wear the splint at night for a few more weeks, to keep from re-injuring it if I rolled over onto my face.

"Gonna do my best, Dave," I said, and shoveled in a few more spoonfuls of chili, only because Rosa was still watching me.

After lunch, Rosa shooed us away from the kitchen.

"Not you, Dave—you can dry the dishes," she said. "But the rest of you—go on, get outside. Take a walk. Ride a horse. Go jump in the pond. Do something fun!"

"It's sixty degrees out there, Rosa," Cody said. "Little chilly for swimming."

"Don't be a baby. You can sit by the fire afterward. Go!"

I asked Cody if he'd mind (ha!) going for a ride with Lily while

I spent some time with Eeyore. The little guy looked so forlorn when I rode off on Trigger or Licorice that I wanted to make it up to him with some extra oats and a good session with the body brush. Dave took great care of him, but I knew Eeyore liked it better when I was the one grooming him.

I hooked his halter to the sides of the grooming stall by two leads. If I kept feeding him carrots and apples at regular intervals, he probably wouldn't bite me—he never had before—but there was no point in taking a chance.

First, I gave him a few handfuls of oats, stroking his velvety black nose as he munched. "You're a good guy, Eeyore. Grumpy, maybe. But reliable."

I picked up the brush and began smoothing it over his back. At least with Eeyore I didn't have to reach up to do it, not like with Trigger and Licorice. Eeyore made me feel tall.

"You'd never smile and tell me everything I want to hear, and then run out on me, would you?" I lifted his long mane and brushed beneath it. He twisted his head around as much as his leads would allow and gave me the eye. I handed him another apple. "Nope, you're a straightforward kind of guy. You tell me what you want, I give it to you. And *you* don't bite me on the ass."

I walked behind to get to his other side, keeping my hand on his rump the whole time so as not to startle him into kicking me. He twisted his head around to eye me again. I gave him a carrot.

"Yes, sir, you might be a mean son of a bitch sometimes, but at least people know where they stand with you." I might have started getting teary-eyed at this point; probably barn dust. "*You* don't act all charming and fun and loving, and then just leave . . ." Okay, yeah. I was crying.

I wiped my eyes on my shoulders and ducked under the lead. Started brushing his forelock. It was long, almost covering his eyes.

Didn't hurt his aim when he lunged for someone, though, so I assumed it didn't interfere with his vision. He butted my chest lightly and held still. I hugged his head. In a rare show of affection, he let me.

Which, of course, made me really turn on the waterworks. But silently, so I wouldn't scare him off. Man, how pathetic must I be if even my asshole pony was being nice to me?

"Howdy? You in there?" Mark's voice startled me upright. Eeyore neighed his disapproval.

I wiped my eyes again, more thoroughly, and adapted away any redness that might be present. "Yeah, back here with Eeyore."

He walked into view from the other side of the barn. "Thanks for the warning," he said with a smile. Even with his spook reflexes, Eeyore had managed to nip him a few times over the years.

"So, what brings you to the Circle C?" I asked, tamping down the dread that was building in the pit of my stomach. If he told me anything had happened to Billy . . .

"I was on this side of the country and thought I'd stop in and see how you're doing." Still smiling. Warm, soft eyes.

I relaxed somewhat. Surely he wouldn't be looking like that if he had anything bad to tell me. I smiled back. Maybe not my biggest and brightest, but, I hoped, a reasonable facsimile. "Hunky-dory. As you can see. Let me put Eeyore in his stall, and we can go to the house. Rosa made a humongous batch of chili, if you're hungry."

"I'd never turn down Rosa's chili," he said. "So, how's Lily-Ann?"

"Fine. Great. She and Cody are out for a ride. It's been fun having her around." I closed Eeyore's stall and went back to the wash area. Mark followed me over and leaned casually against one wall while I hosed off my hands.

"So, Tom tells me he hasn't heard much from you," he said.

"Doesn't Thomas have better things to do than worry about me now that he's married? Or is that why you're here? Playing remote control nanny again?" Funny, but it didn't even make me mad the way it used to. If he wanted to waste his time keeping tabs on me, let him.

"No. He said you sounded good the last time you guys talked. I guess I'm here for me."

I hung up the hose and dried my hands on the back of my jeans. "Well, I'll tell you what I told Thomas." And my mom and dad, and Auntie Mo, and James and Brian and Billy's sisters. "I'm good. Enjoying a much needed vacation, that's all."

We chatted for a while about the ranch. Mundane things, like Dave's new hobby (whittling) and the new curtains Rosa was making for the kitchen.

"You're not even going to ask about him?" Mark said after a particularly long pause.

My heart clutched. "No," I said, and started to leave the barn.

Mark fell in step beside me, saying nothing.

When I got to the door I stopped. "*Damn it.* Tell me. Just tell me and get it over with," I said, bracing myself.

"He's okay, Howdy. I can't tell you where he is or what he's doing, but I want you to know he's all right."

"Does he . . . will he . . ." I swallowed hard. "Has he been in contact with his family?"

"They know he's working a job for me. He's had long assignments before, so I don't think they're especially worried. And you shouldn't be either."

I nodded and started walking. The wind had picked up, and it felt good on my face. Mark kept up easily. I walked faster and faster, past the house, not ready to stop moving yet. If I stopped moving, my thoughts might catch up with me, and I didn't want them in my head.

Mark stuck with me all the way to the small stand of trees near the pond. Licorice and Trigger were tied to a low branch, and in the distance, standing near the water, I saw Cody and Lily-Ann. His hat was on the ground beside them. Her arms were around his waist, and his hands were cradling her face. He was kissing her so gently, so reverently . . .

Seeing it triggered an echo of Itchy's punch to my stomach. I sat down, linking my arms around my legs and resting my head on my knees.

Mark dropped down next to me. "Howdy—"

"Hoo-boy," I interrupted, forcing a laugh. "Guess we walked farther than I thought. Think they'd notice if we took the horses?"

"I don't think they're noticing much of anything except each other."

I took a deep breath and let it out slowly. "I miss him, Mark. I . . . I guess I didn't think it would hurt this bad."

He laid a hand on my shoulder. "I'm sorry."

"It's not your fault. You warned me about him from the beginning."

"Doesn't mean I'm not sorry you're hurting," he said.

"Do you think he ever really loved me? Do you think he would still love me if I hadn't . . . made the mistake"—Mark winced a tiny bit—"I made with you? Is that what it's really about? He said he understood, but what if he can't forget about it?" I shook my head slowly. "Boy, when I fuck things up, I do a bang-up job of it." I quirked my mouth. "No pun intended."

"Ciel, he *does* love you. That's what this is all about. He loves you so much he can't handle the guilt of your getting hurt."

"But it's not his—"

"Fault. Yeah, I know you told him that. But that doesn't mean he's not feeling responsible. Guilt and responsibility—it's kind of a new combination for Billy where the opposite sex is concerned. Give him some time to adjust," Mark said.

"He wasn't this way after I got shot," I said.

Mark smiled wryly. "I think he considered that to be as much my fault as his. And maybe even yours," he said.

"True enough," I said.

He stood and held a hand out to pull me up. "Let's head back. That chili is calling to me."

We walked along in silence for a while. But then I had to ask. "Do you think he will? Adjust, I mean? Or will he just keep on running?"

"I honestly don't know, Howdy."

It wasn't until much later, when Mark was gone, that it hit me. I hadn't melted once the whole time he'd been there.

Chapter 30

A few weeks later I lay on the couch in my condo, one of Auntie Mo's lovingly made, but hideous, afghans tucked around me. I'd just returned from a kick-ass training session with Laura—my third in two days—and I was whipped. Sweet Southern thing she might be, but when she got you in a gym, she was brutal. It was going to be so worth it, though. Current exhaustion notwithstanding, I was already feeling stronger. Physically, at least. And I was sure the rest would follow.

It had better, anyway, if I was going to survive Thanksgiving with the family at the end of the week. I *reeeally* didn't want to go, but I'd promised Mom. If I didn't show, she'd pack up the turkey, drive all the way down here, and force-feed me her special chestnut corn bread stuffing (actually one of her brilliant creations).

I was getting my life back on track. My only job since Hollywood had been completed the morning before, and had gone reasonably well. The first-time mother I'd been filling in for was overwhelmed by the new addition to her family. Her wealthy husband had offered to hire a nurse or a nanny (or both), but New Mommy had been terrified her offspring would bond with the help instead of her. So she hired me to take care of junior—as *her*—while she and New Daddy (who apparently didn't give a fig if the kid bonded with him or not) spent a long weekend in Aruba.

Unfortunately, the kid had colic. I *know.* Dumb move on my part. What had I been thinking? Well, actually, I knew exactly what I'd been thinking. That taking care of a baby with colic would leave me no time—nada, zilch, zip—to think about Billy. And I'd been right about that.

The worst part wasn't even the colic. Honestly, I'd felt sorry for the poor kid. The floor-walking and bouncing and jiggling and lack of sleep hadn't been that horrible, since I knew it was temporary. No, the worst part was that the cook had a spectacularly horrendous cold. And yet still insisted on preparing every single meal for me (she was careful not to breathe on the baby), even though I offered to give her the weekend off. With pay. You can't buy (or buy off, apparently) dedication like that.

Which meant, at the moment, I was unsure whether I was coming down with a cold or if I was about to start crying. Again. The feelings are remarkably similar, as the past month had taught me well. But as long as I stayed too busy to think, I was okay. I could keep it under control.

The trouble always started in the brief moments between frenetic action and falling into an exhausted sleep. That was when the thoughts of Billy hit me like an anvil falling on Wile E. Coyote's head.

He hadn't tried to contact me since he'd left me at Nigel's. I knew he was alive—as of a week ago, anyway—only because Mark had given updates to Auntie Mo, who'd passed them along to my mother, who then overnighted them to me inside insulated packages of frozen casseroles, because I'd absolutely forbidden her to deliver them in person. Thomas had picked the casseroles up from my doorstep while I was on the job.

When the doorbell rang, I ignored it. I was in no mood to see anyone, or, especially, to have anyone see me. Not before I'd regained enough strength to take a long, hot bath and soak the kinks out of my poor, abused muscles.

When I heard the front door open, I might have been nervous, except I knew it had to be a member of my family. The locks were too good for a stranger to get in without breaking through the door, and I was pretty sure doing that would have made more noise. I figured it was probably Thomas with a backlog of creative casseroles. Laura must have told him my job was done, the rat. You'd think a spook would be better at keeping secrets.

"Go away. I have a cold!" I hollered, deciding I liked the idea of that better than the alternative. When I didn't hear the door open and close again right away, I added, "Leave, or I will breathe on you."

"Promise?"

Billy.

I rolled over so fast I almost fell off the couch. I pushed up to a seated position, and held myself steady until the dizziness passed. When I could focus, Billy was still standing across the room, looking uncertain of his welcome.

"Do you still want me to leave?" he said.

I shook my head.

"Hi," he said after what felt like forever, still not approaching me.

"Hi," I said, and waited.

To break the suspense about who was going to move first, I snatched a few tissues from the box on the table beside me, turned my head away, and quickly swiped them across my eyes, covering the action by blowing my nose.

"When did you get back to the States?" I asked.

"About forty-five minutes ago."

"Oh." I waited some more. "So," I said at last, "you look awful." And he did. He was unshaven, sunburned, scratched up, and covered in small red welts. "Are those bee stings or do you have the measles?"

"Africanized honey bees."

"*Killer* bees?"

"Yeah. They get testy if you wander too close to their hive. Territorial little buggers."

I nodded. "Does it hurt?"

"At first. Not so much now." His Adam's apple bobbed up and down. "How's your nose?"

"All better." I blew it again. "Well, the break is healed. It's just kind of runny because . . ." I shrugged.

"Your cold."

I nodded, and nodded some more, until the nodding changed to shaking, and the tears were leaking from my eyes again.

He came to me then. Crawled under the ugly afghan with me and gathered me into his arms. I held on so tight I thought I must be cutting off his breath. He didn't seem to miss it.

"I might not actually have a cold," I said after a time.

He held my head to his chest. His heart was thrumming so fast I could hardly distinguish separate beats. "I just keep hurting you, don't I?" he said hollowly.

I sat up, not letting go of him, and looked into his eyes. "Why did you come here?"

"Well, Mommo said I couldn't come to Thanksgiving dinner without you . . ."

"That's it? I'm your ticket to a turkey dinner?"

"That's not the only reason. Mark told me to sack up and go see you. He said that judging by your workouts with Laura, and the job you took—colicky baby? You really did that?" I nodded. "He said it was obvious you're a masochist, so maybe I was the right guy for you after all."

I laughed. "Reminds me of a joke Dad told me. What did the masochist say when asked why he stayed with the sadist?"

" 'Beats me,' " Billy said. "That's an oldie." His eyes became less guarded, and I saw the shallow indentations of his dimples beginning beneath his scruff of a beard. But only briefly, as if he couldn't—or was afraid to—muster his humor.

"Does this mean you're back?" I said.

"If you'll have me. Ciel, I—"

"Wait. I'm not finished yet." I pushed myself away from him. Looked into his gorgeous blue eyes . . . and punched his face. Didn't pull it either.

He grabbed his jaw. "What the fuck, cuz?"

"You keep acting like you were the one who personally beat me up. Well, I'm showing you I can fight back. Maybe you won't be so worried about me then." I scooted off the couch, slapped the other side of his face, and hopped backward.

"Ha-ha. Very funny. Now stop—"

I jabbed his chest. He stood. Tried to loom. He's normally a good loomer. "I said stop it, cuz—"

"Why should I? If 'you' beat me up, I should get to beat you up, too. Fair is fair." I stepped back and executed one of the maneuvers I'd just learned from Laura.

"Ouch!" he said, and rubbed his arm. I couldn't kick nearly as high as she did, but his bicep was going to have a bruise. "That's enough, Ciel. I get it."

"Do you?" I punched his stomach. Not as hard as I could have, but he felt it.

He reached for me. I ducked under his arms and danced away from him. He followed, a determined look on his face, and maybe . . . yes, definitely a sparkle in his eyes. I rounded the sofa, taunting him with a two-handed come-and-get-me motion.

He lunged for me. Missed. I circled behind him and landed another kick, right on his butt. He whirled and reached for me again, but I was already gone.

"Laura's lessons?" he asked, dimples no longer shy.

"Yup." He came at me one more time. I let him get close enough to grab my shoulders, lifted my arms up between his, hooked my leg behind his knees, and brought him to the floor while breaking his hold on me. He landed with an *oof.*

"She's a good teacher," he wheezed out.

"That's basically the move I used on Itchy in jail. Laura helped me refine it," I said, standing over him. "So, now we're even. You can stop feeling guilty about me. Deal?"

"Deal," he said. "Help me up?"

I took his hand. He gave a quick yank and I was on top of him. He flipped me over and held my legs to the floor with one of his. My arms were pinned, too, but it didn't matter. I wasn't trying to get away.

He was smiling like the Billy I knew. Even with the scruff, scratches, and bee stings (and possibly the beginnings of a bruise on his jaw), he was utterly gorgeous.

"Think you're pretty smart, don't you?" he said.

I grinned, and shrugged as much as my pinned arms would allow. "Smarter than you. Of course, considering the level of intelligence you've displayed recently, that's not saying mu—"

His mouth descended on mine. Several minutes later, when he

finally lifted his head, I said, "Don't ever make me beat you up again."

"I don't know . . . if it ends up like this, it might be worth it. Go ahead, slug me."

I rolled my eyes. "Hey, idiot . . ."

"Yeah?"

"Shut up and take me to bed."

Thanksgiving was in full swing when Billy and I got to the Doyle homestead. It was their turn to host it this year, though I was sure Mom and Dad had been there since morning helping with the preparations. The smells emanating from the kitchen were enough to make my taste buds weep with anticipation. This was a meal the Doyle-Halligan clan had down to a science. It was always as close to perfection as food could get.

My parachute pin was securely attached to the high collar of my green silk sweater. Billy had wrapped me in his arms when he saw it, his embrace soundlessly reinforcing the apologies I'd told him I didn't need to hear anymore. I was sure my new piece of jewelry would be gushed over by every female in the family before we made it to the appetizers.

We were greeted in the entry hall by my brothers, who took our coats jovially enough. I got a hug from each of them in turn.

"Where's everyone else? Are Laura and Devon here?" I asked.

"In the family room. You can see them in a minute," Thomas said. He took Billy's hand to shake it, and pulled him into one of those manly one-armed hugs, clapping him on the back. "You okay?" he asked. "I hear it was a rough job."

"I'm fine," Billy said. "No sweat."

"Good," Thomas said, and punched his left jaw.

"Thomas!" I said, appalled.

"Sorry, bud. But I told you if you ever hurt my sister . . ."

James was next. Greeting, punch (the right jaw), apology. I shoved him aside and reached up to stroke Billy's face. "Are you okay? James, I cannot *believe* you did that."

Thank God Brian was nonviolent. He hugged Billy (both arms—he's always been affectionate), pondered life for a moment, shrugged, and punched Billy's nose. "Sorry, dude. You know how it is with sisters."

I didn't know how to respond. I stared at my youngest brother, absolutely boggled.

Billy didn't seem all that surprised. "We good now, guys?" he asked, cupping his nose with both hands.

"Of course."

"Yeah."

"Sure."

They were all smiling and laughing, as if slugging my boyfriend was the most fun they expected to have all day. And Billy was laughing and grinning along with them, the idiot.

"Excuse me!" I said. "Billy, is your nose okay? Let me check it." I ran my fingers along it gingerly, wiggling it the tiniest bit at the tip.

"Not broken," he said, without so much as a grimace. "Satisfied?"

"Huh. You're lucky Brian hits like a toddler. Um, sorry, Bri," I said when I saw the chagrined look on my brother's face.

"Hey, I can hit him harder if you want. I was going easy on him because he came back to you."

"No, that's okay," I said quickly. "I think he's suffered enough."

Billy nodded. "I couldn't agree more. So, guys, is that it? Anyone waiting to dismember me along with the turkey?"

"I can take a shot at it, if you like," Mark said from across the hall, where he was leaning one shoulder against the wall. There was a genuine smile on his face, and yeah, I did start to melt. Apparently being happy again had relaxed *all* my emotions.

"I think this last assignment already kicked my butt enough," Billy said wryly.

I looked at Billy's battered face and stuffed my residual feelings for Mark back where they belonged—buried deep. I suspected I'd have to deal with them one day, but today was not that day.

Mom and Auntie Mo couldn't hold themselves back any longer, and wedged their way into the hall. Mo engulfed me first, while Mom wrapped her arms around Billy. Then they traded places, and pulled us into the crowd waiting in the den.

Once the general hubbub died down a little, I let loose a piercing whistle (I learned that from Auntie Mo—she seemed impressed) and said, "Everyone, before we eat, I have an important announcement to make."

Billy's eyes got big, but the smile on his face never wavered. Mom and Auntie Mo clutched their chests, expectation lighting their faces. Dad and Uncle Liam cocked their heads and waited.

"I call dibs on a drumstick!" I said, and ran to the dining room, grinning evilly.

Acknowledgments

So, here I am at the end of another book, once more contemplating all the people who have helped me on this crazy journey. Hmm. There's a reason, I believe, writers tend to call this space the "acks." As in "Ack! Who am I forgetting?"

So many people went into the polishing of this book. My critique partners, beta readers, and general support group, for instance, without whom I would never attempt such an enormous undertaking. Elise Skidmore, Tiffany Schmidt, Tawna Fenske, Julie Kentner, Kris Reekie, Emily Hainsworth, Susan Adrian, and—new to the gang with this book—Sarah Meral, you guys are the best! You have my heartfelt thanks, and if you're ever in close enough proximity to me, I will toss in the libation of your choice.

I would like to thank my copy editor, Eva Talmadge, for fixing all those bugs that were obviously added to my manuscript by gremlins during the electronic transmission of it from my computer to Tor's.

Michelle Wolfson, Super Agent, has my eternal gratitude for her continuing belief in Ciel and the gang. And, you know, for handling all the contract stuff that makes my eyes glaze over.

A huge thank-you to Melissa Frain—aka "Melificent"—for her part in whipping my books into shape for the reading public. She does a magnificent job, hence my nickname for her. (However, if there *is* anything you don't like about this book, let's just blame her, shall we? I mean, that's what editors are for, right?) Also, my deep appreciation goes to editorial assistant Amy Stapp for all the things she does, not the least of which is being easily amused by writers who like to think of themselves as funny.

Many thanks to my daughter, Annalisa, and son-in-law, Mike, for the airplane and car info. Any meanderings from fact are strictly due to artistic license on my part, and no fault of theirs. ("Artistic license" means never having to admit you're wrong.)

Special thanks to my son, Sean, for listening to me jabber on about my characters as if they're real people, and for not looking at me like I'm crazy while I do it. (Much.)

And, as always, my everlasting love and gratitude to my husband, Bob. A writer couldn't ask for a more supportive spouse. Thanks for everything, sweet cheeks. Especially for all those reminders that "it's five o'clock somewhere."